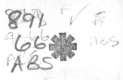
**CITY CENTRE CAMPUS
LEARNING & SKILLS CENTRE**

Other Seren Classics

Rhys Davies: *Print of a Hare's Foot*

Caradoc Evans: *My People*

Margiad Evans: *The Old and the Young*

Christopher Meredith: *Shifts*

Gwyn Thomas: *Selected Short Stories*

Siân James: *A Small Country*

There Was a Young Man from Cardiff

Dannie Abse

seren

seren
is the book imprint of
Poetry Wales Press Ltd
Nolton Street, Bridgend, Wales
www.seren-books.com

First published in 1991
This edition published in 2001

ISBN 1-85411-288-0

A CIP record for this title is available from
the British Library

*The publisher works with the financial assistance of the
Arts Council of Wales*

Printed in Plantin by
CPD Wales, Ebbw Vale

Author's Note

There Was a Young Man from Cardiff is intended to be a companion piece to *Ash on a Young Man's Sleeve* which was first published by Hutchinson in 1954. When Penguin Books reissued *Ash on a Young Man's Sleeve* in 1982 they mistakenly printed 'Autobiography' on the cover. As a result some readers have been deceived into thinking that that book was nonfiction.

Perhaps it is not necessary for me to stress that again, in *There Was a Young Man from Cardiff*, I have attempted to write autobiographical fiction; that once more I have deleted my past and, despite approximate resemblances, substituted it with artifice. If I am disbelieved, so much the better.

D.A.
Ogmore-by-Sea, 1990

Acknowledgements

I wish to thank the editors of those publications where a version of some of the contents of *There Was a Young Man from Cardiff* first appeared: 'Sorry, Miss Crouch' (*Punch*); 'The Scream' (*New Statesman and Society*); 'Knickerbocker Glory' (*The New Welsh Review*); 'My Father's Red Indian' (*Arts Council New Stories 2*); 'An Old Friend' (*A Strong Dose of Myself*).

John Manifold's poem is taken from his *Collected Verse 1978* (University of Queensland Press); and the quotation of Robert Penn Warren is from his *Selected Poems 1923-1975* (Random House, Inc., New York).

Tell me a story

In this century, and moment of mania
Tell me a story

Make it a story of great distance and starlight

The name of the story will be Time
But you must not pronounce its name.

Tell me a story of deep delight.

From *Audubon: A Vision*
by Robert Penn Warren

Contents

PART ONE: *The Name of the Story*
The Pencil Box   13
     Focus 1933: Cardiff   25
Sorry, Miss Crouch   28
Knickerbocker Glory   35
The Power of Love   49
     Focus 1938: Vienna   63
Artificial Flowers   66

PART TWO: *Double Footsteps*
The Secret   99
     Focus 1945: Bridgend   106
The Scream   109
Madagascar   119
     Focus 1953: Near Moscow   168

PART THREE: *Ogmore Elegies*
My Father's Red Indian   175
     Focus 1968: London   185
An Old Friend   187
The White Ship   198
     Focus 1986: Ogmore-by-Sea   214
The Deceived   216

Afterword   230

PART ONE

THE NAME OF THE STORY

The Pencil Box

I was only a small boy when I broke two of the Ten Commandments. I had never heard of the Ten Commandments until Mr Griffith took our class. Our usual teacher, Miss Carey, had to leave. The headmaster came into the classroom and whispered something to Miss Carey. He left the classroom with Miss Carey. We never learnt why Miss Carey disappeared from Marlborough Road Infants School in Roath, Cardiff. Was she a Fugitive from Justice?

Our new teacher, Mr Griffith, usually took the Big Boys. It was hard to understand him because he was a Big Boys' teacher. That first day Mr Griffith came into our class he told us about God's awesome appearance on Mount Sinai.

'Yes, dead quiet it was, children, when Moses heard the enormous voice above the strange cloud on the mountain shout, "*Anoki*".'

Glyn Parr who sat in the desk in front of me shot up his hand immediately and Mr Griffith smiled, nodded, addressed Glyn Parr directly, 'Yes, boy, you wish to know what *Anoki* means? Very good. I will tell you.'

'No, sir,' said Glyn. 'Please sir, can I leave the room?'

Mr Griffith closed his eyes for a long time. Glyn kept his arm raised for a long time. For some reason Mr Griffith was not pleased. Miss Carey would have released Glyn Parr at once. Not grumpy Mr Griffith. For a moment, for several moments, it was as silent in the classroom as it had been on Mount Sinai; silent as the chalked letters A, B, C, on the blackboard; as the goldfish chewing gum in the glass tank; as the tintacks that pinned our crayoned drawings to the cork panel on the wall. I stared at the back of Glyn's head wondering whether my classmate wanted to wee-wee or do big kaka.

At last Mr Griffith revived, opened his eyes and, temporarily, ignored Glyn's strenuously raised arm. He said, '*Anoki* is Egyptian meaning *It is I*. Moses, you see, was an Egyptian. So God spoke directly to him in his own language. If Moses had been English He would have spoken to him in English; if Moses had been Welsh He

13

would have spoken to him in Welsh. God, you see, can speak all seventy languages and, being courteous, addressed Moses in the language of his home-patch. Anyway, the Lord then pronounced the Ten Commandments. That was a long time ago, *thousands* of years ago; but if these Commandments, to this day, are not honoured, are not kept, then beware of God's wrath.'

Because Glyn Parr was, at last, irritably released from the class-room he was the only boy who did not hear Mr Griffith, terrible of countenance, utter the Ten Commandments. After he had named the ten Thou Shalt Nots, he added, 'They are of paramount impor-tance.' Paramount importance – I liked those words.

The late September sun no longer slanted through the tall windows. It had begun to rain. The wind had blown the sun, as mother would say, all the way to Spain. The wind blew the rain against the window-glass, making patterns on it. Soon it would be time to go home, for Mr Griffith to call out, 'Class dismiss'. When it was sunny Keith Thomas and I walked together down Marlborough Road, all by ourselves; but when it rained my mother or Mrs Thomas waited outside the iron gates of the playground with an umbrella.

'Class dismiss,' said Mr Griffith.

My mother allowed Ronnie Moore to shelter under her umbrella beside Keith and me, though Ronnie was not our friend. He was a cissy who wore knickers. Because he took up so much space I was getting wet from the dripping edges of the umbrella. The almost colourless rain delicately arrived on the pavement, darkening it, and dived into the foliage of the front gardens of the Marlborough Road houses. I felt the rain on my wrist, on the back of my neck, felt it scald the skin like the brief touch of ice. This all happened when I was still new in the world, when I could still remember my first memory, not just remember the memory of it: the sound of an aggregate of small rain on the fabric of a pram's hood, the noise that now played on my mother's umbrella.

At home my mother was troubled when I told her the few Commandments I could remember. Thou shalt not wish for your friends' toys; thou shalt not steal; thou shalt not kill. I thought she would like to know. It was of paramount importance and it had been many years since Mama had been to school, in Ystalyfera, in the Swansea Valley. 'You're Jewish,' she said. I don't like you having religious instruction at school. I think you'd better have a word with your Grandfather Shepherd.'

I had two grandmothers but only one grandfather. My grandmother, Doris Abse, was a free-thinker – a 'liberated woman' Mama always said. And her children, my uncles and aunts, were atheists. As was my father. But the Shepherds, especially Grandpa and Grandma, were observant Jews. The Shepherds thought the Abses to be ignorant atheists who did not know the Talmud from the back of a horse; the Abses thought the Shepherds enslaved by piety and superstition. Wilfred, my eldest brother, thought Grandpa Shepherd was a religious nut and I usually agreed with Wilfred who had recently taught me which was my right hand and which was my left. Grandpa Shepherd gave you the feeling that he had known Moses personally.

'You're the third son,' he said, pointing his grey beard at me, 'so here are three pennies for you. God favours the third. The ancestor of all humans was Seth and he was the third of Adam's sons. And of all the Hebrew kings, do you know whom God made the wisest? Solomon. And he was the third Jewish king. As for Moses, he belonged to the tribe of Levis, the third of the tribes. And Moses, let me tell you, was the third child of the family.'

Afterwards, my mother and I waited for a tram to take us back to our house in Albany Road. When we alighted at the White Wall I told my mother that Grandpa had said I was lucky to be the third in the family. She said, protesting, 'I have four children, not three. You're the fourth, the baby, the afterthought. There's your sister, Huldah Rose. You're the third son, but our first-born is Huldah.'

'I think Grandpa thinks girls don't count,' I said.

My mother nodded as if I had said something very, very wise like the third King of Israel, Solomon.

Miss Carey had taught us Letters and Numbers, and songs and stories. I knew the alphabet anyway. My brother Leo had taught me how 'A stands for armaments, the Capitalist's pride, B stands for Bolshie, the thorn in their side'. And Wilfred said, 'Abie, C D goldfish? L M N O goldfish! O S A R.' But Mr Griffith was different from Miss Carey. He was definitely a Big Boys' teacher.

He divided us into teams, Marconi, Edison and Bell, and when one boy or girl gave a correct answer the team got a point. And when the team had ten points the team got a silver star, and when the team had three silver stars they got a gold star. I was glad I was in the Marconi team because I had been to Weston in a boat once and had passed the island of Flatholm. And that's where the first radio message was received, Mr Griffith told us. Marconi had transmitted it from the coast three miles away.

'Yes, while you're here in this classroom,' Mr Griffith said, 'who knows, an event may be taking place right now, faraway in the Tumult of Elsewhere, an event or an invention that could change all our lives and yes, you may leave the room, young Parr, you weak-bladdered boy.'

I saw the pencil box for the first time on Glyn Parr's desk after Glyn had been excused. How odd that Glyn had not boasted of his new treasure. I would have shown it to all my friends. The beautifully patterned enamel lid had been half slid back, revealing pencils of delicate length and fineness. There were black-lead pencils encased in cedar wood and a score of pencils of all colours. I could see on top two yellow pencils – the yellows of different hues like those of a daffodil. I wanted to lift the pencils out of that box, that box with its bright brass hinges, one by one, and claim them as my own. I wanted not only the pencils in the box but the box itself. And I thought, as Glyn Parr returned to his desk, 'Thou shalt not...'

I do not think I would have taken Glyn's pencil box if I had not been wearing Leo's old overcoat. It had such deep pockets – dark places to hide treasure. I had never stolen anything before. In some ways you might say it was that old overcoat's fault.

In our front room, our tidy spick and span room, there was a card table. Its varnished mahogany top was divided into triangular segments, the apex of the triangles meeting at its exact centre. The segments could be lifted up to reveal a green baize covering rather like billiard cloth. Near its edges there were hollows where the card players could keep their money or their counters. More importantly, on each side of the table there were shallow baize-lined drawers and into one of these, next to my father's beribboned medals of the Great War, the war to end all wars, I thrust my forbidden pencil box.

Was it safe from discovery there? The table was hardly ever used. The room itself was usually empty except on those occasions mother welcomed visitors other than relations. Sometimes she would have old friends visit her from the Swansea Valley and then she would speak Welsh and bring out her finest crockery to offer them tea (occasionally sweet Palestinian wine) and Madeira cake. But they would not play cards. Surely nobody ever opened those drawers. Still, supposing...? I began to wish I had never taken the box. One could be cursed by breaking a Commandment like that.

That night, as usual, my mother came up to tuck me into bed. But after she had left, after I had said my prayers, the shadow on the wall moved. Later that same night I woke up, my mouth screaming.

Mr Griffith told us all to make a picture. I observed Glyn Parr busy, head bent, crayoning away. He did not raise his hand and say, 'Please sir, my pencil box is missing'. He showed me his coloured drawing afterwards. 'That's my mother,' he said, 'the lady with a big tummy.'

'What's your mother's name?' I asked.

'Mrs Parr,' he said.

Mr Griffith was going round each desk in turn and saying, 'Well done,' or 'What's that?' or 'Good, good.' I thought that when he came to Glyn's desk he would learn about the pencil box, but Glyn said nothing at all. I had done a nice drawing of Mama and Dada and our house. I was quite proud of it. Mr Griffith said, 'Ye-es. But why are the people you've drawn as big as the house?' So then I knew he would not give me a point. The best artist in Marconi was cissy Ronnie Moore but he was still absent with measles, or a cold or tummy-ache or whatever it was, so I was not surprised Edison won. They received a silver star because Mr Griffith gave so many points to Margaret Thomas who had crayoned trees with their leaves falling. He was always giving points to Swot Margaret Thomas.

After school, Glyn walked down Marlborough Road with Keith Thomas and me. If you were lucky you might see a motor car but usually there was only an occasional horse-and-cart. Glyn seemed sad – as if he had lost something, something very valuable. I felt sorry for him. Keith Thomas said, 'Mr Griffith wears a vest,' and I nodded. I knew that. When he came close you could see the neck of his vest through his shirt. It was a cissy thing to wear a vest but

17

my mother was very keen I should wear one.

At last, Glyn Parr said unhappily, 'I'm going to have a new brother or sister.' I could see he was trying not to think about his pencil box.

'They get Welsh babies from Howells store,' said Keith, 'and English ones from a place called Selfridges in London.'

'No, babies are inside a lady's tummy,' insisted Glyn who could be daft sometimes.

Keith Thomas bent down to do up one of his shoelaces. 'That's how it used to be,' Keith Thomas said when he'd made the bow and stood up straight. 'Babies used to be in a married woman's tummy in the old days. But now it's more convenient to get 'em from Howell's.'

When we reached our house I asked Glyn and Keith to wait at our front gate for a moment. There was something I wanted to give Glyn. I hurried inside and got out my cigarette-card collection. I loved this collection. I had all the photos of the great cricketers of the world. I had all the English team including Jack Hobbs and Walter Hammond. My father smoked Ardath cigarettes especially so that I could have the card which came with each packet. My father smoked thousands of cigarettes so that I could have a good collection.

'I'd like you to have these,' I told Glyn.

'What's wrong with them?' asked Glyn.

He grabbed the cards and peered at them suspiciously. 'This one of Sutcliffe is creased,' he complained.

'I'll have them,' Keith said.

'You want to swap them?' Glyn asked. 'I could give you my blood alleys for them. I've got quite a few blood alleys.'

'No, you can have them for nothing,' I said. 'Not a swap.'

'I don't mind having them,' said Keith.

'I can keep them? Or is it a loan?' asked Glyn.

'Forever,' I said. 'I want you to have them for keeps.'

'But I'm your friend,' Keith said loudly, for some reason annoyed.

The lamp-post man came by to light the gas lamp posts. I had to go in. It was teatime. My mother, when I had gathered my cigarette-cards, was laying the table and said, 'Don't be long now.' The gas hissed like a snake and when the yellow light bloomed the road suddenly darkened. The lamplighter walked on with his long pole and Glyn went home pleased with the gift of my cricket-card collection. Keith Thomas left, too, grumpy and without saying, 'So long' to me. Everybody had to be home before dark.

Inside the house I sneaked into the front room, opened the card-table drawer and felt at the back of it for the pencil box. It was still there. I wished I hadn't taken Glyn's box in the first place. I wished it would go away on its own. I wished there was, at least, a safer hiding place than this card table.

Mother was preparing tea. She put another slice of bread on the long toasting fork and held it towards the redness of the crumbling fire. Sometimes we would have tinned sardines on our toast. Sometimes we would have Welsh rarebit but this my mother prepared in an enamel dish. She would put a little milk in the dish before adding layers of cheese. After the cheese melted in the dish on the gas stove she added a little vinegar and pepper. Sometimes, instead of toast, we had pikelets with Moonraker butter spread on them. And sometimes Mother made Welsh cakes on a bakestone. I liked them better than Mrs Thomas's cakes because my mother put cinnamon in them.

'And what did you do at school today?' my mother asked as she took the toasted bread from the long fork.

'At playtime,' I told her, 'we went into the playground an' near the bicycle shed, one of the girls, Mary Prosser, had a spinning top. She made it whirl round and round with a little whip. So many colours it had. And it hummed. It really hummed. Like when a bluebottle's stuck against a window pane.'

'Now sit up at the table,' said my mother, not listening.

When my father came home he offered me another cigarette-card but I told him I did not collect them any more.

'Ah,' said my father, 'you're growin' up, chief. You're getting to be a big boy.'

On Saturday afternoon I put on Leo's old overcoat again and pushed Glyn's pencil box deep into its pocket. It was no use to me. I could not even try out any of the pencils. Not once. I hated the box. It had to be got rid of like a coffin. It would have to stay out of sight forever. I decided I would just chuck it away somewhere. A good place would be right down Newport Road over the railway bridge where my father took me to see the engines shunting and, best of all, an express train whoosh by. But they would not let me go that far on my own. I was not to go where there was traffic. Unfortunately, so many good secret places were out of bounds. My mother came into the hall carrying a vase of carnations. She was going to take the vase into our front room. Were we going to have visitors? 'Where are you going?' she asked me.

'I'm going to the park,' I said.

'Mind how you cross the road,' she said.

There was a satellite park close to Waterloo Gardens which might have owned an official name but the children of the neighbourhood called it the Fishing Park. A brook ran through it, and if you had a net and you were quick you could catch the darting sticklebacks, especially from where the bank was not too steep, not too far from the small waterfall. Near the Fishing Park railings I met Peter Williams who usually wanted to fight me. He was a year ahead of me at school in Miss Townsend's class, and bigger than I was too so I usually got the worst of it. But now he looked at me pacifically, as if Moonraker butter would not melt in his mouth. He carried a fishing net in one hand and in the other an empty jam jar.

'Come with me if you like,' he invited.

'You goin' to catch fish?' I asked.

'What do you think?' he said.

'You're not goin' to keep them in that jam jar,' I said, 'it's cruel.'

'It's a marmalade jar,' he protested.

'Too small to keep fish in,' I said. 'Definitely. You could get reported to the RSVP.'

Peter Williams was silent for a long time, contemplative. At last he said quite companionably, 'You comin' or not?'

I would have accompanied him but I had a mission, a solitary mission.

'No,' I said.

'Then get stuffed,' he said, and turned to walk through the Fishing Park.

When I was out of sight, the other side of the trees, I bellowed, 'Podge, Podge.' I expect he heard me.

Meeting Peter Williams had given me an idea. The fishing brook continued its slow, glassy progress under the bridge and on through Waterloo Gardens. Just before it quit the Gardens, as it turned at a banana bend, there was a bosky corner where no one could observe you. I had played Cowboys ambushing Indians there once with Keith Thomas. So I crossed the road looking right and left and right again, determined to launch the pencil box into the stream. A coffin going out to sea.

As I passed through the gates of Waterloo Gardens I heard someone distantly playing a cornet. I knew the tune: 'Roses of Picardy'. The melody became louder as I walked down the gravel path between the rhododendron and laurel bushes. There were not many people in the Gardens. There was a dishevelled, unshaven man sitting on a park bench and playing the cornet. The other side of the park I could see the park-keeper in his peaked cap. He did not forbid the cornet player from blowing through his silver instrument. Some leaves were falling from the trees like in Margaret Thomas' picture as the man played.

By the time I had reached the bosky corner the man was playing another tune. I knew it. I had heard my mother sing it – 'Goodbye Dolly, I must leave you'. The strains of it seemed quite far away as I looked right, looked left, looked right again, before extracting the pencil box from my overcoat pocket. It was secretive here behind the bushes, and darker. I could smell the undergrowth and the stream. The flowing water was quite clear so that you could see many stones beneath it. Suddenly, the cornet player stopped and I heard only the nearby bird-whistle and chirrup.

The pencil box did not sink. It moved slowly, slowly, at funeral pace down the minnow-smelling stream. Poor Glyn. He might miss it terribly. I bet he loved that box. Maybe he'd been given it as an expensive birthday present, something he had hoped for, dreamed about, and now, perhaps he was afraid to tell his parents it had gone. The pencil box bobbed against a large stone at the bend, hesitated, before travelling on and on out of Waterloo Gardens, on its way out of Cardiff, towards the sea. It might end up, for all I knew, on the rocks at Flatholm. Anyway, it was far from my vision and beyond my telling. I would never see it again. It was as if it had never existed. 'Sorry, Glyn,' I whispered to God.

After calling the register on Monday morning, including Ronnie Moore now back at school – 'Present, sir. Present, sir.' – Mr Griffith told us that this would be his last week with us. Miss Carey would be returning the following Monday. He had, he said, 'been holding the fort'. (I had a fort of my own. I had been given it on my birthday, and though it was made out of cardboard it looked like Cardiff Castle. It even had a drawbridge where I posted one of my tallest toy soldiers as a sentry.) I was sorry Mr Griffith would be going back to wherever he came from. Back to the Big Boys I supposed. He was more interesting than nice Miss Carey. He knew more.

That morning he told us about Once Upon a Time, how ten years from now in 1940, or even later in 1950, or 1970, or in 3000, *we* would be Once Upon a Time. What was happening now in the classroom, or happening out there at this very moment, perhaps great distances away in London, or Vienna, or Boston in America, would be Once Upon a Time. That was very interesting that was.

'Put your hand in front of your mouth when you yawn,' he suddenly commanded Mary Prosser. 'I was saying about Once Upon a Time...'

After playtime, after we came back into the classroom, I wished it was already Once Upon a Time. Ronnie Moore stood next to Mr Griffith who looked very stern. He hit one of the front desks fiercely with a ruler and shouted, 'Silence!' Ronnie Moore looked pale. He had obviously committed a great crime and Mr Griffith was going to tell us about his misdeeds and make an example of him. Mr Griffith stared at us malevolently and waited until we were all still. He waited for Margaret Thomas to stop coughing, for Keith Thomas to stop shuffling his feet, for Freda Davies to stop fidgeting; and meanwhile Ronnie Moore, the cissy, looked as if he were about to cry.

Then Mr Griffith told us that – surprise, surprise – Ronnie Moore's new pencil box was missing; that while poor Ronnie was sick at home with a feverish cold, someone had opened Ronnie Moore's desk, taken out his new, much loved pencil box which had a strikingly individual enamel cover, and not returned it.

Mr Griffith paused. 'Now I know someone here has just *borrowed* it. Intends to put it back. But it has just slipped his or her mind. Hand up the boy or girl who has just forgotten to return the pencil box.' Nobody put up their hand. Mr Griffith said, 'Now, Ronnie, you wouldn't mind somebody *borrowing* your pencil box, would you, as long as they return it soon?'

'Well, sir,' Ronnie Moore said. 'I do mind.'

'Not if he or she intends to return it,' insisted Mr Griffith.

'Well, sir,' Ronnie started to object – but Mr Griffith quickly interrupted him.

'All of you, close your eyes,' commanded Mr Griffith. 'Close your eyes now, all of you. Yes, you too, Master Moore. That's right. Now the boy or girl who *borrowed* Ronnie's pencil box, the boy or girl who took it out of his desk, put up your hand. Everybody's eyes are closed now, so that whoever puts up his or her hand can be confident that what they have done will be a secret between the borrower and me. Put up your hand whoever took out the pencil box from Ronnie's desk! Put up your hand!'

I lifted my face a little bit to the ceiling to see through my eyelashes whether Glyn Parr, the blighter, had put up his hand. I had taken the pencil box out of his desk, not out of Ronnie Moore's.

He must have taken the pencil box out of Ronnie's desk. No wonder he had not been upset that the box had disappeared. What if he owned up? Mr Griffith would ask him to return the box and I knew that it was now somewhere in the Bristol Channel, bobbing in the waves on the way to the Flatholm Island or even to Weston in Somerset. Maybe there was a seagull perched on it, sneaking a ride.

'All right,' Mr Griffith said. 'Open your eyes. Sit down, Ronnie. It seems it was a magic box and disappeared on its own. But if it doesn't reappear by tomorrow morning all the class will be sorry. I'm asking the boy or girl concerned to return it tomorrow. And I just want to remind you that God can see everything.'

God can see that Glyn Parr has my cigarette-card collection, I thought.

And yet I remained uneasy. After school, after we'd walked down Marlborough Road, after Keith Thomas entered his house, I did not go home at once but walked on beyond the railings of Waterloo Gardens to the point where its stream re-emerged. I followed its small rushing noise along the nearby bicycle path that threaded its way first between the allotments and then, narrowing, over bumpy waste land. I ambled near the flowing, translucent water, keeping my eyes glued to its stony bed just in case the pencil box had not reached the open sea but had sunk instead.

I walked on and on, out of bounds, to where the path disap-peared and where I had never been before. I stopped. The sun had sunk down in the sky behind a line of menacing trees and no one at all was about. Surely I was not in Wales any more, not even in England? I had reached a strange country, one not on the map, and suddenly I was afraid. I felt impelled to look up at the sky. There was a slow cloud passing over, the front of it shaped like a man's huge face – the forehead and the nose and the jaw forming.

Focus 1933: Cardiff

One slow, autumn, chalk-smelling afternoon at Marlborough Road School, Mr Griffith repeated to the Big Boys what he had rhetorically pronounced to the infants three years earlier. 'Boys,' he said, 'you've heard how the grown-ups say, "It's a small world," because a certain Mr A has bumped into a friend of his, Mr B, far from home in London, or abroad, say, in Timbuktu. But it can be a small world because of another reason, because of what I call the Tumult of Elsewhere. Something of consequence could be happening at this very moment, far away, that could alter millions of lives – yours, too, Keith Thomas, put your hands on your desk. Now what was I saying? An event or an invention...'

But Elsewhere for a small boy, ten years of age, who lived in Roath, Cardiff, first in one rented house, then in another just around the corner, Elsewhere was not simply London or improbable Timbuktu. It could be located in equally distant places, some miles away, in the unexplored districts of Cardiff: Splott, Grangetown, Cathays, Canton, Whitchurch, Llandaff, Rhiwbina, Ely, Tiger Bay.

As for the Tumult, some of that, or echoes of it, could be found at home when Leo shouted the odds about Unemployment, Injustice, Freedom, in capital letters. I sometimes heard my seventeen-year-old brother practising oratory in his bedroom behind a locked door. How passionate he sounded: 'It is given to man to live but once and he should so live that dying he might say – All my strength, all my life has been given to the finest cause in the world, the enlightenment and liberation of mankind.'

'The People's Flag is Deepest Red ...'

Leo's Tumult-at-home metamorphosed into the Tumult of Elsewhere when he visited the Hyde Park Corner of Cardiff, Llandaff Fields. He was a public event talking about Public Events. In righteous indignation he would stand, gesticulating, on a grocer's wooden box beneath a candle-coloured sky, surrounded by a crowd no larger than those who gather about a Punch and Judy show. In an electrically charged voice, Leo would broadcast to his comrades

25

in the Labour League of Youth and to a minion of older strangers, including one white dog and one policeman, the scandalous, indisputable truth: how the nation was shameless; how the politicians in power were shameless in shrugging off the responsibility for grim unemployment – nearly half a million in Wales alone, how unjust were the pitiless means test techniques which callously broke up family life.

'What we have here in Cardiff,' he roared hoarsely, 'is a sluggish, do-nothing Council led by purblind and rigid Tory patricians who are served by unimaginative and timorous bureaucrats. Meanwhile, we see more and more listless men, men without hope, gathering at street corners, ill-cared for, ill-clothed, ill-fed, their families at home, desperate. What can they do on a Monday but spit in the air; on a Tuesday, spit on the ground; on a Wednesday...'

'Cut the grass round the cenotaphs,' a sympathetic heckler interjected sadly.

'Yes, remember what all those little grey cenotaphs stand for, all of them, in every village,' Leo responded with magnificent solemnity. 'But think what's happening now, here, in this Land that they once unctuously promised you would be fit for heroes to live in. The pity is in the facts...'

'You're a Bolshevik,' another man in a cellular woven shirt intervened aggressively. 'Are you for the Empire? Let me tell you, son, I fought for King and Country. They gave me medals, they –'

'So they gave you medals,' Leo replied. 'They gave many of you medals. They gave my father medals – medals as useless as are flowers without perfume to the war-blinded. Now they give you the dole...'

'And they've cut that to a pittance,' a woman piped up. 'The kid is right...'

The cloudlight was changing. It waxed brightly, but only for a slow-motion minute. A wind, cold-edged, had come in from the East, perhaps from the refrigerations of Siberia. It pushed forward the neutral, dispersing and re-uniting clouds. Altitudes above the Fields, above the nearby spire of Llandaff Cathedral, the different shades of white, the various grades of grey, opened up their secret chasms, closed them down again. The weightless, buoyant spirits within the clouds exalting, played with and smudged their confluences, wound up the wayward silent machinery of speeding vapours so that the very clouds themselves seemed to strike poses.

The cloudlight continued to alter as the totalitarian wind dived down to invade Llandaff Fields, its tides acoustical in the high trees. The wind bullied the branches to let the leaves go, half a dozen at a time, so that they hurtled obliquely down towards the gathered people hesitating around a youthful orator raised on a grocer's box and gesticulating wildly.

Sorry, Miss Crouch

Whenever my father tucked the violin under his chin and dragged the wavering bow across the strings, his whole countenance would alter. Often with eyes half closed like a lover's, he would lean towards me and play Kreisler's 'Humoresque' with incompetent daring. He was an untutored violinist who, losing patience with himself, would whistle the most difficult bits. I always liked to hear him play the wrong notes and whistle the right ones; and, best of all, I liked his response to my huge, small applause: he would solemnly and elaborately bow. After this surprising theatrical grace he would generally give me an encore.

That August evening he gave me two encores: 'Men of Harlech', and 'Ash Grove'. Afterwards he said, 'You'll be ten next month – wouldn't you like music lessons?'

I was being offered a birthday present. Psss. I wanted a three spring cricket bat, like the one M.J. Turnbull, the captain of Glamorgan, used; not music lessons. I didn't want to play a violin.

'The piano,' my father said. 'We have a first-class piano in the front room and nobody in the house uses it. Duw, it's like having a Rolls-Royce without an engine. Useless. If your mother wants something for decoration she can have an aspidistra.' He replaced his violin in its case. 'Yes,' he continued. 'You can have lessons. You'd like that, wouldn't you, son?'

'No, don't want any,' I said firmly.

'All right,' he said, 'we'll arrange for Miss Crouch to come and give you piano lessons every Thursday.'

When my mother told me I could have a cricket bat as well, I was somewhat mollified. Besides, secretly I was hoping Miss Crouch would look like a film star. Alas, several Thursdays later I discovered I disliked piano lessons intensely and mild, thin, tut-tutting Miss Crouch did not resemble Myrna Loy or Kay Francis. The summer was almost over and on those long Thursday evenings I wanted to be out and about playing cricket with my friends in the park. So, soon, when Miss Crouch was at the front door, her pianist's hand on the bell, I was doing a swift bunk at the back, my right, cunning cricket hand grasping the top of the wall that separated our garden from the back lane. My running footsteps followed me all the way to Waterloo Gardens with its minnow-smelly brook and the pointless shouts of other children in the cool suggestions of a September evening. In the summerhouse my penknife wrote my first poem – I expect it's still there – 'MISS CROUCH IS A SLOUCH'.

My father was uncharacteristically stern about me ditching Miss Crouch. For days he grumbled about my lack of politeness, insensitivity and musical ignorance. 'He's only ten,' my mother defended me. On Sunday, he was so accusatory and touchy that when all the family decided to motor to the seaside I said cleverly, 'Can't come, I have to practise for Miss Crouch on the bloomin' piano.' They laughed, I didn't know why. And now even more annoyed, I resolutely refused to go to Ogmore-by-Sea.

'We'll go to Penarth,' my father said, a little more conciliatory. 'I'll fish from the pier for a change.'

'Got to practise scales,' I said, pushing my luck.

'Right,' my father suddenly snapped. 'The rest of you get ready, that boy's spoilt,' he told my two elder brothers and sister.

My mother, of course, would not hear of them leaving me, the baby of the family, at home on my own. However, I was stubborn and now my father was adamant. Unwilling, my mother, at last, planted a wet kiss on my sulky cheeks and the front door banged with goodbyes and we won't be long. Incredible – hard to believe such malpractice – but they actually took me at my word, left me there in the empty front room, sitting miserably on the piano stool. 'What a rotten lot!' I said out loud and brought my two clenched fists onto the piano keys to make the loudest noise the piano, so far, had ever managed to emit. It seemed minutes before the vibrations fell away, descended, crumbled, into the silence that gathered around the tick of the front-room clock. Then, as I stood up from the piano stool, the front door bell rang and cheerfully I thought, 'They've come back for me. This time I'll let them persuade me to go to Penarth.' I'd settle for special ice cream, a banana split or a peach melba. Maybe I'd go the whole hog and suggest a knicker-bocker glory. Why not? It hadn't been *my* idea to learn the piano as a birthday present. Not only that, *they* had abandoned me, and in their ten minutes of indecision I could have died. I could have been *electrocuted* by a faulty plug. I could have fallen down the stairs and broken *both my legs*. It would have served them right.

I opened the front door to see my tall second cousin. Or was Adam Shepherd my third cousin? Anyway, we were related because he called my mother Auntie Katie and he, in turn, was criticised with a gusto only reserved for relatives. Father had indicated he was the best-looking member of the Shepherd family (excluding my mother, of course), and he was girl-mad. 'Girl-mad,' my mother would echo him. 'He needs bromides.'

Standing there, though, he looked pleasantly sane. And, suddenly, I needed to swallow. I would have cried except big boys don't cry. 'What's the matter?' he asked, coming into the hall, breathing in its sweet biscuity smell. I told him about Miss Crouch and my birthday, about piano scales and how I had scaled the wall, about them leaving me behind, the rotters.

'Get your swimming stuff,' Adam interrupted me. 'We'll go for a swim in Cold Knap, it'll be my birthday present to you.'

'Can we go to Ogmore, Adam?' I asked.

Less than a half-hour later in Adam Shepherd's second-hand bull-nosed Morris we had chugged out of Ely and now were in the open country. Adam was really nice for a grown-up. (He was twenty-one.)

'Why do girls drive you crazy?' I asked him.

It was getting late but people were reluctant to leave the beach. There was going to be one of those spectacular Ogmore sunsets. Adam and I had dressed after our swim and we walked to the edge of the sea. There must still have been a hundred people behind us, spread out like a sparse carnival on the rocks and sand. We were standing close to the small waves collapsing at our feet when suddenly a man began singing a hymn in Welsh. Soon a group around him joined in. Now those on the other side of the beach also began to sing. Everybody on the beach, strangers to each other, all sang together. When the man who had begun singing sang on his own, the hymn sounded sad. Not now. The music was thrilling and I wished I could play the piano – if only one could play without having to practise.

Adam kept telling me that those on the beach were behaving uncharacteristically. 'Like stage Welshmen,' he said. 'This is like a pathetic English B film. It's as if they've been rehearsed.' But then Adam himself joined in the hymn. In no time at all, somehow, he was next to a pretty girl who was singing like billyo. I had noticed how he'd been glancing at that particular girl even before we went swimming.

'You look like a music teacher,' he said to the girl and he winked at me. Consulting me, he continued, 'She doesn't look like Miss Crouch, I bet?'

'Miss Crouch, who's she?' the girl asked.

Their conversation was daft. I gave up listening and threw pebbles into the waves. I thought about what Adam said – about the singing, like a film. I had been to the cinema many times. I'd seen Al Jolson. And between films, when the organ suddenly rose triumphantly from the pit, it changed its colours just like the sky was slowly doing now – the Odeon sky. Amber, pink, green, mauve. My mother had a yellow chiffon scarf, a very yellow scarf, and she sometimes wore with it an amber necklace from Poland. I don't know why I thought of that. I thought of them anyway, my parents, and soon they would be returning from Penarth. It was getting late. I went back to Adam and to the girl whom he now called Sheila. 'I'm hungry, Adam,' I said. 'We ought to go home.'

Adam gave me money to buy ice cream and crisps so I left them on the beach and I climbed up on the worn turf between the ferns and an elephant-grey wall. At the top, on the other side of the road, all round Hardee's Café, sheep were pulling audibly at the turf. One lifted its head momentarily and stared at me. I stared it out.

I took the ice cream and crisps and sat on a green wooden bench conveniently placed outside the Café. Down, far below, the sea was all dazzle, black and gold. Nearer, on the road, the cars, beginning to leave Ogmore now, had their side lamps on. Fords, Austin Sevens, Morris Cowleys, Wolseleys, Rovers, Alvises, Rileys, even a Fiat. I was very good at recognising cars. Then I remembered my parents and felt uneasy. If they returned from Penarth and found me missing, after a while they'd become cross. I'd make it up to them. I'd practise on the piano. I'd tell them about the singing at Ogmore. They'd be interested in that. 'Everybody sang like in a film, honest.'

When I returned to the beach the darkness was coming out of the sea. All the people had quit except Adam and Sheila. It seemed

31

she had lost something because Adam was looking for it in her blouse. They did not seem pleased to see me. Unwillingly they stood up and, for a moment, gazed towards the horizon. A lighthouse explosion became glitteringly visible before being swiftly deleted. It sent no long message to any ship, but another lighthouse, further out at sea, in the distance, nearer the Somerset coast, brightly and briefly replied.

'They'll be worried 'bout me,' I said to Adam.

'They'll be worried about him at home,' Adam told Sheila. She nodded and took Adam's hand. Then my big cousin said in a very odd, gentle voice, 'You go to the car. We'll follow you shortly.'

So I left them and when I looked back it was like the end of a film for they were kissing and any second now the words THE END would appear. I waited inside the car for *hours*. Adam was awful. Earlier he had been nice, driven me to Ogmore, swum with me, messed around, played word games. Ice cream. Crisps. It was the girl, I thought. Because of the girl he had gone mad again, temporarily. When he did eventually turn up at the car, on his own, pulling at his tie, he never even said, 'Sorry'!

Returning to Cardiff from Ogmore usually was like being part of a convoy. There'd be so many cars going down the A48. And we'd sing in our car – 'Stormy Weather' or 'Mad About the Boy' or 'Can't Give You Anything But Love, Baby'. But it was late and there were hardly any cars at all. Adam didn't even hum. He seemed anxious. 'Your father and mother will bawl me out for keeping you up so late,' he said.

Yes, it was *years* after my bedtime. If I hadn't been such a big boy I would have had trouble keeping my eyes open.

'We'll have to tell them we've been to Ogmore,' said Adam gloomily. 'We'll have to say the car broke down, O.K.?'

Near Cowbridge, we overtook a car where someone with a hat pulled down to his ears was sitting in the dickey. We followed its red rear light for a mile or two before passing it. Then we followed our own headlights into the darkness. There was only the sound of the tyres and the insects clicking against the fast windscreen.

Adam wished we were on the phone. So did I. Keith Thomas, my friend, was on the phone. So were Uncle Max and Uncle Joe, but they were doctors. You needed a phone if you were a doctor. People had to ring up and say, 'I'm ill, doctor, I've got measles.' I wished we had a phone rather than a piano.

'Have you a good span?' I asked Adam.

'Mmmm?'

'To play an octave?'

At last we arrived in Cardiff, into its mood of emptiness and Sunday night. Shops dark, cinemas and pubs all closed. At Newport Road we caught up with a late tram, a number 2A, which with its few passengers was bound for the terminus. Blue-white lights sparked from its pulley on the overhead wires. After overtaking it we turned left at the White Wall and passed St Margaret's Church and its graveyard where sometimes Keith Thomas and I would play hide-and-seek.

'Albany Road,' I said.

'Right,' said Adam. 'Don't worry. Don't say too much. I'll come in and explain about us having a puncture.'

'What puncture, Adam?' I asked.

He parked the car, peered at his wristwatch under the poor lamplight. 'Christ, it's twenty to eleven,' he groaned. He needn't worry, I thought. When I told them that from now on I'd practise properly they would let us off with a warning.

When Adam rang the bell the electric quickly went on in the hall to make transparent the coloured glass of the lead lights in the front door. Then the door opened and I saw my mother's face... drastic. At once she grabbed me to her as if I were about to fall down. 'My poor boy,' she half sobbed.

In our living room she explained how worried they had all been. They had made an especial point of returning early from Penarth and I had... 'Gone... gone,' said my mother melodramatically. Later it seemed they had all searched for me in the streets, the back lanes, the park, and she had even called at Keith Thomas's house to see if I was there.

'You didn't have to run off just because you don't like piano lessons,' my mother said, scolding us.

'I don't like piano lessons,' I said, 'but –'

'He didn't run off,' Adam said, interrupting me. 'We had a puncture, Auntie.'

When my mother told Adam that, as a last resort, they had all gone to the police station, and that's where the others were now, Adam became curiously emotional. He even made an exit from our living room backwards. 'Gotter get back,' he muttered, 'I'm sorry, Aunt Katie.' Poor Adam, girl-mad.

Before I went to bed my mother gave me bananas and cream and she mashed up the bananas for me like she used to – as if I were a kid again.

'I'll speak to your father about the piano when he comes in,' my mother said masterfully. 'Whatever he says, no more piano lessons for you. So don't fret. No need to run away again.'

I was in bed and asleep before the family returned from the police station. And over breakfast my father, at first, didn't say anything – not until he had drunk his second cup of tea. Then he declared authoritatively, 'I'm not wasting any more good money on any damn music lessons for you. As for the damn piano, it can be sold.' My father said this looking at my mother with rage as if she might contradict him. 'If this dunce, by 'ere,' he continued, 'can't learn the piano from a nice lady, a capable musician like Miss Crouch, well not even Solomon could teach him.'

My mother laughed mockingly. 'Ha ha ha, Solomon! Solomon was wise but he never played the piano. Ha ha ha, Solomon indeed, ha ha ha. Your father, I don't know.'

'Why are you closing your eyes?' I asked my father.

It was time to go to school. I had to kiss Dad on the cheek. As usual, he smelt of tobacco and his chin was sandpaper rough. But he ruffled my hair, signifying that we were friends once more.

'I hate Mondays,' I said.

'Washing day. I loathe them too,' said my mother.

Miss Crouch never came to our house again. And it was almost a week before Dad took down his violin and played 'Humoresque'. I didn't listen properly. I was waiting for him to finish so that I could ask him if, after we had sold the piano, we could have a telephone installed instead – like they had in Keith Thomas's house.

Knickerbocker Glory

At breakfast I said, 'This'll be my last week at school before we break up.' But this summer I wouldn't be going away. My mother and I would be staying in Cardiff because my father, thanks to the wild, gambling machinations of my Uncle Eddie, had been financially ruined and, worse, my parents were now estranged. 'Your Uncle Eddie,' my mother kept saying umpteen times, 'is a twister. Good night, all he thinks about is fast cars and chorus girls. How your Aunt Hetty puts up with him I don't know. And those mad ideas of his to make a mint. You'd think your father wouldn't have been taken in by him any more.'

My mother had always criticised Uncle Eddie – that he was a glib, dangerous man, that he took unacceptable risks, that through his uninhibited piratical ways he would, one day, come a cropper and, worse, endanger others too. She had been right, too right.

My father, Uncle Eddie and the lawyer, Elwyn Davies, had jointly owned a cinema in Aberaman (which my father had managed), a skating rink in Bridgend, and a dance hall in Swansea (both of which Uncle Eddie had pretended to supervise). Now, that summer of 1937, all three enterprises belonged solely to Mr Elwyn Davies.

'You can join your father in the holidays, if you like, at Ogmore,' my mother said, clearing the breakfast things. 'Now that your sister has gone off with her friend and your brothers have gone hitchhiking, you ought to have a holiday, too.'

My father's Riley, on Sundays and holidays, knew only one route westward from Cardiff. Not only did my parents always aim for Ogmore, where they had once spent their honeymoon, but uncles and aunts, cousins short and tall, would also set out from Cardiff, from Swansea, from Ammanford, for the same destination.

This summer, my grandmother had rented the large bungalow, The Darren, and several of my family, including my father, were already installed there, or were camping nearby in Hardee's Field.

'I'm not going to leave you on your own in Cardiff, Mam,' I said gallantly. And my mother hugged me and yet again plucked the eau-de-cologne handkerchief from her bag. As I walked through Splott, that washing day, that sun-struck Monday morning towards St Illtyd's School I didn't hurry. Happily, along with three Protestant boys I, being Jewish, was barred from the first class of the day – Prayers and Religion. That's why the approaches to St Illtyd's were almost deserted. The rest had already filed into the building, into the chalky classrooms, fingering their rosaries, humming their prayers like busy bees below a crucifix hung on the wall. But near the big iron gates of our school I recognised my father's blue Riley. Its front door opened and my father stood there. 'I've been waiting for you,' he complained.

'All the other kids 'ave gone in. You're late.'

'Religion,' I said, 'the first class is Religion.'

'I thought you might like to come to Ogmore for the day,' he said gently. 'I have to pick up your Uncle Eddie who's sold his car. I thought we'd all go back together. Your Aunt Hetty's there already.'

'Can't,' I said. 'I mean I can't come today. We receive our school reports today.'

'You can mitch for the day,' said my father. 'Duw, we 'aven't seen each other lately. Not for a month. I want to know your news.'

Trying to be a competent gazetteer I said, 'I scored sixteen a week last Saturday when I played for the Junior School team. I hit a four.'

'Get into the car, love, and I'll take you to your grandmother in Ogmore. We'll have a nice day. Go 'ead.'

'Can't,' I said. 'Can't.'

He stared at me puzzled. 'I'll write you a note if that's what you need.'

I felt, somehow, that I would be betraying my mother if I went to Ogmore with him and Uncle Eddie. I was on my mother's side but I couldn't tell him that. We just waited there silently, it seemed forever, an uncomfortable silence. I noticed one of my shoelaces was undone but I did not bend down to do it up.

At last he stretched out his arm, placing his right hand, affectionately, on my left cheek. 'C'mon chief,' he said. 'You're my prize specimen.' Reflexly, I drew my face away and he let his arm fall to his side. Then he went to the car. I had upset him, I could see that, but I made no move and said no word. He opened the car door,

36

and hesitated. He looked thinner than when I saw him last. Saturday evenings, always, he used to take me to Aberaman, to the pictures. He would show me off. 'My prize specimen,' he'd say and all the employees at the cinema would be nice to me because I was the boss's son: the operator in his high compartment above the balcony who aimed the smoke-filled beam at the screen; the aging two-ton Tessie with a fringe who sold the esculent confectionery; all the young usherettes; and that fellow with dyed hair and a waxed moustache who played the organ that, victoriously illuminated, rose from the dark pit, alternating its splendour of loud, fairground colours – Cardiff City blue, bruised purple, blood-alley red, poison green, bold orange – as it squeezed out 'Goodnight Vienna'. Now my father was no longer the boss and somehow he seemed, in his wiry frame, more shrunken, vulnerable.

'Are you hundred per cent sure you don't want to come with me?' he asked, half in, half out of the car.

'Mam said you should...' I stopped, thinking better of it.

'What?' he said.

'Nothing,' I said.

'What, what did your mother say?' he rapped out, like a sentry demanding, 'Friend or Enemy?'

'Mam said... you...'

'Yes?'

'...should get a job.'

He looked as if he'd been bayoneted in the back by that same sentry. I had not wished to say anything. 'Mama says we don't want the Means Test man in our house,' I explained.

The car door slammed and that was that. He manoeuvred a three-point turn without giving me a further glance and drove away until the street was empty. A bird violently flew out of the noisy foliage of a nearby pavement tree. I bent down and tied up my shoelaces before going into school.

Before the bell rang at four o'clock Brother Bonaventure distributed our school reports. I had come fourth. Most of the comments opposite individual subjects and my marks were drivel. *Physics* – Should try harder. *Chemistry* – Did better last term. *History* – Good but could do better. That sort of thing. Ordinarily, my father would inspect my report and sign it. This summer Mother would have to do it.

With the other boys I streamed through the big iron gates and to my surprise saw, yet again, parked up the road, next to a van, my father's Riley. This time not my father but his kid brother, Uncle Eddie, was waiting in it for me. He gave me a comedian's smile.

'Your father says you don't want to come to Ogmore,' he said, moving towards me all friendly and bounce.

'No,' I said. 'I have to go home. Mother will be expecting me.'

'Get in the car then. I'll drive you home.'

'Where's Dad?'

'He's gone to see a man about a dog. Get in,' Uncle said. 'No problem.'

I could see my schoolfriends watching me as they passed the parked car. There didn't seem any option really. I didn't trust Uncle Eddie but there seemed no harm in his giving me a lift home. I'd been told so many stories about him – like the famous family one about his advice soon after my Uncle Max qualified as a doctor and put up his brass plate speculatively in Cowbridge Road. At first, apparently, Uncle Max received very few patients so Eddie pronounced, 'If you want paying customers, Max, you 'ave to get yourself a remarkable reputation. For instance...'

Eddie suggested that after Uncle Max examined a pregnant woman, even if she were only three months pregnant, he should prognosticate authoritatively the sex of the child. 'Fifty-fifty chance I could be right,' Uncle Max grinned.

'Exactly,' Eddie had said. 'If you promise the expectant mother a boy then write down in a big ledger book opposite her name, while she's observing you – a girl.'

Uncle Eddie then argued that what Max had said half the time would be confirmed and the delighted new mother would spread the word of Max's prophetic powers far and wide. As for the rest, well, most mothers wouldn't be bothered anyway, only too pleased that their babies were human. And as for those who might challenge Uncle Max? 'No problem. Just bring out the ledger book, show Mrs Jones her name and what you'd entered. "See for yourself, you're mistaken, Mrs Jones. It's written down there. A girl."'

Eddie became excited about his scheme. 'I'm telling you, Max, all the pregnant women in Wales from Merthyr Mawr to Merthyr Tydfil, from Aberystwyth to Aberthaw, they'll be queuing up at

38

your surgery. And once you 'ave a reputation for prophetic powers you're in, mun. All patients, not just pregnant women, want to know their future, don't they?'

I felt awkward in the driving seat sitting next to Uncle Eddie. Hadn't he ruined my father? A sort of enemy, really. I became alarmed when, instead of driving me home to Sandringham Road, he turned left and took the direction towards town. 'Don't worry,' he said, 'I'll take you to the Dutch Café. You'd like an ice cream before you go home, wouldn't you? They have very interesting ice creams at the Dutch Café.'

Uncle Eddie ordered himself a coffee and lit a Passing Cloud cigarette while I studied the ice cream menu. I couldn't make up my mind whether to order a Patagonian surprise or a knickerbocker glory. I felt uneasy choosing a knickerbocker glory. It was the most expensive of the ice creams but I had never had one before. Dad had let me have a banana split or a peach melba but never a knickerbocker glory.

'What 'ave you got there?' Uncle said after the waitress left.

'My report,' I said, 'I came fourth.'

'Fourth?' said Uncle. 'If a horse comes in first, second or third, you might win something. Fourth, and you get bugger all.'

When the knickerbocker glory arrived Uncle Eddie said to the waitress, 'Thank you, my flower,' and I thought, 'Grandma's probably paying for this'. Uncle Eddie watched me eat the ice cream with a microscopic intensity. You could see he was thinking of something, some sly scheme, no doubt. He kept tapping the ash from his cigarette into his saucer instead of into the nearby ashtray.

'It's no good your mother and father falling out, is it?' Uncle said. 'But your mother's a very stubborn woman.'

'She's not,' I said.

'Your mother,' he repeated, 'she's like a mule.'

'Mam isn't,' I insisted.

'Women,' said Uncle Eddie, 'they've got to be courted all the time, they've got to be given a lotta ice cream.'

'My mother likes Black Magic chocolates,' I said. 'Dad used to give her a box now and then.'

Again Uncle Eddie looked thoughtful. 'That's right,' he said.

And then he called for the bill and I noticed how he left a generous tip on the table for the waitress he called 'my flower' before ambling over to the cashier at the front of the restaurant. As my mother said about Uncle – when it came to money, it was easy come, easy go. 'That's how he put your father on the rocks with his mad schemes.'

Uncle Eddie joked suggestively with the cashier. I could see she was not displeased. I thought he had on too much Brylcreem, or Bay rum or whatever it was. Either side of a vivid parting his hair was plastered down black and shining like patent leather shoes. Dad's hair was nicer, floppy. A young woman with a baby joined the queue and I heard her say proudly to her older companion, 'I put the rattle in his little left hand and you know what, when I looked next the clever boy had got it in his right hand.'

Outside the Dutch Cafe, once more Uncle tried to persuade me. 'Let me take you to Ogmore now. It's only ten past five. Your Grandma would like to see you. And your Dad. He misses you, Christ knows why. I'll see you get home by bedtime. No problem. Is it a deal?'

Having devoured the knickerbocker glory with such relish I felt ungrateful saying 'No' again. Mother would be frantic if I didn't arrive home soon in time for a bit of supper. Besides, I had arranged to go swimming at the Baths later with Nosey Tim Parker. (I had temporarily quarrelled with my friend, Keith Thomas.)

'We could let your mother know,' Uncle said very reasonably. 'I'll telephone.'

'No.'

I had said 'No' louder than I'd intended. I heard my own voice and it had sounded shrill. Once more Uncle Eddie gave me that concentrated, staring look, then he tightened his mouth strangely before commanding me threateningly, 'Get in the car.'

'I'll go home by tram.'

'Get in the car. Think I'm going to kidnap you?' he shouted.

Dubiously I opened the car door and sat in the seat next to the driver's. He drove the car too fast but at least we took the direction towards Sandringham Road. Suddenly he relaxed, put both arms around the driving wheel, hugging it, and leaning forward muttered, 'I wish I hadn't sold my Bentley.' I said, 'You know, Uncle, coming fourth in Form IV Latin is quite good.'

He nodded. After we'd passed someone driving a horse-and-cart he said quietly, as if not wishing to be heard, as if he were telling a momentous national secret, 'My friend Tony Harris is an inventor, a great inventor, and he's almost cracked it, this idea of his of running cars on hydrogen instead of petrol – it's a winner.'

'Hydrogen's inflammable,' I said, 'That airship, the R101, it went –'

'So is petrol,' said Uncle. 'My friend's working on a formula to make hydrogen safer and a better fuel than petrol. There are unlimited quantities of hydrogen in the air. He'll make a fortune an' I'll have a cut of it. I'll be on ten per cent. I've invested.'

By now we had arrived at Sandringham Road. He leant across me to open the door and, instead of saying 'Goodbye', he pronounced without malice, as if it were a statistical fact, 'You're spoilt. Your mother's spoilt you. An' you're as stubborn as she is.'

I didn't inform mother about the knickerbocker glory. I didn't mention anything about Uncle Eddie. I felt disloyal having been in his company. I just recounted how Dad had been waiting for me outside School, how he had tried to persuade me to go to Ogmore with him and I had said 'No'.

'How's your father lookin'?' Mother asked.

'Thin,' I said.

My mother looked troubled. 'Did he have a clean shirt on?'

'I didn't notice,' I said, 'but he looked really thin.'

'Oh.'

'Thin as a matchstick,' I said, almost enjoying myself. 'Skinny.'

'Thin as a matchstick,' my mother repeated.

'I'm in your team,' I said to console her.

Later that evening, after supper, my bathing costume rolled in the towel that I carried under my arm, I decided to walk to the Baths and save the tram fare. I had spent most of my pocket money on Saturday morning when I paid fourpence to see the cowboy film at the Globe. The sultry evening was pavement-grey and I looked up at the clouds hoping it would not rain. My mother said that the imposing, three-storey houses in Newport Road, because of the cost of things, would some day probably be transformed into small hotels or restructured into separate flats. I walked past them and the yellow, swaying, grinding, cymbal-crashing trams passed me with a kind of mindless joy, their long, oblique pulleys striking the palest of bright blue sparks from the overhead wires – the Number 2, on its way to the Pier Head in the dangerous docks, the 2A destined for the terminus beyond Cowbridge Road, the other side of Cardiff at respectable Victoria Park.

Outside the Newport Road Roath Branch Library, near Clifton Road, sprawled a sort of stuffed-up scarecrow. As I approached, I saw he was a long-haired, over-bearded down-and-out. Despite the warm stickiness of the evening he wore a long, shabby overcoat and heavy dusty boots without laces in them. Nor was he wearing socks. He lay jackknifed silently against the wall of the library. He said nothing but his mean eyes followed me like those of a portrait painting in an art gallery. He made me feel uneasy but I didn't say 'Hello' or even nod. Perhaps I should have handed him the pennies I was saving by walking to the Baths?

There was many a down-and-out in Cardiff. There was sloth and unemployment and depression in the Welsh valleys, and the Prince of Wales had said poshly, uselessly, 'Something must be done.' But nothing had been done. That's why I was a revolutionary like Leo, why one day I would grow up and vote Labour. It was strange to think that my father was now one of the unemployed. And Uncle Eddie too. He had even sold his Bentley.

The other side of City Road, my back to the Glossop Terrace Hospital where babies were born, I put on my green and gold schoolcap for I had to pass the huge house where the Christian brothers lived. At St Illtyd's the boys, out of doors, had to wear caps. 'You have to be proud of your school,' Brother Gilbert had shouted. 'Green and Gold, Green and Gold, strong be your heart and bold.' The Brothers were a reactionary lot. General Franco supporters to a man. I passed the house with the many windows. wondering what they were all doing in there: Brother Gilbert, Brother Patrick, Brother Coleman, Brother Bonaventure. Brother Vincent, Brother David, men without women, playing billiards perhaps, or ping-pong, or on their knees possibly, or drinking sherry and muttering about the rape of nuns in Spain. And then there was Brother Anthony who was something else, who truly believed devils were incarnated in human form and that some of them were in his class. He tried, virtuously, to beat the hell out of us. Still, we would be breaking up soon and next term he wouldn't be teaching me in Form V Latin.

At the Baths I squeezed into the unpleasant, damp, little cubicle and changed into my swimming costume. When I came out into the echoing artificial light I observed Tim Parker talking to Gus Parry's sister. Cathy. They stood near the deep end and if I hadn't felt somewhat tired after my long walk I would have dived into the chlorine water and swum towards them over the restless, zig-zagging black lines on the green-blue tiled bottom of the Baths. But as I hesitated – neither of them had seen me – I could not help noticing how Cathy smiled up at Nosey, alertly attentive to whatever he was saying. Then Nosey Parker gave her a push and she tottered on the brink before falling into the forged greenness of the water with a flat splash. She did not seem to mind Tim Parker horsing around for, floating, she smiled up at him from the water before striking out in a stylish backcrawl. At once Nosey dived in with a stinging whoosh, trying to catch her up as they raced, all volts and energy, among the shouts and blank explosions of the Baths towards the shallow end. I lowered myself into the water, taking care not to let my head go under, for when wet my hair went straight and I knew I looked bad enough already what with the pimples on the left side of my forehead. Besides, my father always discouraged me from diving – 'bad for the ears' he would opine.

Afterwards, the three of us stood near the cubicles and Cathy removed her bathing cap to let her rich brown hair fall gorgeously around her shoulders. I was unostentatiously aware of the soft curve of her breasts. They were having a strange conversation. Cathy said that she thought the eyes were the windows of the soul. I could not help, at this point, looking at Nosey Tim Parker's eyes. They were small and pink: chlorine-irritated.

'I went to the pictures Saturday morning,' I said, 'and when Gary Cooper's mate got shot do you know what he did? He closed his eyes. That's what they do with dead people. Close their eyes. Do you think it's something to do with the soul?' I turned to Cathy, triumphantly.

'He's barmy,' said Nosey Parker and then proceeded to boast how he got into the Olympia cinema for nothing. He also swanked about how he got free meals in cafés by adding a dead caterpillar to his almost empty plate.

'You crazy,' said Cathy, laughing, impressed.

'I do it all the time, it never fails,' boasted Tim Parker though I knew he was bloody well lying.

There was something of Uncle Eddie in Nosey Parker I decided. He was fascinating Cathy though. Well, Mother had said Uncle Eddie was a ladies' man – 'Him and your cousin Adam Shepherd are a fine pair. They both need buckets of cold water over them to cool their ardour,' Mother had said frequently.

Cathy Parry was giving Tim Parker her full attention as he continued his tall stories remorselessly. Anyway, I became interested in the man on the high diving board. Not only because I had never seen anyone so indisputably tattooed – almost every bit of his skin on arms, chest and back – but because he began performing spectacular diving somersaults. Bad for his ears, no doubt.

Gradually, such was his skill, people came out of the water just to watch him. He must have been a professional acrobat. 'Terrific, extraordinary,' I said, but Nosey and Cathy seemed oblivious of things beyond themselves. How could they ignore the stunning circus aerial performance of the tattooed man? It was wonderful the way he abruptly flung himself into the air, did a sort of slow loop the loop before crashing in perfect equipoise through a small, imaginary, hyaline hole in the water. Once again, afterwards, the tattooed man climbed to the high springboard and, curiously, the whole Baths became silent. It was like a silence at a concert during an interval between two movements of music except nobody was coughing – and by now even Cathy and Nosey had turned to watch him. Nobody was swimming in the water any more. We all stood around the edge watching the tattooed man on the high springboard.

He stretched his arms out horizontally, the palms of his hands facing each other. Then, evidently, he saw something of the future at the other end of the Baths. For his eyes perceptibly widened until you could see the whites. He let his arms fall and like the other spectators I followed his gaze towards the shallow end where, now, two policemen had stepped forward.

For a second the policemen were still, the man on the springboard utterly still, the spectators eerily quiet. Then the tattooed man hurled himself up into the air, somersaulted twice and straightened himself into a graceful swallow dive; yet it was less a man diving than a man flying, yes, flying ecstatically free through the air. When he rose to the surface, the tattooed man, doing a butterfly stroke, walloped his way to the shallow end, to the shining, big, black shoes of the waiting policemen. Then, with the tattoos rippling on his muscles he drew himself out of the water and everybody heard him say, 'I'll just get my clothes on.'

One person began to clap and, shortly after, we all applauded. The tattooed man, standing smaller between the two uniformed policemen, seemed peculiarly unclothed but he put up his right arm to acknowledge the applause and, momentarily, the clapping grew louder.

'I've never seen anyone arrested before,' Cathy said.

'It was beautiful the way he flew. He flew into the water,' I said.

After the tattooed man left with the policemen we all went into the cubicles to change. I noticed how the skin on my fingers had wrinkled. Soon the Baths attendant would be blowing his whistle for closing time.

As I dressed I thought about the tattooed man, how he had come a cropper – as my mother would have put it. Perhaps it was because he had done something forbidden, soared to illicit heights – as if a man who could fly would steal the ambrosia of the gods! Uncle Eddie, too, was a high diver in his own way and took exciting risks. My mother was sensible, had always urged Dad to take care, not to be like his reckless young brother, Eddie. But what was better? To be safe and dull? Or to gamble, to violate taboos, to dive thrillingly – and so win much or lose all? Those Elizabethan heroes that we learnt about at school – the Drakes, the Raleighs – they weren't accountants sitting on their fat bums, they weren't careful grocers, cautious candlestick makers. No, they were ruthless men, pirates prepared to be bold, prepared to gamble. They won and they lost. Drake took a million pounds of plunder off the coast of Peru; Raleigh languished in the Tower of London.

When I came out of the cubicle Nosey, already there, said, 'C'mon.' He obviously didn't intend to wait for Cathy Parry to return from the Ladies' Changing Room. 'Aren't you going to take her home?' I queried.

'Christ, mun, she lives in Llandaff,' Nosey said. Llandaff was miles from Roath.

'She's neat,' I said.

'One day I'll do 'er,' Nosey boasted, 'but not tonight.'

While we were inside the Baths there must have been a shower for the pavements gleamed wetly under the lamplight which had just jerked on. Nosey seemed in a hurry to reach the tram stop. I think he was afraid Cathy might catch us up.

'I wonder why they arrested that tattooed man,' I said.

'Murder, I expect,' guessed Nosey Parker. 'There's been lots of murders lately.'

That was true. I had read in the *South Wales Echo* reports about Mahon, the Mumbles murderer. 'And that tailor, Maltby,' said Nosey, 'you know, the one who'd made a suicide pact with his wife.' The wife, it seemed, had killed herself but the tailor couldn't go through with it. After her death Maltby had dined quietly in the bathroom each night, bringing in candles, his wife all the time propped up stiffly in the bath.

Upstairs, in the undulating 2A tramcar, Nosey shrieked, 'I wonder if Maltby let the water out,' and laughed, making a noise like an active bicycle pump, and couldn't stop. Nor could I. Other passengers on the top deck grinned at us because of Nosey's squeaky laughter.

At the White Wall we alighted and listened to our own footsteps till Nosey said, 'That tattooed guy, like you said, sorta flies through the air.'

'My Dad's against diving,' I said. 'Says it's bad for the ears, very bad.'

'I wouldn't mind being a Life Guard one day,' Nosey pronounced. 'Diving in to save people aint 'alf a bad job.'

'My father's unemployed now,' I said. 'Half the world's unemployed. Mam says we're broke.'

'Go on, your Dad's on the dole?' In sympathy, he added, 'You can come round and listen to my records some time, if you like. My new ones are the Mills Brothers singing "Stardust" and Duke Ellington's "Concerto for Cootie".'

'All right,' I said.

I left him at the corner of St Margaret's Church. He lived in Southminster Road. I walked beside the wall of the graveyard towards Waterloo Gardens. Only yards away from me were the graves with their little monuments or stone angels covering the dead whose eyes had been closed and whose mouths were open probably, dumbstruck in the dark night. It was spooky. I turned down the empty, shining, black street with all its innuendoes of

46

loneliness and danger. As I passed successive lamp-posts I observed my own shadow getting longer and longer and then shorter and focused. God knows how many murderers, child-killers, maniacs with hatchets, at this very moment, were roaming the streets of Cardiff or hiding in the bushes of Waterloo Gardens waiting to pounce. I crossed the road away from Waterloo Gardens thinking how the tattooed man couldn't have been a murderer. No, not one who could fly like that.

Why, if I could somersault, loop the loop, and fly-dive like the Figure of Eight at Porthcawl, I would give exhibitions all over Wales – hundreds would come to watch me, thousands even, including Cathy Parry. How Cathy would applaud, how every-body would. Modestly, I would listen to their eulogies, and the money I'd earn from giving such exhibitions I would pass on to my mother. I looked up at the sky as if a fellow-diver, someone up there, an angel in spotlight, was about to swallow-dive. I saw the moon racing one way and, below it, a procession of grey clouds moving fast in the opposite direction. Then I knew what I had to do, I knew with the certainty of revelation: I couldn't somersault or fly, of course not, but like Michael O'Brian in my class, that white, clown-faced boy who always came late, I could earn money by going on a newspaper round this August.

I wouldn't give all the money I earned to my mother. I'd keep just a little bit back, just enough to buy myself, before school began again, another knickerbocker glory. No, no – it would all be for mother. That would help to quell her fears about the Means Test man. Was I not taught, did not the rabbis teach, 'If I am not for myself who will be for me? But if I am only for myself, what am I?'

Suddenly I felt strangely happy. The flying moon, the fleeing clouds above, were authentic witnesses of my inspired decision and I ran, and I ran faster over the half-dry pavements, past those houses that were utterly dark and those houses that were awake with lights behind curtains, past the pavement trees with the active wind in them, past the sentries of lamp-posts shining in their vigil – not because of marauding Cardiff murderers, but because I was blessed and pure and generous and needed to relate, at once, the good news I had to impart to my mother. How long would it take to earn a golden sovereign, like the amateur rugby players were reputed to find in their socks in the dressing room after an important game? Or better still, a guinea, such as doctors like Uncle Max could earn?

When I reached the corner of Sandringham Road I ceased running. Disappointed, surprised, I saw once more my father's Riley, parked outside our semi-detached house. I walked to our gate. Had Dad come to take me to Ogmore? Or was he back home for good? Grandma wasn't such a good cook as my mother. Or maybe only Uncle Eddie waited with my mother inside the house? Or perhaps both of them were there, a box of Black Magic chocolates open, lying on a cushion on the sofa?

A little breathless, I walked up the pathway, aware of the secretive aroma of the damp black foliage of our front garden, before I banged the knocker of the door truly hard. Foiled, I would keep my plan of a summer job to myself; instead I would tell them all about the man who could fly. It seemed ages before the hall light went on behind the safe coloured glass of our front door.

The Power of Love

Keith Thomas, my best friend, decided that he was a fourteen-and-a-half-year-old Welsh Christian Atheist and that I was a fourteen-and-a-half year-old Welsh Jewish Atheist. We had founded The Ethical Atheist Party. So far only Keith and I were Party members. We had not agreed yet who would be President, who Vice-President. We staged a secret vote but it had been a draw.

Keith had become an atheist because of his father. Mr Thomas when drunk, which was often, would become maniacally religious. He would shout out, 'O Jesus Christ, happy is the man that trusteth in Thee' and 'The Fear of the Lord is pure, enduring forever'. Keith often grumbled, 'It makes me sick. He's got so much worse over the last few years, ever since my mother died.' Keith rarely mentioned his mother though sometimes he sighed, 'I wish I had older brothers like you have. I could do with a bit of help with my Dad.'

Truth to tell, I wasn't so totally convinced about the non-existence of God as Keith was, but I loathed going to synagogue, disliked, for the most part, Jewish ritualistic custom and all its restrictions. It was so much more *convenient* to be an E...... Atheist, more interesting to walk through the holy outdoor pageant of springtime on a breezy, air-delighted Saturday morning than to worship in an oppressive, stuffy enclosed building. Places of worship with their man-made configurations of tamed stone, pillar and wood, their man-made windows of colour, glass, pattern, these were but spacious sanctuaries from all that was barbarously wild and unknown outside. They were Theatres of Escape where the trembling stars at night, and the eighth invisible colour during the blaze of day, could be forgotten.

'What do you mean the eighth colour?' disagreed Keith. 'There are only seven colours.'

'You can't be sure,' I protested weakly.

'Are you an Atheist or not?' challenged Keith.

'Yes,' I hesitated.

Keith and I had marked our outrageous apostasy by visiting the old railway tunnel near the back of Cardiff High School's cricket ground, which was decorated with graffiti mainly about the war in Spain: END FARCE OF NON-INTERVENTION; VIVA POTATO JONES; NO PASARAN. Oddly someone had added his private slogan also: LOVE ONLY ME. There, in the tunnel itself, under its high, brick, curved roof, a thrown voice would echo and echo and echo. First Keith had bravely shouted out, 'I don't believe in You... believe in You... You... You.' Then, worryingly, it had been my turn.

Things had gone badly since that day – a coincidence, no doubt. The weather in Cardiff had been continuously lousy so that all its arcades smelt of wet mackintoshes and umbrellas; the Bluebirds (Cardiff City F.C.) had kept on losing; Keith had been caught smoking near the quarry by his headmaster and had had to suffer six of the worst. As for me, a rash of blackheads had visited my forehead like a plague from Egypt.

Not only that. The World got worse. That Haman, Hitler, had presented an ultimatum to Austria, threatening to invade unless Schuschnigg, the ductile Austrian Chancellor, resigned. And Franco's fleet of sinister Heinkels and Junkers was bombing the breath out of Barcelona. It made me wonder whether I should recant.

Worse news was yet to come. For Keith, grinning like a greyhound, told me, 'I saw Lydia Pike yesterday evening walking with Llewelyn Rees at Roath Park lake. They were leaning over the railings, romantically looking down at the swans near the waterfall. They were that close together.'

'I don't know what you find amusing,' I protested.

I wished now that I had not confided to Keith how I felt about Lydia Pike. Though I had only spoken to Lydia twice, briefly, she often occupied my most wayward thoughts. As for Llewelyn Rees, that tinkling cymbal, it was scandalous that she should go out with him. He was seventeen, much too old for her. And he had a nasty, irritating habit of vigorously rattling two coins in his pocket when he addressed you.

'Yes,' agreed Keith. 'He's cynical to the extreme.'

Last summer, at grassy Arms Park, when Keith and I were watching Glamorgan play, Rees had told us, 'When it comes to sleeping with women you have to think of three dangers. Babies,

VD and Emotional Entanglements.' We had pondered on this till Keith, who had been trying to read a philosopher called Nietzsche, had replied with slow, studied wisdom, 'When you go to a woman, take a whip with you.'

'Aye,' Llewellyn Rees had said, rattling the coins in his pocket, 'you're right there, sonny.'

As we walked along I kicked a discarded pipe tobacco tin in front of me. Sometimes, when it grittily slid to Keith's side of the noisy pavement, he would take a turn at kicking it. At last, Keith said, 'Llewelyn Rees, I must say, is very goodlooking.'

'He looks like the back of a bus,' I said. 'That's my honest opinion.'

'He's very fast with women, fast as Larwood,' said Keith who, inexplicably, seemed very cheerful. 'I wouldn't be surprised if Lydia Pike let him.'

'What do you mean?' I said, annoyed.

'She often wears dresses with a zip up them.'

'So what?'

'Zips that go all the way down from top to bottom.'

'What are you getting at?' I said. I kicked the tin strenuously. It went into the gutter.

'Buttons are harder than zips,' said Keith, who appeared to be really enjoying himself – so much so that I almost decided to quit the Ethical Atheist Party.

'Body-line bowling, I bet Llewelyn Rees goes in for,' Keith added, 'middle and leg.'

'I don't care,' I affirmed. 'Don't care a damn, one way or the other. I think Lydia Pike's stupid anyway. When I asked her what she thought of the Show Trials in Moscow she thought I was talking about sheepdogs.'

We weren't too far from the echoing railway tunnel. Sometimes I loathed Keith. Perhaps I should suggest we should walk there and shout out for luck, 'I believe in You... You... You.' Besides, just supposing that slogan of extreme narcissism, LOVE ONLY ME, had appeared on the wall like in the Book of Daniel? Like a proxy signature of God?

But Keith suddenly looked depressed. 'You and Lydia,' he said, 'it's hormones, that's all it is, hormones.'

One of my brothers, Leo, was ill in bed with a febrile cold and cough. He would be twenty-one in a month's time. I could not afford to buy a proper present for him so I offered to undertake a favour for him if he so wished. 'You can return these overdue library books for me,' he pronounced. So on the Saturday morning, instead of meeting Keith Thomas, Basil Parr and that gang to kick a football around at the Rec. where they had erected real goalposts, I nobly carried a couple of books to the Roath Branch Library in Newport Road. The titles of the books were *Soviet Democracy* by Pat Sloan and *Freud or Marx, a Dialectical Study* by R. Osborn. Snappy titles, I thought.

Keith in particular would wonder why I had not turned up that windy March morning to play football under the panorama of a mobile blue and white sky (the Cardiff City colours). I would explain things to him later. Going on an errand for a sick elder brother was an exercise in practical ethical atheism, I would argue. So much more valuable than mumbling mumbo-jumbo, droning Hebrew prayers like a window-clinging bee in a humourless sabbath synagogue.

My good deed was rewarded by... by Fate... for Lydia Pike herself happened to be in the foyer of the red-brick library, reading an advertisement on the notice board. My luck was changing. I felt it in my air-filled bones. I approached her, trying to remain cool, but I felt unsafe like water cupped in the hands. Over her shoulder, I observed that the leaflet pinned to the notice board's green billiard cloth advertised THE POWER OF LOVE, *a lecture by the Rev. Trefor Taylor at 8 pm, 12th March.*

'That's tonight,' I dared myself to say out loud, 'sounds quite interesting.'

Lydia Pike turned around, startled. I had never stood so close to her before. I could almost sense the 98.4 degrees Fahrenheit temperature of her body. The book she held in her hand (such an elegant small hand, though she obviously bit her fingernails) was *Sown Among Thorns* by Ethel M. Dell.

'You like that romantic stuff?' I asked.

She focused on what she thought I had been reading and she looked crushed. I wished that I had read a few pages of Leo's books but I merely said, 'I'm just returning these. They're a good read though I don't agree with everything Osborn says about Freud or Marx.'

She nodded. 'I must be going,' she said. 'It's nearly lunchtime.'

'Some romantic novels are better than others,' I said generously.

'Yes. But I expect this one is mush.'

She was about to leave. I released the brakes. I allowed myself to go almost out of control downhill. 'Come with me to this lecture here tonight,' I heard my own voice say impulsively. I was amazed at my own recklessness.

She hesitated. I listened to the residue of silence and a dog outside in the street distantly barking and barking. 'I'm going to wash my hair tonight.'

'Looks clean to me,' I said.

'It is clean,' Lydia said.

'Then what do you want to wash it for?'

The sun must have edged away from a cloud for the library foyer bloomed warmly with spring sunlight. Lydia looked terrific. Even the ordinary seemed beautiful. People with books were clattering in and out of the library, opening and shutting the glass doors. The dog outside stopped barking. I was trying to think of something persuasive to say, a bombshell of a remark. 'Pity,' I said, 'pity that brains and beauty, don't go together.'

'What do you mean?' she asked.

'I mean it's obvious. You're beautiful, but have you got brains as well? Beauty is commonplace. Brains are rare.'

She did not seem offended. She smiled and patted her clean hair.

'I suppose you'd think me brainy if I accept your invitation?' she said.

'Exactly.'

The foyer darkened again. Outside squadrons of clouds must have been racing over like billyo.

'How's Llewelyn Rees?' I asked.

Her eyes widened. 'He's a beast,' she said.

'You're not going out with him any more?'

'How do you know I went out with Llewelyn?'

'I have my spies,' I swanked. 'I've posted 'em up Leckworth Hill, up Cyncoed, down the docks, Victoria Park, Roath Park, behind every bush actually, just to spy on you.'

I could tell by the way she looked at me that I was winning.

'Cardiff's a small place,' she complained. 'You only have to go out with a boy in town and people ask if you're engaged.'

'We don't have to be engaged just to go to a lecture together,' I persuaded her.

'I should learn my lines. I'm playing Jacques in the school play,' she boasted. 'You know – William Shakespeare's *As You Like It*.'

'I don't know it very well,' I fenced. 'We're doing *Macbeth* in our class.'

I would have liked to have asked her to come and see Ginger Rogers and Fred Astaire at the Park Hall but I did not have enough money to splash out on that. The lecture was free and, afterwards, I could afford to buy us both some chips from the fish and chip shop in Clifton Road.

'I'll come if you call off all your spies,' Lydia relented.

'O.K. Great. I'll see you here just before eight.'

After Lydia left the library I wanted to run somewhere – on the pavement, on grass, on sand by the sea, up a rocky mountain, around the block, anywhere. Instead I went through the swing doors like a swaggering, victorious cowboy entering a Hollywood saloon. In the library proper, a tall, bored-looking girl behind the veneered wood of a counter was stamping books with unnecessary vehemence. To my surprise, under a notice, SILENCE PLEASE, I saw my moth-bearded, unkempt Uncle Isidore slumped in a chair asleep. He had a book on his lap.

My Uncle Isidore was a distant foreign relative, not always distant. He was connected to our family by marriage. This lemon-tea Bolshevik, who never did any work, visited members of the family from time to time. Once, my cousin Adam Shepherd had asked him what he did every day. 'Nothing,' Uncle Isidore had replied. 'And I don't do that until after lunch.' My Uncle Max, my Uncle Bertie, young Uncle Eddie and my Dad, all of whom gave him a coin or two after he had eaten a meal, grumbled about his visits for he emitted a distinct smell like a continuous signal. Moreover, he was given to uttering cryptic Talmudic or kabbalistic remarks like, 'What is below is above and what is inside is outside so the circle closes before and behind' or 'By dawn, the golem turns back to dust', even though nobody had said anything to prompt such an opinion. Most of the family agreed that he, though erudite, was meshuggah, a bit off his head. Sometimes, Uncle Isidore would play a tune on my father's violin. He had to be heard to be believed. He must have been the worst violin player in the world. Tone deaf, he made my father's playing sound like Yehudi Menuhin's. Uncle made dead catgut sound like live cat when he scraped out 'My Yiddisher Momma' or 'The Red Flag'. I was certainly glad he did not exit from the library while I was talking to Lydia. She would have thought him to be a tramp. He would not, repeat not, have made a good impression on Lydia Pike.

Quickly, I took a novel for myself so that it should be stamped before he woke up. I chose Llewelyn Powys' *Apples be Ripe* because of the epigraph on the flyleaf:

Apples be ripe
Nuts be brown
Petticoats up
Trousers down.

The girl behind the counter gave the book a knock-out blow with her stamp.

After supper I went up the stairs (two at a time) to ask Leo if he wanted anything. 'Justice,' he said. Then I went into the bathroom to spruce myself up before meeting Lydia Pike. The healthiest smell in the world, my mother frequently opined, especially after a visit from Uncle Isidore, is the smell of Lifebuoy soap. Maybe yes, maybe no. Anyway I gave the Palmolive soap a go under my armpits before putting my shirt back on. Afterwards I made faces at the mercilessly tactless mirror. What a shame I wasn't better-looking. How nice to be handsome like Cary Grant or Ray Milland or Ronald Colman or even Llewelyn Rees.

My mother was the eye-catching one in our house. As she never tired of telling her four children, when she first walked out with my father the whole population of the Swansea village of Ystalyfera cried out in fearful unison, 'There goes Beauty and the Beast.' I wished I looked more like Mam and less like Dad.

I was trying to delete a prominent blackhead on my forehead when I heard the bell ring again downstairs. All through supper there had been front door interruptions. First some gypsies had come, trying to sell their wooden pegs; then, a very short man, wearing a cap and carrying strings of onions over his shoulders, chatted to my mother in his Breton patois. She responded in Welsh. Johnny Onions and she understood each other to a T. Now, though, from the hall I could hear Keith's voice. 'He's upstairs,' I heard my mother say.

My Mam always welcomed Keith warmly ever since my friend's mother had died. She was very sentimental about 'Keith, poor boy', and very condemnatory of his father's drinking habits. Now I could hear them having a desultory conversation about the vase of daffodils next to the telephone on the hallstand. Aren't they nice?' Keith said, pie-in-his-mouth. 'From the garden?'

'My favourite flowers,' my mother said. 'They're very pleasant. This lot look as if they could fly off like canaries, don't you think?' Then my mother called my name. 'Keith's here,' she shouted.

It was my turn to grin like a greyhound for I had news for Keith. I could not go out on a Saturday-night loafing expedition with him, promenading up and down past the closed but lit shop windows opposite Albany Road School, hoping against hope that we might meet somebody interesting or that we would witness something extraordinary happen – a house on fire maybe, or a huge, white, riderless horse bolting towards City Road. No, none of that. I had an appointment. Within one hour I would be sitting, happy as blancmange, jelly and trifle, next to Lydia Pike, no less, listening to a sexy-minded (with luck) priest expound on The Power of Love. Still, Keith, if he wished, could walk me part of the way down Newport Road.

'Gosh, you look tidy,' my mother said when I came down the stairs. 'Have you got warm enough things on? It's cold outside and I don't want you to catch a flu like Leo.'

'There's an icy wind,' Keith agreed.

'Have you got your vest on?' my mother probed.

I could see Keith smirking superiorly. 'Don't fuss, Mam,' I said.

'All right,' she said, 'but don't slam that front door when you leave. You make it slam like a cannon every time you go out these days.'

I shut the front door behind me, softly as a burglar. Outside I felt free – like a smile restored. Soon we were walking past the White Wall, past the three-storeyed houses with their smoking chimneys, past the tall bare trees of Newport Road and the accusatory lit lamp-posts. Keith had looked glum when I told him my news but suddenly he seemed to cheer up. 'I wouldn't mind hearing this lecture myself,' he said, inspired.

'No,' I said.

'It's a free country.'

'No,' I said.

'Why not?'

'No.'

'I won't sit next to you, honest.'

'No.'

A light became active in the front room of one of the houses. We looked through the shocking transparency of the windows. We were two spies working for the British Secret Service, Ethical Atheist Division. A man crouched on the carpet, crouched mending something. Or praying? What was he doing? We could not see his face, only the top of his head. Perhaps Keith and I had been fated to walk this way, at this moment, merely to corroborate some story? An old woman appeared at the window. She was dressed in Mediterranean black. She pulled the curtains, blinding us like a cataract to whatever illuminating event was being enacted within.

We walked on under a sky tremendous with stars, past the railings and hedges of dark front gardens. 'You know what makes women go wild?' said Keith, after a thoughtful silence.

'What?'

'Their ears,' Keith said. 'Kiss their ears and they go wild.'

'Lips are best,' I said.

Keith stopped, looked upwards. Above us the clouds sped over the moon – broken like ectoplasm in the night sky. 'If I were you, given 'alf a chance,' Keith advised me solemnly, 'I'd kiss Lydia's ears. Women's ears are very sensitive.'

'Who told you that?'

'I've heard.'

I'd never seen Cary Grant or Ray Milland kiss Myrna Loy's ears. Not once. 'Rubbish,' I said.

The lit jewellery of a tram rocked by, the top of its long diagonal pole sparking a gunpowder plot on the overhead wires.

'Stick your tongue in her ears,' Keith said. 'She'll go bonkers.'

'What?'

'Stick your tongue in her ear.'

'Ach y fee,' I said.

We were getting quite near to the library. I was beginning to feel nervous like when I opened the batting for St Illtyd's Junior XI. Or like that elongated moment before an important school examination when the appointed invigilator stares at you with unfounded suspicion. 'She's really neat,' I said of Lydia, reminding myself how fortunate I was.

'She's got a fat bum,' said Keith.

'She hasn't.'

'Quite a fat bum.'

'I like fat bums,' I said. 'Anyway she hasn't got one.'

Keith shrugged his shoulders, turned. I thought for a moment that he was going to shake hands with me – as if I were about to undertake some dangerous mission, a reconnoitre into mine-planted enemy territory. Instead he said, 'Don't do anything I wouldn't do.'

'What?'

'If you can't be good be careful.'

Then he walked back the way we had come. I felt sorry for him. His father was probably at the pub. It was Saturday night and he had nowhere to go. I walked on... to my Destiny. I heard him whistling in the distance the tune of 'Alone. Alone on this night meant for two. Alone.'

The lecture took place in the high cavernous Reading Room where rows of chairs had been arranged between the newspaper stacks, their titles boldly displayed: *Daily Mail, Daily Herald, Western Mail, News Chronicle, Manchester Guardian.* Lydia and I sat down at the back. I counted only seventeen people in front of us. Then I was dismayed to see Uncle Isidore taking a seat near the front. He must have stayed at the library most of the day. One way to keep warm perhaps? I hoped he would not turn round and recognise me. I wondered whether, prophylactically, I should explain to Lydia my relationship to him. I called him Uncle but he wasn't really an uncle – he was not a brother of either my mother or father. I knew there was something shameful about wanting to disown him – yet what would Lydia think if he approached me familiarly, emitting his amazingly noxious body odours and stale tobacco intimacies and uttering some baffling idiotic remark like, 'The end is in the beginning just as the flame is attached to the coal.'? I did not wish Lydia to think there was lunacy in the family; and just supposing, just supposing she happened to be a teeny-weeny bit anti-semitic? If so,

I could say goodbye to my present compulsive ambition in life – which was to kiss Lydia smack on the lips – Keith and his ear theory notwithstanding.

The chairman briefly introduced the Rev. Trefor Taylor who had an extraordinary complexion. The skin on his cheeks looked as if it had been grafted from his scrotum. 'The power of love,' the priest began, 'the power of love, divine or profane, can be illustrated by so many scriptural and historical examples.' He then proceeded to reel off at length half a dozen from each of those sources. He only became interesting after about half an hour when he spoke about Philippe Pinel who was to become Napoleon's doctor.

It seemed that, in 1793, the insane were chained and abused dreadfully. (I glanced at Uncle Isidore to see how he was taking that bit of information.) Dr Pinel, to demonstrate the power of love, unchained a certain English captain whose history nobody knew but who had been chained in his cell for forty years. The keepers kept their distance from him for, in a fury, he had already killed one of them with a blow from his manacles. 'Pinel entered the cell unattended,' the Rev. Trefor Taylor told us. At this point, in order to engender suspense, the scrotum-faced priest reached for the glass of water on the table, lifted it to his mouth, sipped from it deliberately, swallowed so that his Adam's apple rose like a yo-yo, before returning the glass to the table. He continued in the persona of Dr Pinel. 'Captain, I'll order your chains to be taken off and give you liberty if you promise not to harm anyone.'

It was now that I took Lydia's hand in mine. She did not withdraw it, she was too absorbed by the priest's dramatic presentation of how the maniac's chains were removed, how Dr Pinel left without closing the cell door behind him. She leant forward, her chin lifted, her eyes staring at the platform. She was wearing a blouse and skirt – not a zip in sight.

'The maniac raised himself several times from his chair but fell back each time,' the Rev. Taylor declared, 'for he'd been in a sedentary position so long he'd lost the use of his legs. It took him a quarter of an hour to stand up and keep his balance. Then he tottered to the door of his dark cell. He looked up at the sky and uttered, "How beautiful, how beautiful." All day he kept moving outside his cell, exclaiming his delight and wonder till, in the evening, of his own free will, he returned to the cell to sleep tranquilly. Yes. That little act of love by Dr Pinel counted for so much that...'

'The power of love,' shouted out Uncle Isidore.

'Exactly right,' the priest said, not wishing to be interrupted.

My hand was getting very hot and sticky but Lydia did not seem to mind. Unfortunately, when the meeting concluded and a vote of thanks had been uttered by the chairman (who some time in his life had been irrevocably demagnetised), Uncle Isidore rose and stood by the door, pulling at the bird's nest of his beard. He continued to stand there like a bloody doorman. He had seen me all right. As we shuffled towards the exit I bent my head down, staring at my shoes as if there were something wrong with them. Lydia was by my side. As we approached, Uncle's marshy odour became notice-able. I kept my head down but Uncle gargled, 'Hello, Dan.' I looked up in the opposite direction, towards Lydia who, however, seemed to be staring at my rags-and-bones uncle. We had just about passed him when he called out a little louder, 'At dawn, Dan, the golem turns back to dust.'

Outside in the street Lydia said, 'Who was that funny old tramp? He knew you.'

'I don't think so,' I said.

'He called you by name, I think.'

'What name?'

'Your name.'

'No, no,' I said. 'Let's get some chips.'

After we had eaten our chips, before we reached Lydia's house in Colchester Avenue, I mentioned casually that I was Jewish.

'Jews are being persecuted in Germany,' said Lydia, as if this were not generally known. Then, immediately, she asked me, 'How did you know I went out with Llewelyn Rees? Really. Did he tell you?'

Considering she had decided he was a vile beast and that she would never see him again ever, he did seem to fascinate her. She kept bringing him into our conversation. I kept on thinking of the graffito in the railway tunnel, LOVE ONLY ME. When next she happened to mention that squirt Rees I changed the conversation in the blink of an eye. 'Do you enjoy acting in Shakespeare?' I asked.

'S all right,' she said. 'But I keep forgetting the lines.'

'They're good lines though,' I said. 'Definitely.'

'Yes,' agreed Lydia.

Suddenly she stopped walking. 'It's ten o'clock...' she said.

'No, it isn't,' I said, startled. 'Not yet.'

'It is ten o'clock,' she recited, 'thus may we see – quoth he – how the world wags: 'Tis but an hour ago since it was nine. And after one hour more 'twill be eleven: And so, from hour to hour, we ripe and ripe, And then from hour to hour, we rot and rot. And thereby hangs a tale.'

'Brilliant,' I said. 'Absolutely brilliant. I think you'd make an excellent actress.'

'Thank you,' she said.

At her front gate in Colchester Avenue she hesitated for a while but I received no clear signals. Still, I arranged to see her again before she turned and went into the house. At the porch she waved. That was it.

Keith would probably ask me if I had kissed her goodnight, if I had had a go at her ears.

'No,' I would tell him. 'Slowly, slowly. I'm going fishing with a big net for this brilliant actress. It'll take time before she joins our Ethical Atheist Party.'

God, if he was there, was not pleased with me. For, while we were eating our Sunday lunch who should ring the front doorbell but Uncle Isidore. Mother made a place for him at the table and he sipped noisily at the knaidlach and chicken soup as if he were a deaf man. He spoilt my dinner because I feared he might tell the family how I had snubbed him. When he put down his spoon he said, 'I've been thinking. I've been thinking how all human history begins with exile, with Adam's banishment from Paradise. But soup like this, Kate, comes from Paradise itself.'

'It's Wilfred's favourite,' my mother said. 'Pity he's not home to have some.'

'Wilfred?' asked Uncle Isidore, puzzled.

'My eldest brother,' I reminded him.

I wished I had not spoken. He turned his hairy face towards mine and fixed me with his moist, accusatory, chocolate eyes. He was going to spill the beans, surely? But he hardly spoke during the rest of the meal, not until mother served us raisin and *lokshen* pudding.

Then, addressing me directly, he said, 'A golem is mute. A golem that speaks might bring about the death of God.'

'Leo's in bed with flu,' my father replied, obviously feeling he had to respond in some way.

'Flu!' Uncle Isidore pronounced contemptuously. 'Flu! That comes and goes but my arthritis, it's getting worse. Worse and worse. In the mornings I'm stiff as a poker. I know how old Job felt at dawn. Leo's lucky. We should all get our illnesses when we're young and healthy.'

The meal over, Uncle Isidore took his lemon tea away from the table and to my father's dismay sat in his chair. 'Get your violin out,' said Uncle Isidore. 'Do you feel like a bit of music?'

'Oy gevalt,' my mother said.

'Some strings are broken,' Dad lied.

'Strings? Who needs all the strings?' said Uncle, dribbling on his beard. 'It's an imperfect world.'

My father rose from the table and pushed a chair towards Uncle Isidore. 'Sit here, it's comfortable,' my father said.

'Don't worry yourself,' my uncle replied.

My father stood indecisively, his face a blank. 'Sit down,' Uncle continued.

'Dad likes the chair you're sitting on,' I explained".

Uncle Isidore sighed. '*Pace*, your father wants. *Pace*. He'll have his chair back soon enough. A little patience. If nothing else, four thousand years of Jewish history should have taught him patience.'

Later that afternoon, when I was seeing Uncle Isidore out, when we were alone in the hall, near the front door, he said to me softly, 'You needn't have been ashamed of my seeing you with that young girl. I'm broadminded, you know. Just because she had a lot of make-up on doesn't necessarily make me think she's a slut. Look, my boy, be yourself, never pretend to be other than you are. Don't be ashamed of things.'

'You're right, Uncle,' I said, grinning like a greyhound, 'you're absolutely right.'

'The power of love,' Uncle Isidore said, winking. 'I understand.'

Focus 1938: Vienna

The tall corpulent man wearing an extraordinarily ornate, heavy blue dressing gown was restlessly returning to the bookcase, arranging and re-arranging files, manuscripts, photographs of death masks. He was interrupted in this obsessional occupation, a ridiculous one in view of what was about to happen, by his housekeeper, Hermine, who asked, 'Dr Friedell, shall I take Schnack for a walk?'

Egon Friedell's career had been unpredictable. He kept changing disguises. He had studied philosophy but he became a cabaret turn, a sophisticated comic in Vienna's nightclubs; then he became an actor in the legitimate theatre; then, after he wrote his five-act play, *The Judas Tragedy*, he had been labelled The Austrian Shaw. More recently, he had become celebrated as the author of the three thick volumes that now lay on his desk, *A Cultural History of the Modern Age*.

As soon as his housekeeper had left the apartment with the dog, Egon Friedell, with trembling hands, locked the door. He knew the SS men would arrive this night. Hopeless, it was hopeless. He felt hot and cold at the same time. Though sweating, he shivered. The other side of the door, on the landing, as Hermine went down the stairs, he could hear Schnack barking. Absurdly, he recalled that engraving which had been so beloved by Schopenhauer, the one that portrayed a soldier about to be despatched by a firing squad selflessly waving a cloth to frighten away his dog from the line of fire.

It was Schopenhauer who had written that the whole civilised world was but a masquerade. And for him, Egon Friedell PhD, had it not all been one endless dissimulation? Masks! Masks! Not only as an actor had he worn them. Even when he had been a student at Heidelberg studying philosophy and natural science, he had had a deep interest in deceptions, in things and creatures that were not what they seemed – like the whale, that hunted mammal posing as a fish. Besides, did not the gods themselves wear masks? When Jupiter was in love he came disguised as a bull, as a shower of gold, as a singing swan, as a cloud – yet never, never, would Jupiter come as Jupiter. But now it was time for him to take off the last mask.

'Revealing what?' he asked out loud and heard the bitterness in his own voice.

His mother, when he had changed his name to Friedell, when he had ceased to be a Jew, when he had become a Christian – out of belief, not convenience, he had insisted – when he had defended the Gospel against Mosaic subversion, had simply said softly, without accusation, 'You've put a knife in your father's heart. You're neither fish nor fowl.'

Those in Vienna – they thought of him as 'a character' because of his noisy presence; because he affected a monocle and a huge, twirling pipe; because he drank so much, ate so much; because he had trained his dog to tear any newspaper which carried an adverse notice of his theatre performance into small pieces; because he demanded that, on the playbills, they added PhD after his name; because on his recent sixtieth birthday he had sent to each of his friends who had remembered the occasion a printed card with an identical message on it: *Of all congratulations received, yours has pleased me most.* Yes, they thought him a character because they did not know what his true character was.

Egon Friedell, in abject misery, but a little calmer now, moved to the window. It was dark outside, the light snow on the ground hardening. Two evenings earlier on Friday, down in the street, lorry after lorry had passed by, open lorries with hooligan Nazis, Austrians, waving swastika banners, shouting, faces naked below helmets, faces wearing peaked caps, screaming, 'Kill the Jews, kill the Jews, Juda Verreke...'. And now that the Germans had invaded Austria, many of Friedell's neighbours had already joined the torch-light procession to Vienna's centre, had thrust out Nazi Party flags from their high windows.

'*Sieg Heil. Heil Hitler. Ein Volk, ein Reich, ein Fuhrer.*' The mindless, terrible roar of it.

Only a few weeks earlier, the day before his sixtieth birthday, he had told his friend Alfred Polgar at the coffee house, that no no no, he would not try to escape if the unthinkable happened, if Austria was invaded. He had made up his mind. 'I feel so guilty,' he had added quietly.

'You're depressed because you're sixty tomorrow. Egon, you must prepare. You pay no attention to reality. You prefer to take a walk into the Past.'

The unthinkable had happened. And yes, he had made up his mind – to take a walk – had made up his mind weeks ago. He would take a walk through the open window now facing him. He would walk until he dropped down past four floors in the silence between one heartbeat and the next. How true those lines of Rilke:

We are all falling. This hand's falling too –
all have this falling sickness none withstands.
And yet there's One whose gently-holding hands
this universal falling can't fall through.

Down below, a car's oncoming headlights. The car stopped precisely outside his front door. The window glass on which he had been breathing had partly misted over. With his finger he wrote on it, as he had when a child, his authentic name: EGON FRIED-MAN. He was crying, he could not stop crying. He was crying, a grown man crying and crying. They were breaking down the door when he opened the window.

Artificial Flowers

That moonless February night I was on the wrong side of Roath Park Lake when the undulating air-raid hooter groaned on and on. It was like an eerie, gigantic howl of an animal, not of this world, that had suffered terrible and irrevocable loss. In the dark, I passed a silent middle-aged couple who carried a black-out torch and, soon after, the Ack Ack guns began to conduct their noisy, insane orchestration of dissonant explosions as they aimed at some distant, hesitant drone hardly audible in the sky.

The small railings and large gates of the Park had been dismantled, taken away, iron for the war effort. Entering the blackness of the park I walked homeward faster as the long white verticals of the searchlights hunted in panic for the oncoming bombers. Nobody else seemed to be about. I used to like leaning, at night, on the railings overlooking the lake, listening to the occasional forlorn cry of nightfowl and to the rushing of the water as it descended down the long waterfalls.

By the time I reached the west side of the lake and ascended the sloping, dark, narrow back lanes, I was running; for, alarmed, I could hear great menacing cracks and clangs of metal hitting metal. It was shrapnel, I presumed, striking the dustbins that had been placed outside the back doors of the houses of Lake Road West. I ran through the lonely blackness of the lane awkwardly – awkwardly because my right arm was in a sling, my collarbone having been broken the previous Saturday morning while playing rugby for the school. I jogged the joint as I ran so that my shoulder ached; but now the heavy iron clamour of guns and bombs, indistinguishable from each other, became tremendous.

My father, who had gone to visit my Uncle Bertie and Aunt Cecile, had not yet come home. Since my cousin Clive had been missing at Dunkirk my father went to see them much more often. And my mother who did not approve of Uncle Bertie because of his pugnacity and willingness to get into fights – real fights, bare-fisted fights – had even softened towards him. But now she was annoyed that my father had delayed at his brother's house in

Llandaff. She was awaiting our return anxiously, and because of the explosions our black mongrel, Caliban, had settled himself under the side-board, rolling a white eye now and again. The smash of rooted and aerial explosions subsided but the All Clear did not sound. Mother served me a bit of supper and Caliban, with minimal enthusiasm, wagged his tail a few times when he emerged from his cwtch.

'There was shrapnel falling out of the sky, hitting the dustbins in the lane,' I said. 'Several times. Clang, clang, clang. I hate to think...'

'It's bad enough me worrying about them,' my mother said, nodding at the sideboard that carried photographs of my two brothers, Wilfred in army uniform and Leo in the RAF. 'You shouldn't have been out, a night like this. Stupid. Your father has a duty to see Bertie and Cecile now that Cecile is in such a state with Clive lost. But where've you been? Chasing girls? What for?'

I knew what for.

'I'm in now,' I said.

'And your arm in a sling. You're seventeen. You may be the baby of the family but you don't have to behave like one.'

'Well, I'm home now.'

'You could have been killed. I'm going to speak to your father. Night-prowling during air raids is ridiculous.'

'The air-raid warning hadn't sounded when I went out,' I argued rationally.

'Good night, with a broken collarbone, you should be taking it easy.' My mother relented. 'You want some more soup?' she asked.

I nodded and reached for a Penguin I was reading.

My father felt it was my own fault that I had broken my collarbone. He rarely scolded me. But when he'd returned to the house last Saturday to find me sorry for myself, in some discomfort, my arm in a sling, he had gone off the handle. He'd shouted, 'You're useless. You shouldn't play rugby if you're no good. You can't be any good if you get injured all the time. Daft, you are. Hopeless.' And, crazily, he strode out of the room slamming the door emphatically behind him. It was as if *he* had been injured. 'He doesn't mean it,' my mother said. 'He's just worried about you.'

Perhaps he was right about me not being skilful enough at rugby. On that frosty Saturday morning when St Illtyd's played Canton

High School, the whistle had signalled a scrum. The packs in their coloured jerseys, their multiple breaths all visibly fleeing in the air, had bent down, locked themselves together, heaved, and the ball had come out sweetly. I must have called out 'Kevin' as I darted forward on the blind side to receive the oval against my chest with my right hand. Too slow. Even though I accelerated I had been tackled high, my arms pinned so that I had fallen on the frosted ground on my right shoulder. I had heard clearly a noise that I had never heard before: the queer distinct click of a human bone snapping, my own bone snapping.

Mother kept glancing at the clock. She was worried about my father. Supposing this, supposing that? He should have been home for supper by now, ready to listen to Lord Haw Haw on the wireless afterwards and to mutter, 'Damned liar'. He was late. He was very late. My mother had her hands over her face. On a Friday night, when she lit the Sabbath candles, she would shut her eyes, put her two hands over her face, and say a prayer. Was that what she was doing now? Praying that her husband would be home soon, safe and sound; that the war would be over and won, so that my sister Huldah in London would not have to endure more air raids and that my two elder brothers would be demobilised and back in Wales? Maybe she was even thanking God that her youngest son had not just been struck by shrapnel.

Not that my mother was a worrying person. About most things she was absurdly optimistic. She had the confidence of a woman who, all her life, had been flattered because of her physical appearance. She told us all, often enough, how everybody agreed that she had once been the most beautiful girl in the Swansea Valley. 'Now I'm the wreck of the *Hesperus*,' she was fond of adding, confident that she would be contradicted.

My mother took her hands away from her face. 'That Hitler,' she said, 'that swine. So many, so many people, children too, little children maimed or killed because of him and his evil gang.'

I resumed reading *Penguin New Writing* (No 2) which had just been published. I read the poems first: 'June Thunder' by Louis MacNeice; 'For Me There is No Dismay' by C. Day Lewis; and 'Huesca' by John Cornford whom I knew had been killed while fighting for the International Brigade in Spain. I admired their poems. I wrote poems too, not as good as these of course, but my

English master at school reckoned that when I wrote essays I had a style of my own. I kept my poetry writing a secret. I had a reputation to keep up. I played rugby for the 1st XV and poetry was thought by my friends to be a cissy thing. I turned to an autobiographical piece in *Penguin New Writing* by B.L. Coombes about colliers going on night shift, going up to the colliery mouth. Then I heard the noise of the front door being opened. My mother immediately went into the kitchen to fetch my father's supper.

My father, hugely excited, said to me, 'Come outside. Good God, you've never seen anything like it.'

Inside our blacked-out living room we had no awareness of the quality of the light outside. I expected to see long searchlights once more probing the occasional cloud, and the stars above them, as usual, neutral, imperturbable. But outside the stars were not visible – it was too light. It was a strange, green, phosphorescent light – the flares dropped by German bombers so bright that everything, every detail of every image could be seen as in daylight. The moon – where was it? – poured itself out a sickly green. As in some eerie dream, the houses of Windermere Avenue stood there in this peculiar green light, and the road too, gutters and pavement and all, waited artificially green. That green, counterfeited, intensified light, had it been spawned by simple flares? Or had green firebombs been dropped? Or had the German's discovered some secret, terrible, green weapon? Green deathrays?

'Come in, you two,' my mother at the front door was shouting. 'Come in, are you mad?'

And Mr Davies, our neighbour the air-raid warden who had suddenly appeared, also urged us to take shelter. 'Look,' Dad said. 'Look at the lake, it's green.' It seemed the Germans had mistaken the water of Roath Park Lake for the docks. Anyway, the bombs were soon whistling down and we sat under the staircase while Caliban resumed his position beneath the sideboard.

After a bomb exploded perilously close my father struggled to pin up his raincoat against the wall window, sensibly concerned about flying glass. I watched him uselessly, my arm in a sling. No sooner had my father rejoined us under the stairs than we heard the whistle-whine that did not seem to stop but continued on and on, nearer and nearer, louder and louder until I was flung, I think – as no doubt my parents were – yards into the air. I don't know how long it was before I felt wetness against my face. It was Caliban licking me.

It was silent. As if something had been strangulated. What was wrong? What had happened to the blackout? I could see a circum-scribed green, stange light that should not have been there. Obviously there was a hole, a large gap in the wall. Also part of the ceiling had collapsed. Now, outside, someone was thinly screaming. That greenness, that peculiar, unlikely, threatening light, I could not at first make it out. It was as if gangrene had come into our dazed house. 'Are you alright?' I heard my mother call and then my father's voice answering, steady, reassuring us.

The cottage hospital, on the outskirts of Cardiff, had only two small wards – one male, one female; in fact, the male area with its five beds was less a ward than an odd-shaped alcove. A long polished table which carried vases of flowers divided three beds from the two occupied by Rod and myself. From a stretch of parquet floor the walls lifted vertically white and undecorated to a whiter ceiling. 'Ah, the serenity of a blank wall,' Dr Pike would utter. A window opposite my bed overlooked a bare, utterly still, winter tree and the top of a grey wall that one would expect a cat to walk along. Above and beyond it, distantly, a sky usually as grey as the wall. Alas, I could not stare that way easily as I had been elastically bandaged up, my right hand flat against my left chest, and ordered to lie back, a sandbag between my shoulders. So my best view was of the ceiling. It seemed a radical form of treatment for one with only a broken collarbone and mere transient bruises. I was told by Sister Tomlinson, though, that I was very privileged to have such treat-ment. I would have a nice, healed, straight collarbone, without any disfigurement, without any ugly bumps in it, she promised me. 'They give this sort of beauty treatment to those Hollywood cowboys who fall off their horses and break their clavicles,' she said. 'Tom Mix and Gary Cooper, their collarbones are straight as die now because they had the same sandbag treatment as you.'

Dr Pike, who was waiting to be called up into the Forces, was also pleased with me. I was his first war casualty. When he discov-ered that in the Sixth Form I was studying the pre-medical subjects, biology, chemistry and physics, and planned one day to be a doctor like my brother Wilfred, like my uncle Max, and that I was already

70

saving up money to buy thousands of sandbags for future patients with broken clavicles, he delayed at my bedside to explain 'The knitting of broken bones, when the ends are placed in opposition and set – do you follow me? – remains one of the mysteries of the healing process.' He jabbed a finger at me as if I were taking an oral examination. 'How do the bone cells know they must manufacture extra cells to bridge the breaks to form a callus? And by what token do they know when to stop proliferating?'

'I don't know,' I admitted.

'Exactly,' he said. And rose, smiling, victorious, to turn to speak to Rodney Price who lay in a grotesquely tortured posture in the next bed to me.

'And how's Rod today?' I heard Dr Pike say. 'On the mend, eh? Are you comfortable?'

Rodney Price hardly looked comfortable. Compared with him I was floating on water. His right leg swathed in a Hodgen splint had been hoisted up by a pulley affair to an angle of forty degrees. His bed seemed more a vehicle than a bed, what with its uprights, pulleys and weights. Moreover, it had been tilted, the farther end raised up a foot from the parquet floor and surrounded by a Balkan frame; so that if someone had fired a starting gun surely Rod, one leg in the air, his right foot dorsi-flexed in a stirrup, would have taken off, across the polished table, above the three beds opposite, and smashed through the window to fly in his bed over the grey wall and zoom over Glamorgan.

'I'm browned off, Doctor,' I heard Rod say.

'Aye, exactly,' said Dr Pike wisely. 'I bet you won't be in a hurry to get on your motorbike again.'

After Dr Pike quit the ward, Rod Price spoke to me for the first time. 'That doctor is pig-ignorant,' he said. 'How long did 'e say you'd be by 'ere?'

'It takes weeks for a collarbone to heal,' I said.

'Six months for a femur,' Rod groaned. 'I've been 'ere venyer three months now. According to 'im I have a nasty fracture of the shaft of my femur. But anatomically speaking I doubt if 'e knows 'is 'ead from 'is arse. 'E's pompous as 'ell too.'

'Six months!' I said, sympathetically.

'After three months,' Rod said mournfully, 'you feel you could fuck a stoat. Ah that bloody Wolseley, driven by some berk of a colonel in civvy clothes, coming round the bend of Leckwith Hill on the wrong side of the road. An' you?'

'Air raid,' I said proudly. 'Our house got bombed.'

'Anybody killed?' asked Rodney Price, somewhat hopefully I thought.

'My mother and father only got bruised. But the ARP warden, our neighbour, had it.'

'Got killed?'

'Yes.'

'I wish they'd bomb this bloody place,' said Rod, suddenly seething.

He scowled round the ward and unpredictably shouted out, ''Itler, do us a favour an' bomb us all to smithereens.'

At the other side of the polished table the man they called Ginger sat upright in his bed and called back, 'Shut your 'ead. We're all fed up with you. Boastin' all the time and tellin' lies.'

I could see Rod flush. 'You,' he screamed. 'You. If I wasn't shackled by 'ere I'd bloody do you.'

Ginger laughed. 'You and what army,' he said, just like a kid.

'The Salvation Army,' shouted Rod.

The bed in the corner being empty, there were only four of us in the ward: Rodney Price; Iowerth 'Ginger' Morgan who always looked as happy as a guillotine; old deaf Dai Davies, an ex-miner; and myself. Every morning Rod would shout out to old Dai, 'How are you this mornin', Dai?' and every morning he would reply, 'Duw, my breath is bad today.' Otherwise, being almost totally deaf, he hardly joined in the occasional disconnected conversations and desultory quarrels of mornings, afternoons, long evenings. He never responded when the clock-ticking silence was punctuated by the general quipping of Sister Tomlinson or straight-backed Nurse James who was known as 'the Iceberg', or the very English nurse, Dorothy Briggs who, according to Rod, looked like an 'orse. 'Like an 'orse, definitely.'

White-faced, haggard Ginger Morgan and conventionally hand-some Rodney Price seemed to hate each other. Ginger's starved appearance was the result of his being, until recently, on a milk drip because of a troublesome duodenal ulcer. Milk, only milk, and then more milk had been dripped into his stomach. But after Dr Pike had taken the tubes out and he had been allowed solid nourishment, his

72

old bellicosity had returned, prompt and red-haired. Once he even quarrelled about Rodney's name. 'With a name like that you can't be real Welsh,' Ginger megaphoned. 'If you were Welsh you'd be called Rhodri, spelt R,H,O,D,R,I.'

'I know how to spell my own name, you git,' cried Rod. 'Mind you, if I had a name like Iowerth I'd be glad to be called Ginger.'

Rodney's laugh was made of bile. He only stopped laughing when Ginger Morgan got out of bed and shuffled around the long table.

''Ere I come, 'ere I come, 'ere I come to get you,' he chanted.

'You come by 'ere, Frankenstein,' yelled Rod, 'an' you'll be buried without honours.'

''Ere I come, 'ere I come –'

Sister Tomlinson entered the ward at this moment, so sheepishly Ginger shuffled back to bed again as Sister Tomlinson watched him, her hand on her hip.

'He was goin' to ask me for a dance, I think,' murmured Rod to me. 'A tango or a rhumba. Know that song? "'Twas all over my jeal-ous-y." Ta-ra-ra-ra.'

Since our beds were quite close to each other I chatted, when I chatted at all, mostly to Rod. Though I was still only a schoolboy he seemed anxious to tell me about his girlfriends. 'If this leg don't mend soon some other swine will be shaggin' 'em,' he sighed. He told me about Betty and Gwen and Sandra who worked with him in the munitions factory at Bridgend. 'They think I look like Alan Ladd,' he smirked.

One evening he pulled out from his wallet a sheaf of snapshots of girls – not only of Betty who apparently was an heiress of some sort – though that was a secret – and Gwen, whom he had once saved from drowning at Lavernock and Sandra, who, it seemed, excitedly frothed at the mouth whenever he came near her, but also photos of all his 'ex's' as he called them. My mother said my cousin Adam Shepherd was so mad about girls he needed bromides, and my Uncle Eddie had the reputation of knowing too many chorus girls, but obviously they were relatively celibate monks compared with Rod.

I stared enviously at girls complacent in ATS uniform, girls in bathing costumes, landgirls, girls in close-up, girls reclining on grass looking at Rod's camera rather expectantly. And I wished I was as good-looking as Rod and didn't have this repeated tendency to have pimples appear on my forehead.

'All these are ex-girlfriends?' I asked.

'Yes,' he said. 'I've shagged the lot.'

'This is a pretty one,' I said.

'Mmm,' he said, 'but 'er vagina's too short.'

I handed the snapshots back. I remembered how Ginger had said Rod was the biggest liar west of Chepstow. All the same those girls in their different poses did have an invitingly friendly, soft, moist, post-coital look about them. 'You'll see Betty or Gwen or Sandra on Sunday afternoon,' Rod said. They sometimes take it in turns to visit me. I used to take it in turns to visit 'em.' And again he laughed until Ginger shouted out, 'Don't believe a word he says. Been showing you photos, has he? Next thing he'll be telling you about what' e found once in a dustbin. Go on, tell the kid what you found in a dustbin.'

'I'll tell 'im what I like,' Rod said.

''E's incredible, utterly incredible,' Ginger appealed to deaf Dai Davies.

For a moment or two the ward was silent. But then Rodney Price, lowering his voice, murmured, 'I shouldn't 'ave told 'im. I just said that my leg is no more useful than a leg I found last April in a dustbin.'

'A leg you found in a dustbin?' I repeated.

'I did,' Rod said. 'They're building a camp, a special camp for the girls working at the munitions factory in Bridgend. Well, there was an explosion, see. Anyway, I can't go into it, I'm sworn to secrecy. That's why it's 'ardly believable, fair play. But I'll tell you this, mun, if the war wasn't on it would 'ave been front page news like. An' it was me that set this investigation off.'

'What investigation?' I asked.

'Can't tell you any more,' said Rod discreetly. 'And when Gwen or Sandra or Betty visits me next Sunday, mum's the word, OK? I shouldn't 'ave said anything. It's all 'ush 'ush. We don't want to 'elp the bloody Germans, do we?'

We did not see any visitors on Sunday afternoon for Geraint Griffiths was admitted to the ward on Saturday morning and, at once, screens were placed around his corner bed. After Dr Pike came in to examine him, he told us that because Mr Griffiths had a suspected viral meningitis the ward would be in quarantine.

'Though a viral meningitis, unlike a bacterial meningitis, is benign,' Dr Pike said, 'Better to be on the safe side. So no visitors for the present.'

After he left, followed dutifully by Sister Tomlinson, Rod muttered to me, 'This is a blow. This is a personal blow to me. It don't matter to them. They don't get any visitors worth speakin' about anyway. Who'd want to visit that Ginger git by there? But me, every Sunday afternoon I look forward to seein' one of my 'arem.'

'I was hoping to see my mother and father,' I said.

'That's not the same, is it?' Rod said, and he lapsed for a moment into a depressive silence before continuing, 'I been thinkin'. This isn't the first time that pig-ignorant doctor do stop visitors comin'. 'Avin' no visitors makes it easier for the staff, see. At the drop of an 'at, 'e stops visitors. 'E should be in the SS, that bloody doctor.'

Gradually Rodney Price worked himself into a blinding temper so that his voice rose roughly like an orator's. 'We're fighting for freedom, aren't we? My mates are workin' down the mines like billyo, aren't they? Or in the Forces. Or doin' their stint at the Bridgend Arsenal, right? No sacrifice too great. But this white coated ponce keeps us incarcerated as if we were bloody convicts. An' allowed no rights, no visitors, nothin'.'

''Ave you 'ad your say?' called Ginger.

''E's more of a screw than a doctor,' continued Rod.

'I've been in this ward three weeks,' interrupted Ginger, 'and you've only had one visitor since I been 'ere.'

'Talking to me?' Dai Davies suddenly asked.

'You came in on a Monday, what you talkin' about?' responded Rodney, ignoring Dai. 'You've only been in this ward two Sundays and one of 'em you must 'ave slept through. Sleepin' Beauty, you are. Sandra came last Sunday an' Gwen the week before.'

'Gwen didn't come the week before.'

'Gwen came the week before.'

'That Sandra looks like the back of a bus,' said Ginger, addressing me.

'Shurrup,' screamed Rod so loudly that the nurse, Dorothy Briggs, came rushing in to scold both of them. 'We have a patient here with suspected meningitis,' she pronounced in her rather Oxford accent. 'We can't have all this hooligan shouting.'

'Gwen came to see me the Sunday before last,' Rod said to me quietly, importantly.

On Sunday afternoon, visitor-less, Rodney Price revealed to me his secret. He was in love. He loved someone called Joyce.

Unrequited love. She would have nothing to do with him. 'Show me her photo,' I said. 'Which one is it?'

'I haven't shown you her photo,' Rodney admitted. 'That's the one photo I 'aven't shown you. I don't let anybody 'ave a dekko at that. It's private.'

'And she never visits you,' I said.

'No,' said Rod glumly. 'I writes to 'er but she don't answer. Love letters, mun. Never done that before. French letters yes, but love letters no. She don't answer. Not once.' Almost whispering, he continued, 'To be honest, I'm not much of a letter writer. I'm not Charles Dickens, if you know what I mean and, besides, it's bloody 'ard, writin' anything when you're strung up like this.'

'I'll write one for you,' I said promptly, not thinking.

'This is solitary confinement, this is,' Rodney complained.

'I mean I'll dictate one for you. I'm good at English. Last year when I did my matric. I got a distinction for English literature. My English teacher, at St Illtyd's, reckons I've got a style of my own. Yes, I'll write a good letter, a love letter to Joyce for you.'

'Don't be daft,' he said. 'You're a kid. A virgin, betcher. You dictate a love letter for me? You're 'ardly outa nappies. You're outa your mind, son.'

Day after featureless day Dr Pike hardly visited us, though he did come in one morning to do a lumbar puncture on Geraint Griffiths behind the screens. Over the next two weeks those screens, on and off, stayed around the meningitis patient though he was gradually recovering. Old Dai Davies kept on smiling when directly addressed, or when teased, countered by saying, 'You cheeky devil.' Meanwhile huckstering Rodney Price and Ginger Morgan, who was now able to sally forth a little more athletically from his bed, traded their occasional malevolent insults. And we received our news of the outside world from the nurses, Nurse Briggs or the Iceberg: how Swansea had been destroyed after three successive nights of massive bombing; how, with all the casualties resulting, we in that little cottage hospital were lucky to be occupying beds; how the USA might help us with something they called Lease-Lend. I thought how Churchill on the wireless had said, 'We shall not fail nor falter. We shall not weaken or starve. Neither the sudden shock of battle, nor the long-drawn-out trial of vigilance and exertion will wear us down. Give us the tools and we will finish the job', and my mother had remarked, 'He's got a mouth on him, Churchill. Good as our Leo.'

Yet, as I lay on that hospital bed – horizontal, a sandbag between my shoulder blades, fed-up, longing to turn, if only for a moment on my right or left side – that world at war, out there, seemed unreal. Real was the itch from the elastic banding around my chest. What a joy it would be to have that elastic bandaging removed, to be beautifully liberated, so that I could scratch my skin there and here and there. That itch, I fear, distressed me more acutely than the abstract knowledge of probable millions being murdered at that very moment in Europe. I often had to remind myself of Rod Price's long-term plight in the next bed to me and to remember my mother's often uttered cliché, 'Count your blessings, son'. At least I was allowed to leave my bed for essential needs and gradually to sit up for longer periods each day. I happened to look across idly at the polished table, at the liquid light like wet silver on its surface, at the vase of cut flowers uprooted from the earth. And then it occurred to me. Those flowers were too perfect, unchanged. They appeared to be the same as when I had first noticed them weeks ago when I had first been admitted to the ward. They had not withered at all.

'They're artificial,' I said out loud.

'Whassat?' asked Rod.

'Those flowers, they're artificial, Rod.'

'Oh, aye.'

'I thought they were real.'

'When I first came in 'ere old Les was in your bed. A commercial traveller. 'E went round floggin' artificial plants to all the big institutions. 'E'd been out weeks but come Christmas the bleeder sends Sister Tomlinson that 'orrible lot. I 'ates 'em.'

What was real, I wondered? One of my brothers, Wilfred or Leo, had once told me that a stallion tried to mount a mare painted by Apelles and that the Greek workmen who were carrying a statue aboard Lord Elgin's ship heard it sob for it knew it was going into exile. And had I dreamed that scene last night when I became aware of scufflings and whispers close by; so close that I turned my head and saw, or thought I saw, the Iceberg, Nurse James, on night duty, bending over and kissing Rod tenderly as Rod fondled her clothed breasts? Had I truly woken for a moment? Or was it a fleeting fragment of a dream?

Now that it was evening again the black-out blinds of the ward had been pulled down, making our ward the only real place in the world, somehow even smaller, more intimate. Soon Nurse James, once more on night duty, came in pushing the noise of a trolley across the parquet floor and handing out our suppers. If Rod had truly experienced a tender, amorous frustrating interlude with the Iceberg the previous night, neither he nor she showed any sign of it. Scowling insubordinately, his suppressed rage at nothing in particular reappearing in one more guise, he groaned, 'Chris', Nurse, not more dried eggs again.'

After supper I lay back trying to imagine that other unlikely world outside: the dark wet rooftops of Cardiff, perhaps just visible in a little moonlight to any bombers going over; the doors of all the dark houses closed, the curtains of the dark, secretive streets drawn. Which friends of mine, right now, were walking with their black-out torches in town as the occasional buses and trams, lit by a ghostly floating blue light, like so many rumours threaded their way down Queen Street or St Mary's Street? And what were my father and mother doing? And my dog, Caliban? 'That table,' Rod called to me, 'that table with the artificial flowers on it, is a sort of frontier, doncha think?'

'How do you mean?' I asked:

'It's them and us,' he said.

'Them and us?'

'To be candid, I can't bear that Iowerth, see. If I could spit that far I would.'

I wondered if Ginger could hear what Rod was saying and whether, as a result, we would have yet another quarrel. 'You know why 'e 'ates me?' continued Rod more loudly. 'Because of Betty and Gwen and Sandra. 'E's green-eyed, know what I mean? 'E just said Sandra didn't look great because nobody visited 'im that Sunday.'

78

'That Sandra. She's a bag,' Ginger called out suddenly and delightedly, obviously glad a quarrel was about to begin.

Rod paused. He turned to Dai Davies as if Dai were an umpire and in a loud voice addressed him earnestly. 'What did you think of my visitor a couple of Sundays ago, Dai?'

'Eh?'

'That young woman who visited me. Wasn't she tidy?' Rod appealed.

'She was that,' said Dai unexpectedly.

'Caw, he's blind as well as deaf,' yelled Ginger.

'All women are a beautiful sight,' said Dai. 'Beaut-iful.'

'I saw a marvellous sight in Ogmore last summer,' I said. 'I was with a friend, Keith Thomas. We happened to be looking out to sea and the sun was behind us. But coming towards us was a wall of rain, and it was travelling at about twenty miles an hour. You sometimes see this in the Bristol Channel and it's a most extra-ordinary sight...'

'I seen it,' interrupted Rod.

'But this time, in front of the wall of rain was a rainbow, coming towards us at about twenty miles an hour, and we saw one side landing on the sandhills and the other on the other side of the river; and this all happened at a terrific pace, within a minute. And it came at this great pace from Devonshire or Somerset or wherever it was. You don't often see racing rainbows! Then finally, in the middle of it, most remarkable thing of all, there was a seagull going right through the arc of the rainbow. It reappeared the other side, and one half-expected it to be coloured.'

It was the longest peroration in that ward that I had embarked on and it seemed, for some reason, to have stunned Iowerth and Rod. The quarrel that had been brewing never materialised. So I lay back in the resumed silence inordinately and complacently pleased with myself. Then I became aware once more of how much I itched and how much I wanted to scratch and scratch.

Rodney Price must have been brooding about it. For the next morning he tentatively asked me to help him write a letter to Joyce. I think it was my description of the travelling rainbow that must have impressed him, made him think that I might be of use in suggesting a phrase or two. 'You 'ave to praise a girl to get anywhere,' he declared, 'and, to be honest, I've run out of words. Joyce don't answer any of my notes to her.' I thought of the seventeenth-century Welsh poet, Huw Morus, who had written a poem in praise of his girl: how he had called her the brightest foam on the sea, the sweetest of lotions, a purest rose, an unflawed pearl, a heart-ache, and a white-breasted paragon, etc.

'Not bad for a start,' nodded Rod, 'plenty of flannel there. I might use one of them phrases. You read a lot of poetry, do you?'

'Yes.'

'An' you write it, too?'

'Yes.'

'Recite me one of your own then,' he said. 'I'm bored enough even to listen to poetry.'

'I don't know any off by heart.'

'Don't know his own stuff by 'eart,' repeated Rod sneeringly.

There was a four-liner I had written. I could remember that. A self-mocking four-liner about me standing alone on the cliffs at Ogmore-by-Sea. I had thought of offering it to the school magazine but I had not decided on a title. Various titles had come to mind, apart from 'On the Cliffs'. For instance, 'Ego'; or 'Sur la Plage'; or 'Narcissus at the Seaside'. I was aware, though, that all these titles sounded pretentious.

'Forget the bloody title,' commanded Rod. 'Let's hear it.'

I glanced around the ward. Dai was reading a newspaper. The screens enclosed Geraint Griffiths and Ginger Iowerth's bed was abandoned – he must have shuffled off to the lavatory. So I recited:

> A beautiful woman
> Should be looking at me
> As I think big thoughts
> And stare at the sea.

I waited for Rod's ugly criticism.

'Go on,' he said.

'That's it,' I said.

'That's it?'

'Yes.'

He paused. He said, 'Well, it isn't Charles Dickens, is it?' Then he asked me to say the quatrain again. Afterwards he repeated it to himself before remarking, 'Fair play. Quite catching, atcherly.'

'It's self-mocking,' I said.

''Ow do you mean?'

Soon Rodney Price began writing a letter. I assumed it was to Joyce. I might have been wrong but I guessed he was writing how he, Rod Price, had begun writing verse, and had composed, for example, a poem; just a short poem, only four lines actually, about standing on the cliffs at Ogmore-by-Sea. The beautiful woman, of course, he would write, would be no other than Joyce, the sweetest of lotions, that unflawed pearl and purest rose. 'Am I right?' I asked Rod. He did not answer. He went on writing; but then, a coincidence, for in came Ginger carrying the morning post: a letter from my mother and one for Rodney Price, Esquire which Ginger handed over to him with ostentatious distaste. 'A summons, I expect,' said Ginger with a guillotine smile.

Rod put the letter he was writing to one side and stared at the newly delivered envelope with a kind of scientific curiosity. He examined the handwriting and the postmark. 'That's a bit bloody odd,' he said, 'it's from Joyce. The first time I've 'eard from 'er since I've been admitted 'ere.' Strangely, though, he seemed loath to open it.

'And you were just writing to her?' I said.

'No,' he said, 'I was just writin' a note to my brother askin' 'im to send me another pair of pyjamas.'

I opened my own letter. I held it up parallel to the ceiling as I tried to read it from my horizontal position. 'I'll read it for you if you like,' I was surprised to hear Rod say. His voice was unaccountably gentle. 'I mean you tried to 'elp me, see, so I should try to 'elp you.'

'It's O.K.' I said. 'I can manage.'

Rod stared down, as if defeated, at the unopened letter from Joyce on his lap. Perhaps it wasn't from Joyce, I thought. Maybe that was just one more of his lies. But I was more interested in my own letter. 'Dear son,' my mother wrote, 'We think of you all the time and hope that you are comfortable. You'll find the house patched up when you return and you, God willing, your own healthy self again. All's well this end though Uncle Bertie and Aunt Cecile are living with us at present, being homeless. A magnetic land mine fell in Llandaff during an air raid. It fell in a front garden a few doors away from your Uncle's house. It didn't go off but it was dangerous apparently, though all the neighbours had thought it was a dud. The expert bomb disposal team appeared and they were very brave. But after the leader examined it he said that unfortunately the fuse was beneath the mine. So they decided to try and shift it over gently to reveal the fuse by putting a wire cable around one of its projections and cautiously pulling it over a little with the help of one of the municipal steamrollers. They had Uncle and Aunt and all their neighbours lined up about a hundred yards away while they went through this manoeuvre, just in case. One of the men reassured Uncle Bertie that it was unlikely to blow up and if it did probably only windows would be smashed. But when the steamroller moved only a few inches it did explode, like a volcano. Terrific, your Aunt Cecile says. And all the houses, including your Uncle's, went up into the air in thousands of pieces. Cecile says there was so much dust everything looked vague for a moment, like in a London fog. But when the dust settled and the air cleared, they could see all the houses were utterly destroyed. Naturally, all the householders were furious. And you know Uncle Bertie. He went tamping mad and tried to fight the bomb disposal man...'

I stopped reading my letter for I heard a choked cry from nearby.

'Oh no, oh no, oh no,' Rodney Price was muttering. The letter was open in front of him. In a kind of panic he said to me, 'She wants a divorce. God, she wants a divorce.'

'From her husband?' I said. 'Now you'll be in trouble. A court case.'

I had read often enough in newspapers how X was cited as a co-respondent. Reporters always wrote, 'Intimacy took place'.

Now Rodney Price would be Mr X.

'You doan understand,' he said. 'From me. Joyce wants to divorce me.'

'Are you married?' I said. 'To Joyce?'

He did not reply. Tears started in his eyes and he turned his face away.

Now that the screens had been permanently taken down from around Geraint Griffiths' bed and, day by day, he obviously became stronger, we all wanted to know when we would be allowed to have visitors.

'When is this ward out of quarantine?' demanded Ginger of the Iceberg.

'You'll have to speak to Dr Pike,' she responded.

But Dr Pike had not been seen for over a week. When we asked about him the nursing staff gave us evasive answers.

'Sister Tomlinson's in bed with flu,' the Iceberg reiterated.

'Yes, but where's Dr Pike?' Ginger persisted.

'In bed with 'er?' asked Rod.

Had Dr Pike been called up? Gone down with flu or meningitis? Got married? Had an accident? Gone on holiday? Been struck off the medical register? 'Chris',' said Rod, 'we could all be dyin' practically. And no one, no expert like that is, comes to see us. And those artificial flowers, I'm fed up of lookin' at them. It's March, isn't it? There must be loads of daffodils around. At least you could bring in some daffs or somethin'.'

'Now you just relax,' countered the Iceberg. 'You just lower your voice, please.'

'Well, those artificial flowers are very average,' agreed Ginger.

'We could go on strike,' I suggested. For some reason this set off all the ward (except Dai Davies who did not hear what was going on) into a prolonged volley of laughter. The more we laughed, the more we laughed, so that Nurse Briggs came into the ward to see what was going on.

But nothing was going on, nothing at all and soon we were not laughing any more. 'You know somethin',' said Rod to me confidentially, 'I've lost 'ope.'

'What?'

'I've lost 'ope.'

I did not know what to say. He had lost hope and I believed that at that moment he was uttering the truth, the whole truth and nothing but the truth.

The day Dr Pike reappeared and sent me for an X-ray and told Ginger that he could go home on Saturday, providing he kept strictly to a diet he would prescribe, and, yes, visitors would be allowed in on Sunday, was the day we had a series of unremarkable air-raids. The air-raid siren would release its wounded, prolonged howl and half an hour later the All Clear would sound, though in the interim we had heard neither the ragged drone of heavy bombers going over nor the stutter of any Ack-Ack gunfire. It happened several times: first the air-raid warning then eventually the All Clear. Moreover, because of the way the wind was blowing the blaring hooter could be heard duplicated three times. The warning would sound near loudly, then another could be heard fainter and further off and faintest of all, a third siren, as if what was audible was being reflected in huge parallel mirrors.

'False alarm again,' said Geraint Griffiths as once more the All Clear was sounded.

'They're just practising,' said Ginger.

I was not surprised that Ginger Morgan was going to be discharged. His very stature had changed and he did not shuffle now when he walked. Some colour had returned to his cheeks so he looked less haggard, less a victim about to be guillotined than a solemn, carrot-haired executioner. In his dressing gown he would quit the ward to help the nurses bring in the trolleys or the odd cup of tea, or he would act as a messenger for one of us should the occasion arise. He even made a friendly overture to Rod – astonishing all of us

'Anything you want, Rod,' he declared omnipotently, 'just ask me.'

'You can get rid of those artificial flowers for a start,' said Rod, inspired after only a small hesitation.

'All right, I will then.'

'Go on, then.'

'Where shall I put 'em?'

'Up yours.'

I thought we were in for another old row. But Ginger Morgan just shook his head sadly.

'Well you arst me if I wanted anything and I want them flowers out,' bullied Rod.

'They're doing no harm,' called Geraint Griffiths.

It seemed the end of that conversation but ten minutes later Rod moaned, 'If I could walk, them artificial flowers would be out by there. I'd plant 'em outside.'

'You stupid. They won't grow,' said Ginger.

'Course they won't grow. I know that. It's you who's stupid. It's camouflage, see.'

'Once we're allowed visitors we'll probably get masses of flowers,' said Geraint, trying to defuse the argument. 'Flowers that breathe out oxygen in the daytime and carbon dioxide at night.'

'Are you a fuckin' chemist?' asked Rod. 'Now shurrup all of you. I 'ave to write a lotta postcards to let the girls know they can visit me on Sunday.'

That same night we experienced an air raid in earnest. No fake alarm this time. The lights of the ward had been extinguished and I had fallen asleep almost at once. In my dream I was walking through a wood during a storm. I saw lightning, heard thunder, then I awoke to the real noise of gunfire or bombs or both. Somewhat late, the air-raid warning sounded.

'Chris',' said Rod, 'they've been messin' around all day with them 'ooters. It's been 'ooters, 'ooters, 'ooters but when a real blitz 'appens they're too slow to get their sticky fingers out.'

It was only half past ten. The whole ward was awake and a general conversation began that included Dai Davies – and this meant we all had to talk loudly. It brought in Nurse Briggs who was on duty. 'All this talking,' she said. 'What a lot you are. You remind me of that story about St Peter. When there was a sudden influx of the Welsh into heaven, a very uncharacteristic happening, he was nearly driven mad by the chatter, chatter, chatter.'

'Bet the choir singing got better too,' said Geraint.

'And the 'arp playing,' said Rod.

'I'm not ready for heaven,' said Ginger but just then the chatter was interrupted by further bangings and rocketings of near enough bombs and gunfire.

When all the noise subsided, Dai said very loudly, 'It'll be the night shift beginning back 'ome. My son, and 'undreds of 'is butties, right now, air raid or no air raid, carrying their tin boxes, their tea-jacks, will be stumblin' up the slope of the mountain to the colliery mouth in complete darkness.'

It seemed years since I had read that autobiographical sketch in *Penguin New Writing* (No 2) by B.L. Coombes. 'And they'll be whistling as they go up,' I said.

'How do you mean?' asked Ginger.

'Because a thousand men will be coming down from that hole in the mountain in a hell of a hurry as the others are going up in the darkness. So they whistle to let people know where they are,' I explained. 'Right, Dai?,

'I don't know about whistlin',' Dai said, 'but, good 'eavens, it's lighter down in the pit, the cold light in the pit, than on those narrow, stony, mountain slopes leadin' to the unlit streets below.'

Another heavy crunch of gunfire began. 'Safer down by there in the deep pit,' cried Rod. 'Not 'alf.'

'Whassat?' asked Dai.

'An' quieter too,' Rod said.

'I can't hear it distinctly,' said Dai. 'Not distinctly, but I can feel it.'

'What?' asked Ginger.

'At the top,' said Dai, almost shouting now as if we were all deaf. 'At the top, where the big machines are. You can feel the quiver, the vibrations of the big pumps that compress the air right down into the far fathoms of underground workings.'

'Dig for Victory,' said Geraint inanely.

'I'll make you all some cocoa. Would you all like some cocoa?' asked Nurse Briggs.

In the almost darkness (a light was slanting in from the corridor), with the common threat from outside there was a curious sense of community now in our small ward – perhaps like there is in a mining village during a strike, or an air raid, or, indeed, most of the time. We were all on the same side – and even Dai, usually so handicapped by his sealed and isolating deafness, seemed uncharacteristically sociable and keen to join in the general friendly conversation.

Soon after we had drunk our cocoa the All Clear wailed. We settled down once more to go to sleep. All of us, that is, except Ginger. For he ambled over to Rod's bed and whispered, 'Those artificial flowers, mun. They won't be there in the mornin'.'

When I closed my eyes I could see the silhouettes of hundreds of colliers in their cloth caps, climbing the ridge on the mountain, dark figures in twos or in single file stumbling up the black, twisting paths, all whistling as they climbed. The whole mountain was full with their wonderful whistling – like at a rugby international at Cardiff Arms Park: *Hen wlad fy nhadau...* whistling it, not singing it, and all together, one for all and all for one, whistling it harmoniously until they reached the top and the whistling was drowned by the increasing noise of the vibrating pit gears.

When I woke up next morning the artificial flowers had gone, had been replaced by real, living, trumpeting, yellow daffodils. Somebody, during the night, when we were all asleep, must have crept out of the ward into the garden behind our cottage hospital and, in the dark, dumped the artificial ones then carefully picked these beautiful things.

'I've spoken to the doctor,' said my mother, 'an' they'll be taking that bandaging off tomorrow so you'll soon be home.'

'It'll be a full house what with Uncle and Aunt staying too,' I said.

'No, no,' my mother told me. They've gone to London. Crazy. Your Uncle Eddie, you know what he's like.'

It seemed that my Uncle Eddie had persuaded my bombed-out Uncle Bertie to buy a small hotel, a glorified boarding house actually, in Ladbroke Grove, London. The three-storeyed, dilapidated house was 'going for a song' because of the blitz. So, though many were running away from dangerous London, my Uncle Bertie and Aunt Cecile hurried to the great metropolis to become Manager and Manageress of a more or less empty 'Hotel'.

'Your Uncle Eddie and his mad schemes,' complained my mother. 'I may tell you he tried to get your father to invest too. Dirt cheap, he reckoned. Dirt, I says, it soon could be rubble. Am I right, son?'

That Sunday afternoon our ward had been transformed. The visitors had brought in more living flowers. A blaze of yellow. Either side of the artificial flowers that had been mysteriously discovered in one of the lavatories, daffodils or yellow tulips, in several vases, leaned over to gaze at their smudged reflections in the highly polished table.

'Yellow's my favourite colour,' my mother told Rod who, impudently, was listening to our conversation.

Earlier Rod had gazed at the empty bed which Ginger had irrevocably vacated; at Geraint's brother, a corporal evidently home on a forty-eight-hour pass; at grey-haired, bunned Mrs Davies who sat next to Dai's bed, leaning forward so that her head was only inches away when she addressed him. And now he scrutinised my mother with the intensity of a scientist gazing down a microscope. For some reason he addressed her as 'Madam'. Then I recalled that he had told me he had once worked in a store in Cardiff, Howell's.

At first I felt sorry for Rod. He had spruced himself up, shaved carefully, Brylcreemed his thrice-combed hair until he did indeed look rather like that film star Alan Ladd. But no Sandra, no Betty, no Gwen entered the ward and one could discern his dismay when first Mrs Davies arrived, then my mother, then Geraint's brother. Finally, it seemed, he became resigned to having no visitors so he gave his intrusive attention to my mother instead. He was sweet as pie to her, practising his charms for a better day. In training, like a professional, he dared to say to me, 'You're right. You've certainly got a good-looking mother.' My mother was only temporarily taken aback by this flattery. She turned to him and said, 'Poor man, what's happened to your leg? You can't be comfortable like that.' And she smiled graciously as if she were the Queen visiting the wounded.

'I'm not at all comfortable, Madam,' agreed Rod. 'But it's no good complainin' like, is it? Fate's fate. But we 'ave to bear our sorrows bravely.'

'We do that,' said my mother. 'Son, these Welsh cakes I've brought you. You must share them with this unfortunate gentleman.'

Rod became so smarmy, it was unbelievable – Moonraker butter in his mouth as he thanked my mother and continued to flatter her. At one point I began to wonder whether she was visiting me or Rod! At last she looked my way and said, 'I hope you're getting some fruit. I suppose they're short of things here like everywhere else but...'

'I've a contact,' interrupted Rod again, 'who can get you anything. Salmon, meat, anything. Not just whale steak but the real thing like. 'E can get you a bunch of bananas. Now 'ave you seen a banana, Madam, this la st year or two? No, you' aven't. Well, I play poker with 'im regular an' the bananas I've won from 'im. To be honest, 'e's not much of a poker player an' no kiddin', Madam, I'm a bit of a dab 'and at it.'

He had gone over the top. My mother would see through him now surely. She was nodding her head. I could see she was trying to think of something to say. At last she said, 'My boy here is the baby of the family, you know...'

'You must 'ave started a family very young,' interrupted Rod smartly.

'And he used to love bananas,' mother continued. 'Loved them. Bananas and cream. Didn't you, son? Until he was quite old I had to mash them up for him.'

'I wasn't that old,' I said, irritated.

'Quite a big boy he was. I had to practically feed him.'

'Go on,' said Rod sympathetically.

The afternoon dragged on with my mother embarrassing me and Rod paying my mother unsubtle compliments until the visiting hour was over. Then she bent over to kiss me and afterwards turned to Rod Price and said solemnly: 'Count your blessings, young man.'

''Ow do you mean, Madam?'

'Well, you could have broken both legs,' my mother confided with enormous sincerity.

The sticking plaster had been taken off on Monday and I had been allowed to have a bath. Oh, the uplifting wonder of a delayed bath, the soothing warmth of the soft, soapy, comforting water, the rising steam misting the mirrors and the conclusion, surely, of that itching impulse to scratch, scratch, scratch! But the warmth and steam of the bath combined to open the capillaries in my skin and this, along with my unaccustomed posture, caused me to faint – to mist up like the mirror. The first time in my life that I had fainted. The ignominy of it! Seventeen years old and naked in the bath, helpless as a baby, to be hauled out by nurses and returned to the safe cocoon of the bed. And, worse, then to listen to the hectoring, raucous, dirty remarks of Rodney Price who called me a 'flasher'.

No matter: things were definitely moving. Both Rod and I had been X-rayed again and now we wondered when Dr Pike would come to tell us how we were progressing. Lately he had visited the cottage hospital only once a week – on Wednesdays. 'Playin' golf most of the time,' grumbled Rod. 'An' when 'e's exhausted with that, 'e'll be playin' ludo, betcher.'

At his next ward round, though, momentous decisions were made. Geraint and I could both go home at the weekend. At Geraint's bed he declaimed in an official voice so that the whole ward (except Dai) could hear him, 'You've had what is called a benign viral lymphocytic meningitis. Complete recovery without any treatment is usual. So you can convalesce at home.'

'Thank you, Doctor,' said Geraint.

'Don't thank me,' said Dr Pike. 'Thank the Devil for handing you the virus in the first place and God for curing you.'

At my bedside, after he had looked at the X-ray and told me I, too, could go home on Saturday, he embarked on another tutorial. He could not get it out of his mind that I hoped to be a medical student. He spoke quietly so that no one else could hear him apart from myself and Sister Tomlinson who stood by in attendance.

'Our friend over there who's recovering from a viral meningitis – his cerebrospinal fluid contained an excess of lymphocytes – so that lumbar puncture helped me to establish the diagnosis. That and the history, of course, of sudden onset and the clinical features of severe headache, photophobia, pyrexia. Did you notice, when he was admitted, how he lay on his side, the vertebral column extended and the legs drawn up in flexion at the hips and knees to loosen tension on the inflamed nerve roots...?' He stopped in full flow. Perhaps he read the blank look on my face.

'You idiot,' I thought. 'I was lying flat on my back and Geraint had screens round him so how the hell would I observe anything?' My lack of understanding and of response seemed to make him ill-tempered. For after he had scrutinised Rod's X-rays he turned belligerently to Sister Tomlinson. 'He has two pillows, Sister,' he growled.

'I don't know how he wangled another pillow,' muttered Sister.

'You know he should only have one.'

'Yes, I know.'

'With two pillows the weight of his body won't effect the traction necessary. You know he should only have one. Get rid of that pillow. And look at his quadroceps. Good God, look at that muscle wasting. Atrophied. Is he having regular massage and faradism?'

He went around the ward like a commanding officer. It was a wonder he did not draw a finger over the top of the door to see if it was dust-free. At Dai's bed he was shouting, 'C'mon, Dad, breathe in, breathe out.' At last he left, without offering us one friendly 'Cheerio', to continue his self-important progress through the women's ward.

'He's in a helluva temper today,' I remarked.

'My leg's broken and the world out there's broken,' responded Rod philosophically.

The Iceberg who had overheard my remark, said, 'He's just had his calling-up papers. And Sister's just given him a terrific ticking off for complaining about her in front of one of you lot.' She began to take out the daffodils and tulips which had now withered.

'I'll help you,' called Geraint, 'with the flowers.'

The Iceberg had gone ahead and was out of the ward by the time Geraint Griffiths had put on his dressing gown and picked up a couple of vases.

'You creep,' said Rod, suddenly abusing Geraint. 'You creep. You're always trying to get round the nurses. Yes Sister, no Sister, can I do that for you, Sister.'

'Ever since Ginger left you've been starting to quarrel with me,' objected Geraint. 'What's the matter with you?'

'Get out of it,' responded Rod unreasonably. 'You disgust me.' Geraint Griffiths stood there, a vase of withered yellow tulips in one hand, a vase of withered daffodils in the other. He hesitated, muttered, 'You're cuckoo,' then turned and left the ward, leaving one forlorn yellow tulip petal on the floor behind him.

'I miss Ginger,' said Rod, by way of explanation.

Later, with all the vases gone from the table except the one containing the artificial flowers, and with Geraint Griffiths returned to his bed, Rod told me how he had changed his mind about artificial flowers. 'They're sort of permanent, not like the daffs, right? I don't 'ate them at all. Really nice they are, atcherly.'

He obviously began to consider the meaning, significance, symbolism of artificial flowers, for some minutes later he asked a favour of me. He would give me some money and when I was 'released from this dump' perhaps I would buy some artificial flowers and take them to Church Street, which was off Stacey Road in Splott. 'I want you to give them to Joyce from me as a sign of – well, the holiness, the beauty of permanence like. To remind 'er, see, of 'er marriage vows. To 'ave and to 'old, in sickness and in 'ealth.'

'Well...' I began.

'Definitely,' he said.

'Look,' I said, 'I don't...'

'I'll write a note and you give 'er the note and the artificial flowers. OK?'

'It's a nice gesture, Rod, but...'

''Ow much do you think artificial flowers would cost? They wouldn't cost a bomb, would they?'

'I've no idea.'

'They wouldn't cost a bomb, betcher.'

'I don't know where to buy artificial flowers,' I said.

'There'll be a shop in town,' said Rod.

"It's wartime, Rod.'

'So what? Everything is ersatz these day. No problem. C'mon, it's not a big thing I'm askin'.'

'I'll try.'

'Ta,' he said. 'Mind you, you could nick them flowers on the table, see. Save us some money –'

The Iceberg came into the ward with some electrical apparatus. She was going to administer very small shocks to the quadroceps muscle above Rod's right knee, to stimulate it. 'I need stimulation,' said Rod meaningfully. She took one pillow away.

'You goin' to massage it too?' asked Rod cheerfully.

'Yes,' the Iceberg said. 'And you keep your hands to yourself.'

After lunch, when the ward was quiet, infolded, Rod reached for a hand mirror from his side-locker. The afternoon light streamed obliquely through the side window, and dust that had become strangely visible was climbing up and down a sunbeam. Rod angled the small mirror so that a luminous blob was reflected on the ceiling. He twisted the mirror this way and that so the evanescent circle seemed to come to life. It whizzed in panic from ceiling to wall and from wall to ceiling. Somewhere else floated the great sun, some 870,000 miles in diameter, but here it was shrunken to a few, flying, vivid inches. Rod rotated the mirror to aim this dazzling nucleus of sunlight at Geraint Griffiths. He searched out his face, trying to irritate, scandalously provoke Geraint who, after all, so recently could not even bear ordinary dull daylight. It seemed Rod needed an enemy. Yet, when Geraint eventually cried out, 'Put a sock in it,' Rod did so. He put his irksome mirror away and said to me quietly, 'God, I'm bored. I'm so bored.'

Because Geraint had a raised temperature and felt groggy on Wednesday evening Sister Tomlinson decided he'd suffered a relapse. So I was the only one to be discharged from the hospital on Saturday. Worse, from Rodney Price's point of view, visitors had again been banned. 'Pity,' he declared. 'It's a cryin' shame. Otherwise Sandra and Betty and Gwen, sure as eggs, would 'ave give me the once-over tomorrow.' He extracted some notes from his wallet so that I could buy the artificial flowers for Joyce. Generously, he remarked, 'Keep any change for yourself, mun, and buy yourself a pint.'

Dai was taking his morning walk, twice around the ward, on the arm of Nurse Briggs. At the window he complained, 'I'm puffed.' He always left his bed unwillingly but the medical staff ensured he was up and about some part of the day lest he lose too much calcium from his bones, or experience a postural pneumonia from being in bed all the time. 'Especially at your age,' they warned him. But now, gazing out of the window, Dai became agitated. A drama was obviously taking place out there in the anterior open space of the cottage hospital.

'Duw, look at that, Nurse,' cried out Dai, so that both Rod and I paid attention. (Screens were once more around Geraint's bed.) 'Crikey. Isn't that typical of the whole world outside?'

Apparently he had observed a blackbird pecking at a small snail that had been stranded on the front path of the hospital – the yellow beak pecked pecked pecked, until it had smashed through the snail shell.

Rodney Price ignored the small distraction. He had further business with me. He had written a letter to his wife the previous evening and now he handed it to me, a reluctant messenger, to take to his home in Church Street. The envelope had not been stuck down. 'You can read it if you like,' he said.

''S all right,' I said.

'No, read it,' he persuaded me. 'Check the spellin', there's a sport. I know it's I before E 'cept after C but I've allers been a bit of a dunce at spellin', see.'

He was covertly proud of his literary effort. I sensed he wanted approval from me who had weeks ago impressed him with a poem I had written. Knowing Rod, perhaps he had now stolen the four lines of mine and claimed them as his own. Hesitantly, I pulled the letter out of the envelope and read Rod's remarkably large, simple handwriting. Like a child's. Can one discern anything about character from a person's handwriting? I believed one could tell a good restaurant by the quality of its chips; a good bookshop by the range and stock of its slim volumes of poetry; the civilisation or lack of it in a country from the state of its prisons – but handwriting? Rod was more complex, than this handwriting.

'Go on,' said Rod. 'Read it out loud.'

He wanted the joy of hearing his own creation declaimed out loud but meanly I read it to myself: 'Dear, darling Joyce,' Rod had written:

> I received your letter. Don't even think that way. Visit me. We can work things out. OK lovely? I'm stuck in this dump. I keep remembering. That picknic on Cowbridge Common. That boarding house in Barry. That time we left Bindles in Cold Knapp on my bike. Don't listen to Emily. She's hysterical. You know that. Forget me not – as you said at St Mellons. Keep these flowers in your bedroom. They will last. They will last.
> Your sincerely XXX
> Rod

When I looked up I could see that Rod was staring at me anxiously. 'There's a spelling mistake and you've left out a couple of apostrophes,' I pronounced, giving him my professional opinion. But the price of reading his letter was praise, pure praise. He wanted unadulterated applause with no 'ifs' or 'buts'.

'So what?' he said disgruntled. 'Stick it down. Who cares about a spellin' mistake? Joyce isn't a schoolteacher, see. Stick it down.'

'It's a very nice letter, Rod.'

'Yes,' he agreed. 'Did you like the repetition of they will last, they will last?'

'Very apt,' I said.

He nodded, partly satisfied, 'As you can see, like, I've just written on the envelope – To Joyce.'

'Like a dedication,' I said.

'So you go to Church Street with the artificial flowers and this letter,' he said. 'Right?'

'I'll ask for Mrs Price,' I said.

'Oh no,' he said. 'I mean... just ask for Joyce.' He brought his left arm towards his face and sniffed at his hand. 'Look,' he continued at last. 'Fact is, I 'ave to tell you, there's another family livin' in that' ouse in Church Street apart from Joyce and the baby...'

'You have a baby?' I asked.

'Yes,' he said. 'Couldn't you tell I'm a family man? Anyway, the strange thing is, see, is that the other family upstairs is named Price too. I mean there's another Mrs Price apart from Joyce. That's why it's no good you askin' for Mrs Price. No no. Just ask for Joyce.'

I felt he was making more than half of this up. Another lie. Why he should fabricate into existence another Mrs Price puzzled me. Surely it wasn't true. He could see I had doubts about his story for he added, 'Of course, the other Mrs Price spells it differently like. PRYS. But it sounds the same, aye. 'Er first name is Emily and to tell you the truth it's complicated. She'd been givin' me the come on, know what I mean? Before the accident, that is. So for Chris' sake, ask for Joyce. That's the safest. Blow me, I don't want the artificial flowers to go to the wrong woman, do I?' And he laughed without conviction.

While I was waiting in the foyer of the cottage hospital and saying goodbye to the nurses, I learnt about Rodney Price's probable transfer to a hospital in Oswestry where some highly regarded orthopaedic surgeons worked. I had said '*Au revoir*' to the Iceberg and to Nurse Briggs – *au revoir*, not goodbye, because one Sunday afternoon I intended to return and see Rod. I felt he could do with a visitor. 'You'd better phone first,' Nurse Briggs advised. 'I think Rodney may be admitted to another hospital for he may need an operation. Dr Pike is making the arrangements before he's called up.'

It was over. It was almost noon. My father had arrived. He took the small suitcase from me and I followed him through the front doors of the cottage hospital into the sudden, pleasing shock of fresh, lyrical air, into liberty. April Fools' Day had come and gone and I was about to resume my life. I felt for a moment almost bodiless, the oxygen in the very hollow of my bones. The mysterious other side of light was everywhere, amongst the overgrown grass of the front lawn and in the trees' leaves and those in blossom. I would have broken into a run if my father had not been accompanying me, if I had not been convalescent. I would have run fast, very fast, for the wild pleasure of it, with all the zest of a seventeen-year-old. There was no sign of the snail shell on the pathway, no sign of the snail itself.

I did not look back. The building that was receding as the car moved forward was the least of my losses.

'Do you know where to buy artificial flowers, Dad?' I asked.

'Artificial flowers?'

'Yes.'

'Artificial... what do you want artificial flowers for?'

'To keep a promise... they're a sort of trophy,' I added.

'Not for your mother then?'

'No, no,' I said. 'I promised one of the patients at the hospital. He gave me money.'

'You could try Cardiff market,' said my father, uncomprehendingly. 'But there's plenty of real flowers about now. No need to get artificial ones. At least they haven't rationed flowers yet.'

PART TWO

DOUBLE FOOTSTEPS

The Secret

I telephoned this number and that unsuccessfully. 'Lunch is ready,' my mother called. 'Leave that telephone alone.' My stay in Cardiff would only be for a few days and not one of my friends, ♂ or ♀ seemed to be about on a weekend, forty-eight-hour pass from the Army, Navy or RAF.

As my mother sat down at the table she said, 'So good to have you home, son. Please God the war'll be over soon and then your brothers will be back too. There's a letter from Wilfred on the sideboard.' I picked up the blue air letter from India, where my eldest brother had been posted.

After lunch I walked down Queen Street aimlessly, passing strangers, many in uniform. I tried the Kardomah. I knew no one. The Continental. Not one familiar face. Then I recalled how, on Saturdays, there used to be a tea-dance during the summer at Roath Park Lake. Who knows, perhaps they were still going on, the band would be playing Joe Loss's 'In the Mood' or something slow like 'Smoke gets in your eyes' and an ash-blonde WAAF would be waiting for me to ask her to dance.

As I stood at the bus stop that afternoon, outside the operatic decor of Cardiff Castle, waiting for transport to Roath Park Lake, I looked up at the sky, an unaccustomed, peaceful Cardiff sky. No buzz-bombs floated over. For the last three months so many 'doodle bugs' had been launched towards London that I had become accustomed to a spluttering note overhead suddenly cutting to a long-held, accentuated silence before an explosion. The shell debris and flying glass often lanced unlucky bystanders to pieces.

A cloud released an astonished sun so that athletic shadows raced across the busy thoroughfare. When the bus arrived the woman in the queue in front of me shuffled forward and said to her small son, 'Don't put that dirty penny in your mouth, that's 'ow you get cancer.'

I arrived too early for any possible tea-dance so I stood at the rail where the lake flowed to make its exit down several steep man-made waterfalls. I listened to the decibels of energy, the consistent machinery noise of unending turbulence. I felt peculiarly lonely, and, as couples passed by, I remembered how Walt Whitman had declared how he did not envy the generals their victories, or the President his presidency, or the rich man in his great house, but when he saw two lovers together, arms linked, then he confessed he became pensive and filled with sour envy.

It was then that I espied, some sixty yards away, my Uncle Isidore sitting on one of the prom's park benches which overlooked the lake. Having nothing better to do, I retreated from the insistent sound of the waterfalls and sat down beside him. He was more hairy-faced, more dishevelled than ever.

'Hullo,' I said.

He looked towards me joylessly, expressing no surprise at my sudden appearance. It was as if we had a long-standing, Saturday afternoon, 3 p.m., August 1944 appointment and I had arrived only two minutes late.

'You're home then,' he said at last. 'They tell me you're working in a hospital.'

'Westminster Hospital,' I said.

Two pigeons flirted near his big black boots and he kicked at them so that they shot away, the jerky pistons in their heads busy.

'I was only supposed to begin walking the wards this coming autumn,' I explained, 'but because of the buzz-bombs I've been helping out in Casualty. They're short of doctors, you see.'

'Your father and mother,' he grumbled, 'they've forgotten.'

'What?' I asked.

'My birthday. I'm seventy today.'

As I began to mumble apologies on my parents' behalf he inter-rupted me. 'I was thinking, I was thinking before you came, I was thinking who were the greatest sinners? The generation of the Great Flood or the generation of the Tower of Babel? Or our lot? If it wasn't for Joe Stalin we'd be lost.'

A girl, a delicious girl in a yellow dress, a girl on her own, one who reminded me of someone I used to go out with, Lydia Pike, passed by. I watched her walking gracefully towards the waterfalls as Uncle Isidore droned on, 'All things turn over and revolve and are changed, the head to the foot and the foot to the head, this into that and that into this, right?'

I shrugged my shoulders. He shuffled nearer to me and I became aware of the smell of ear wax.

'You want to give me a birthday present?' he asked.

'What?' I said, feeling the half crown in my pocket.

The girl in the yellow dress had stopped to look at and listen to the waterfalls. Would she be at the tea-dance, I wondered?

'Take me out on the lake,' Uncle said.

'Mmm?'

'You row, don't you? On a day like this I'd like to be in a skiff. Isn't it a lovely day? When I gaze at that sky I feel like a peasant observing a king.'

Truly, it was a lyric day, all swans and water, reflections and water-colour; but what a way to spend one's rare, precious free Saturday, I thought, as I rowed my old Uncle Isidore in a shifty boat across the placid surface of Roath Park Lake while he steered incompetently and despotically ordered me to go slower, to go faster, to rest on the oars a while.

'If I didn't have such rheumatism, such pains in my bones, I'd row,' Uncle said. 'You have to be very young to be healthy in this country. Once you're over thirty you cough, you sneeze, you get sore throats, nose catarrh. Your joints creak, your bones ache whatever the weather. You suffer the afflictions of Job. Job could have been a Britisher.'

'The boring pains in his bones could have been a symptom of syphilis,' I said, boasting my medical student knowledge.

At this he became agitated. The once stable, dainty boat rocked alarmingly.

'Sit down, Uncle,' I said, fearful that the boat would tip.

'A specialist we've got,' he shouted at me. 'If silence is good for wise men, how much better it must be for fools.'

Gradually he and the boat calmed and I feathered the boat silkily around the whitewashed mock lighthouse that had been built as a memorial to Captain Scott, the Antarctic explorer who had sailed from Cardiff and had perished near the South Pole in 1912.

Skirting the swimming area, we made for the far small islands. As I rowed, I saw at the landing stage the girl in the yellow dress accompanied by a GI. They were settling into a skiff. The Yanks in their smart uniforms, and flush and flash with smarter dollars, you could hardly compete with them. Uncle was quiet for a while.

101

There was just the small creak of the oars and the soft splash in the water as they dipped. In the distance there was the occasional piercing cry of some water-fowl or the crazed laughter of ducks. I had taken the skiff out for an hour. There would just be time to round the islands before returning the boat to the landing stage.

It was on our journey back, when we were leaving the inward brooding reflections of the islands' trees for the more open surface glitter, that he began criticising individual members of our family, this uncle, that aunt. 'I hope you'll become a better doctor than your Uncle Max,' he said. 'A horse doctor he should be. The more I tell him how I suffer the more he complains. A doctor should be sensitive but I don't think your Uncle Max has got a nervous system. The medicine he's prescribed me – tastes like ostrich's piss.'

Of Uncle Eddie he said, 'A single coin in a shaken box makes a great noise. Only when the tin is full of coins, it's quiet, right?' His querulous soliloquy, studded with Talmudic proverbs, amused me enough until he started on my father. 'Rudy,' he said bitterly, 'is too comfortable in life. He's an uneducated man. He doesn't deserve a home, a wife, children, good fortune, everything I haven't got.'

I rowed on, passing the white question-mark profiles of two swans, without at first responding to Uncle Isidore's less than benign remarks. But then he, unconstrained, slanderously began to tell me about my parents' previous marital travail.

'You mean when Dad was unemployed for a while,' I said uneasily. 'Yes, he left home for a short time, I remember.'

'No, no. Earlier. Much earlier. Just before you were born. Ye-es. It wasn't always apples and spice. Your mother had to drink bitter water, bitter water mingled with dust.' He hesitated. 'There was a rap on the front door, an imperative rap on the front door. Oi!' Uncle continued dramatically.

'How do you mean?'

'Your mother, nine months pregnant with you, right? She opens the door, she sees a woman outside, a woman she's never seen before in her life, a woman very pregnant like her. Do you understand? A woman in shame who says, "I'm afraid I must speak to you urgently, Mrs Abse." '

I let the boat glide forward. My Uncle Isidore seemed eager to be telling me all this. Aware of my riveted attention his eyes in his hairy face had brightened. 'Your father wasn't at home when you were born,' he said triumphantly.

Never had anyone, uncle, aunt, cousin, elder siblings, anyone ever, indicated that such a discomforting gloomy drama had taken place at the house in Cardiff where I was to be born. Such news. Such old, terrible news. I pictured the two women big with child facing each other. I could see clearly my mother's beautiful face, distressed and angry. The other woman's I could not imagine.

At the landing stage I helped Uncle Isidore out of the unsteady boat, feeling angry with him. Ageing, he seemed to have changed altogether. He did not even thank me for taking him on the lake. I could hear a distant band playing a tango: 'It was all over my jealousy'. Disenchanted, somehow feeling guilty like a furtive eaves-dropper, I no longer wished to go to some trivial tea-dance. Instead I went home.

As I approached my parents' flat I wondered if I dared probe them about the whereabouts of any half-brother or half-sister. Was Isidore's story true? Or was it a wicked confabulation? In any case, when I saw my mother and father together in their usual compan-ionable, teasing, bantering, conversational harmony I knew it was not for me to finger, like an inept surgeon, some old, healed wound – if wound there ever was. What had Uncle Isidore uttered about silence? How it's good for wise men and even better for fools! Besides, my father and mother were so evidently pleasured by having one of their sons home I would have had to be a vandal to disturb their serenity. I did mention, though, that I had bumped into Uncle Isidore.

'Ah,' my father said, 'all he talks about these days is how great Joe Stalin is and how terrible everybody else is. He's getting old and soft in the 'ead. He'll be seventy-five next week, see.'

'He's seventy today,' I said. 'He told me so.'

'No, no,' my mother laughed, 'he's seventy-five on September first. The family's getting together to give him a treat.'

Two hours later, when we were sitting at the table about to begin our evening meal, the front doorbell rang. My mother looked at my father who looked at me.

'Perhaps it's one of your friends learnt that you're 'ome,' my father said. ''Spect you'd like to have some company on a Saturday night.'

'Dinner first,' my mother said.

I rose and as I walked into the hall I heard my father, who was so frequently considerate, telling my mother they couldn't expect to monopolise me; that I was young and it was Saturday night.

For a moment I thought of the girl in the yellow dress. Through the glass of the door I could see the dark silhouette of a man. It was Uncle Isidore. He stood there, shabby, unsmiling, swaying a little. 'Me again,' he announced mournfully. He almost staggered into the hall and it was easy to guess he had been celebrating his mythical birthday.

He must have read my thoughts. 'This wartime hooch,' he complained, 'it would give Noah an ulcer. Tipple a little of it and you get so you can't distinguish between "Cursed is Hitler" and "Blessed be Stalin" '.

My mother must have heard Isidore's voice for when we entered the living room she was bringing in an extra bowl of soup from the kitchen. Isidore slumped into a seat, picked up a spoon, dipped and drank some of the soup noisily without even greeting my parents.

'How are you, Isidore?' asked my mother.

He swallowed more soup, closed his eyes, opened them, then remarked in a melancholy chant, 'What's below is above and what's inside is outside so that the circle closes before and behind.'

'Exactly,' my father muttered.

At last Uncle sat up and said accusingly, 'It's my birthday.'

'Not till September first,' mother said.

'It is September first,' Uncle said loudly.

'No, it isn't,' said my father.

'No?' asked Isidore, more quietly.

'No,' mother said. 'Next week.'

Still looking utterly depressed, Uncle dipped for more soup before saying despondently, 'Well, it ought to be. The dead flesh in the living body doesn't feel the lancet.'

My mother addressed my father as if Isidore was not present: 'I feel sorry for him. He's not the man he was.' (My mother was not the most tactful person in the world.) At the end of the meal Uncle said in sepulchral tones, 'I'll have to go soon because of the black-out. But first can I have a word with you, Rudy?'

My father at once began to put his hand in his pocket but Isidore interjected, 'No, no. A word in private, please.' He stared at me meaningfully, his eyes the liquid eyes of an invalid, before continuing, 'I have a confession to make, Rudy.'

I realised now why he had come to our house that evening. It was not because he had mistaken the date of his birthday; simply he had regretted, surely, telling me what I should not have known. It was as if he had violated some ancient taboo so that now I was irrevocably privy to a secret, a secret that had been deeply concealed, not even hinted at these score of years.

Uncle and my father rose from the table and mother watched them blankly. 'What's this?' she asked. 'A conference?'

Isidore followed my father into the hall on their way to another room, presumably to stammer out his embarrassed confession.

'I'll make some tea,' my mother said. 'God knows what Isidore's been up to now, he seems very depressed. The war gets everyone down.'

When they returned it was my father who appeared tamed and gloomy, while Isidore seemed boisterous. Isidore spoke to me directly, 'It's written that he who reveals a secret can cause bloodshed.' Then he turned to my father, 'But it's all right, isn't it, Rudy?'

Father didn't say anything. He just looked away. When mother came in from the kitchen and poured out tea, Isidore said to her, 'You're as beautiful as ever, Kate.' I knew how she would respond. She would say, 'Go on with you. These days I look like the wreck of the *Hesperus*.'

She put down the teapot, smiling, and said, 'I used to be beautiful. Now I'm the wreck of the *Hesperus*.'

'You're still beautiful,' mumbled my father.

Genuinely startled by my father's rare compliment, my mother said, 'What's the matter with you, Rudy? Are you ill?'

Uncle Isidore cackled and declared almost jubilantly, 'That meal did me good, Kate. I feel more like sixty than seventy.'

'You're seventy-five,' I said unkindly. 'You're seventy-five next week. September first.'

I had spoken louder than I meant to. My father lit a cigarette and, afterwards, the room for a moment was hushed. I could hear the measured tick of the big clock on the mantelpiece.

Focus 1945: Bridgend, Glamorgan

Should you come this way, having walked a mile or so from Bridgend railway station, past the roundabout on the A48, you would find – not too far from the small, douce, almost traffic-free village of Merthyr Mawr with its barbered, thatched roofs and slim, bell-towered, grey-stoned church – some mysterious acre criss-crossed by crumbling pathways and half-hidden, weed-flecked narrow roads. Between these, you might be startled to observe hundreds of very long, low, one-storey concrete structures. Row upon row of them. How sinister they look! The iron gate to the stretched fields is invitingly open, half flung aside, though notices read KEEP OUT.

Ignore the signs. Enter. Look closer. No one is about. Behind you the sagging, rusted, barbed wire. In front you can see, as you advance, that the doors of these concrete structures are askew, on their hinges, or more often simply absent. The windows, too, are broken or completely without glass, revealing the abandoned darkness trapped within. Some of these grey concrete structures still have fading, white-painted, identification numbers on them: 83, or 22, or 47, or other numerals. The whole vandalised, sorry acres are half-concealed by the invincible grass, bereft scrub, strangling weeds and ivy, wild bushes.

The wind, too, is invincible. Listen. You will not hear, now, guttural voices nor the sound of marching feet, nor the hoarse male singing of '*Deutschland über Alles*' as prisoners of war jackboot their way down Merthyr Mawr Road between the high hedges. But the sagging wire about these derelict fields marked, more than forty years ago, the perimeter of Special Camp Eleven.

During the last months of the war, more and more high-ranking German officers had been brought here to Special Camp Eleven, to our own backyard, our home-patch. Many of the prisoners were war criminals, later to be hanged. All had bloody hands though few were bent down with the graves they carried. If the register had been called, the *Sieg Heil* response and clicking of heels would have been from some of Hitler's favoured: inventors of the Blitzkrieg tactic as savagely practised first in Poland; scientists who had, with clean fingernails, constructed the V2 rockets; and those sombre men who had worked for the Intelligence Service of the SS, whose simple responsibility had been to exterminate those hostile to the Third Reich because of political belief, nationality, race or religion. Among the officers on the register with their arms raised, *Sieg Heil,* would be counted Field Marshal von Brauchitsch, Major General Behrens, Major General Dornberger, Field Marshal von Kleist, Field Marshal von Manstein, Field Marshal von Rundstedt, Admiral Hans Voss...

The stationmaster, Mr Hill, of Bridgend railway station knew all about Camp Eleven and its inmates. He happened to be in his office one late spring evening when yet another batch of high-ranking German officers arrived. He heard the loud, stuttering, steamy noise of the engine outside his black-out window. He held a cup of tea in his right hand and hesitated for only a moment, listening to the train coming to a halt, before bringing the china cup up to his lips. He did not need to be involved with the arrival of this new batch of Nazis as they alighted from the train with their kitbags and suitcases. A number of these prisoners, he knew, belonged to the Waffen SS. A small military escort awaited them on the darkening platform. They would handle it. A few Bridgend policemen were in attendance, too, under the command of Superintendent Fitzpatrick. Outside, the doors of the train compartments were being slammed, one by one, like a disseminated sequence of rifle shots.

Before he finished drinking his cup of tea, Mr Hill heard the train move out of the station, the same, familiar, shattering, steamy noise again. He glanced at the circle of the large plain clock on the shining, utilitarian painted wall. In half an hour he would be off duty, free to cycle home. By then the prisoners would have long departed, been marched out of the station, down the hill into Bridgend on their way to Special Camp Eleven, probably singing like the earlier fanatics who had arrived there, 'We will fight and die for the Führer.'

Twenty minutes later, though, Mr Hill learnt from a porter that the prisoners were still standing next to their baggage on the platform. It seemed that they stood there, haughty, sullen, in their peaked caps, dressed in their officers' uniforms that had been earlier stripped of Nazi medals and insignia. They would not move. They would not march out of the station.

'Not an inch. They won't budge. They complain they 'aven't been met by any officer, any British officer of 'igh enough rank,' the porter explained.

Moreover, they refused to carry their own luggage. 'Where's the transport?' one of the generals had shouted at Superintendent Fitzpatrick. 'How far is the Camp? More than a mile! Who's going to carry our things?'

Mr Hill turned on the cold water tap to clean out the cup. Afterwards, deliberately, he put on his Great Western Railway stationmaster's round peaked cap, knocked the light off, opened the door for the porter, shut it behind him, locked it, before strolling on to the twilit platform. He saw the Nazis in their uniforms standing in line, luggage at their feet. He observed the puzzled dismay remarkably expressed on Superintendent Fitzpatrick's face.

It was not too dark. The prisoners saw Mr Hill slowly coming towards them with that dignified, imposing air of his. They saw gold braid on his cap, the rich gold braid on his frock coat. They did not realise they beheld a man in the superb, resplendent glory of a British stationmaster's uniform. They believed that, at last, an army officer of great importance, a Goering amongst men, had arrived to meet them.

'Pick up your bags,' yelled Stationmaster Hill and, docile, they obeyed.

Without any further trouble whatsoever they marched out of the station accompanied by the small, baffled army escort and the few policemen. Disciplined, they goose-stepped down the hill into Bridgend, through Merthyr Mawr Road, onward to Special Camp Eleven.

By the time they arrived at the tall barbed-wire fence that skirted the A48, and could see the four high watch-towers silhouetted against the last light in the sky, Mr Hill was already home, parking his bike down the side path of his house. Soon, after removing his bicycle clips, he was able to tell his wife about the minor local difficulty at the station. 'Pick up your bags,' I shouted. 'Duw, that's all. Pick 'em up. An' know what, love. They picked them up, see. The whole bloody lot of them. Generals too. Easy as winking.'

The Scream

I had thought it best to walk to the main Bridgend-Cardiff Road where a lorry, or a jeep, or a rare private car would, in those petrol-rationed days, pick me up and take me on to Cardiff; but now that the hints of advancing night had become unambiguous I felt uneasy and worried about being stranded nowhere. For who would stop for a stranger once darkness had fallen? I could hardly turn back to Ogmore, return to the shelter and seductive excitements of Gwen's tent in Hardee's Field, having boasted that I would be assisting that celebrated chest surgeon Mr Emyr James the next morning at Cardiff's Royal Infirmary. Besides, now I was more than six miles from Ogmore.

I wished I hadn't fortuitously thumbed the surgeon's car a week earlier when I had set out to meet Gwen. 'You're Max's nephew, aren't you?' he had said. 'And a medical student too? At which hospital?'

When I told him I was at Westminster Hospital in London and had been on a surgical firm he asked me if I would like to observe him operate, 'maybe help out a bit', the following Tuesday. So here I was, nearly seven miles from Ogmore that Monday evening, after one short lift in a farmer's van to Ewenny. Only one vehicle had passed by since, an army lorry with its headlights already on, but it did not even slow down as I hitchhikerly gesticulated and later cursed its occupants. I watched its red rear light disappear past the abandoned quarry beyond the far curving hedge. Afterwards, the engine and tyre noise dying away, the lane became more silent, darker, lonelier, more inhospitable and by the time I reached the A48 only the Western sky behind me retained the residue of daylight.

Each evening, at Ogmore, there had been remarkable chemical sunsets but here the sky, generally, had collapsed into darkness though without a cloud in sight. The weather of 1947 would surely be starred in the record books: first the freezing winter and lately this prolonged summer heat wave. Where I stood, the straight 'golden mile', as this part of the A48 was called, ceased and before me rose the long, long slope of Crack Hill, aiming at the sky. Empty Crack Hill, not a sound or sign of traffic.

During the war, in the cinemas of Cardiff, a peremptory notice would sometimes appear on the screen, interrupting the film: 'An air raid has sounded. BE BRITISH. DON'T PANIC.' Now, as I began to walk up Crack Hill I muttered that slogan to myself. It would have been pointless to loiter at the bottom of the hill. A driver, assessing the gradually increasing incline, would speed up reflexly, be more likely to put his foot down on the accelerator rather than brake.

Half way up the hill I turned to see the lights of Bridgend in the distance below. Two years earlier, not one would have been visible because of the total black-out. But at least the armaments factory next to the Golden Mile, though camouflaged and dark, would have been humming with indefatigable activity, vehicles coming and going, wheels turning. Now all those distant sinister one storey constructions were deserted – like the road below, like the road above. The nameless birds, the birds nameless to me, were flying home, mysterious smudges in the sky, as the stars, punctual as ever, took up, like sentries, their appointed positions. On the crest of Crack Hill I waited yet still no traffic appeared, neither from the West, nor from the East. Small, in the immense splendour of a halcyon summer night, I should have felt awe and humility and gratitude for the gift of being alive. Instead, I experienced a sense of dread – but a dread of what? Perdition, annihilation, Nothing itself? When I observed, at last, headlights moving up the Golden Mile toward Crack Hill I felt as if I had awoken from some terrible but already unremembered dream.

The lorry halted a hundred yards ahead of me. Relieved, I ran towards it but it suddenly began to move away as if the driver had changed his mind about picking me up. Further down the road, though, it stopped again. Surprised, I walked quickly towards the lorry, half expecting it to take off once more. This time it waited in the near darkness, bulky, its engine drumming away, a tarpaulin stretched over some unseen cargo. As I drew near, I noticed the lorry bore no identifying lettering anywhere on it. I looked up at the anonymous driver. 'Cardiff?' I queried.

I had the sense of being observed intensely before the driver eventually nodded. I climbed up into the cabin beside him and after I had thanked him for stopping, without saying one word, he released the brake and drove off into the encroaching darkness. 'Damn-all traffic on the road,' I opined, trying to make a polite connection with the driver. He did not speak but stared ahead as his headlights created, too realistically, hedge, gate, a wall, tree, hedge, and always the empty road. Though he was sitting down I could tell he was a big man. I glanced curiously to my right at his sensitive profile when suddenly he turned towards me.

'Aven't you enough dough to take a train from Bridgend?' he said. His overblown full face did not match his profile. His accent was not local.

'No,' I said. He took a packet of Players from his pocket but he did not offer me one.

'A light?' he asked.

I fumbled in my pocket for matches but I must have left them in Gwen's tent in Hardee's Field. 'Sorry,' I said.

He slowed down the lorry until it was travelling at only ten miles an hour. He kept at this speed for several minutes. 'Anything wrong?' I asked. He did not reply but stared ahead, the unlit cigarette in his mouth, as the lorry crawled forward. I now began to feel a rational anxiety instead of the unfocused unease I had experienced at the crest of Crack Hill, especially when he began a staccato interrogation in which he clumsily attempted to discover how much money I had on me.

'If I hadn't picked you up you'd 'ave to 'ave paid for a night's lodging, right?'

'It would have been a problem. I would just have waited until I got a lift.'

'You've got no money at all?'

He took the cigarette out of his mouth, then put it back again. I could almost *hear* him thinking. At last he asked, 'Are you on the dole?'

'I'm a student.'

'Don't your Dad give you any money?'

'I'm broke. That's why I'm hitchhiking.'

Just then I saw a dead animal on the road, in the headlights. Though we moved towards it almost in slow motion I could not identify it. It had been run over already – a rat or a fox, I wasn't sure. I assumed he had seen it. The dead animal went under the lorry and behind us it was dark. He said nothing. When I repeated, after another mile, 'Why are you going so slowly?' he stopped the lorry. He opened the lorry door though there was no house or building in sight. I didn't know where we were – close, I guessed, to the village of Pentre Meyrick. He began to climb down. I sat still wondering what was going to happen; sat very still not wishing to display my anxiety.

'Don't you want a pee?' he said.

'No.'

Tall, burly, he looked up at me unsmiling, and I felt, perhaps wrongly, that it would be dangerous if I got out of the lorry.

'Better to have a piss,' he grunted. Then, 'Please yourself,' before he moved off into the darkness, away from the headlights. I sat in the cabin, alert, tense, while a crazed insect clicked arhythmically inside the windscreen and the engine thrummed away. He was out somewhere behind the lorry for a long time. Suddenly, two cars appeared, one following the other, one whoosh, then another, as they hurtled past the lorry, their headlights probing the hedges well beyond the lorry's own illumination. I wished I'd been outside to flag down one of those cars and so gain for myself a comfortable, unprovoking lift.

At last, I heard the lorry driver's footsteps and, to my surprise, I saw that his cigarette was now lit. So he'd had a match all the time. He pulled at his cigarette before we set off again, this time travelling at a more normal speed. When we passed through the few houses of Pentre Meyrick he said, 'I'll 'ave to turn off soon. We'll stop for five minutes before we go on to Cardiff.' I didn't understand but as I turned to interrogate him a car coming from the opposite direction momentarily lit his face and I decided to say nothing. I decided it would be best not to ask any questions at all, not even when, a few miles further on, we turned down a narrow country lane – unsignposted, of course, because during the war all the signposts had been taken down lest the Germans should invade us and know where they were!

'I won't be long,' the lorry driver said, throwing his dibby out of the window. 'You'll be able to get a cuppa tea 'ere. You've enough dough for a cuppa tea, haven't you?' And he laughed. His bleak laugh was that of a practical joker. Could he have been having me on all the time, deliberately making me feel threatened, playing me for his own mindless amusement, like a fish at the end of a line? Right from the beginning, hadn't he cruelly teased me, driving the lorry on from its stationary position as I ran up to it? Was he still acting a part when he warned me, 'At this place, keep yer mouth shut, just say you're with me.' Or was he involved in some illegality? Why, I wondered, were there no markings of identification on the lorry itself, and what was hidden under the tarpaulin?

The hedges of the country lane seemed to converge but suddenly they fanned open to reveal electric lights from windows behind the trees. He slowed the lorry down and turned it through an open gate into a small, bumpy yard. As we lowered ourselves down from the cabin I heard a dog barking in the darkness and I sensed that I was about to cross stepping stones into the unexpected. I followed the tall figure of the lorry driver through trees that looked carbon-black against the lighter darkness of the sky. He led me towards the silhouette of a building that resembled a large Nissen hut.

The door opened into its main space without the ceremony of a corridor. The radio was on, tuned to the Light Programme – Much-Binding-in-the-Marsh. It was an impoverished café with a rundown bar. Some B.C. spam sandwiches and what looked like half a blackberry tart lay behind a glass front next to a large metal tea-urn. And in the bar itself there were not too many bottles of beer on a shelf behind the head of the bartender, to whom the lorry driver now spoke quietly. Evidently they knew each other. I looked around at this embodiment of the ordinary and took a seat at one of the white oilcloth-covered tables beneath a flaked ad for Brains beer. At the other side of the room sat the only other occupants – a young woman and a much older man with glasses in front of them that contained what could have been water or gin.

'Tony, give this kid a cuppa tea,' I heard the lorry driver say. He then disappeared through a door next to a stove. I don't know why I kept looking at that stove. It had a large pipe going straight up through the ceiling. It reminded me of some other place but I couldn't recall which or what. The barman called to ask if I took sugar. When I replied, 'Just one, please,' I sensed the couple at the far table were staring at me. I turned towards them but their heads, like lovers or those hatching a conspiracy, were bent towards each other. I had been mistaken. The fair young woman's make-up was over the top: clown-powdered and rouged and bleeding lipstick. She was too thin. Her balding partner, who wore an army surplus jacket, could have been old enough to have fathered her. Above their heads, underneath rickety struts, flies ceaselessly performed their rituals around their god, the lampshade. Then I forgot the vanished lorry driver, the couple whispering together, the bored barman listening to the frequency of the radio, the stove with its wide, upright pipe, and I wondered simply, what am I doing here? What the hell am I doing here? My life was somewhere else.

I could not say I looked forward to observing Emyr James operate. A privilege it might have been, but I had no intention of becoming a surgeon. In the operating theatre I felt inept. Mr MacNab was right when he said that surgery was not my forte. I recalled my blunders the first time I had assisted him two months earlier. Mr MacNab, holding the glinting, silver-coloured scalpel had firmly made an incision near the groin which he carried upward for inches. The blood welled up and I seemed merely to get in the surgeon's way. After he had cut through the external oblique muscle he signalled that the muscle he had divided should be pulled apart, in order that the wound could gape wider. I was too tentative. No wonder MacNab's blue, bluebell-coloured eyes scolded me above his mask.

Soon, with exquisite skill, the divided peritoneum, on either side of the wound, was neatly picked up with forceps and as these were drawn upon they acted as a retractor. Now, open to MacNab, was that clandestine darkness that had been trapped there in the chasm of the abdominal cavity since the beginning. Two fingers of MacNab's gloved right hand disappeared as he felt for the caecum. He called for a blunt dissector. How clumsy I had been. I was a stranger in a foreign land who did not speak the language. So many misunderstandings. Yet in no time at all the peritoneum was sewn up again with a continuous catgut suture. After the muscles and skin had been stitched together, Mr MacNab had said to me cheerfully, 'Never mind. Some people are good at one thing, others at another.'

I drank the dregs of the stewed tea I had been given. I glanced at my watch. It was getting late. I needed to have a good sleep if I was to 'help out' during Emyr James' list in the morning. Would he expect me to assist at all or would I just be a spectator? Emyr James, it was rumoured, attended the royal family and had refused a knighthood. He certainly had the reputation of being a fast and remarkable surgeon. In fact, he was to surgery what Stanley Matthews was to football.

The programme on the radio had changed. Geraldo and his Orchestra featured. The balding fellow at the far table was reading *The South Wales Echo* and I observed the young girl crush the end of her cigarette into an ashtray as if she hated it. Where was the lorry driver? How much longer had I to wait? I did not fancy walking the length of the country lane back to the A48 and trying, this time of night, to obtain a different lift.

Suddenly I heard the girl cry out, 'C'mon, let's dance.' Her partner rudely continued to read the *Echo*. She rose to her feet, energetically pushed one of the drab tables aside, then another, to make room for dancing. 'C'mon,' she repeated. Her older companion would not dance or could not dance. 'Chris', Betty,' he grumbled. 'You,' she said imperatively. I half turned to see if she were speaking to the barman. He seemed busy. He was striking matches. He struck one, watched the small flame leap before dying out in an ash tray, then he struck another one and I knew he would repeat the whole process over and over. 'You, no, you,' she insisted. I hesitated. The barman called out, imitating Tommy Trinder, 'You lucky people.'

There was hardly room enough to dance. I put my arm around her waist and, immediately, she brought both her arms around my neck and with provoking intimacy pressed her thin body close to mine as Geraldo's Orchestra played, 'When the Deep Purple Falls'. Her hair tickled my cheek and, curiously, I gazed over her shoulder at the balding man with the *Echo* in his hand. He merely glanced up at me unsurprised, unperturbed. 'Fair dos, she fancies you,' he said. If she was trying to make him jealous obviously she was not succeeding.

'Do you come here often?' I joked, somewhat desperately, but the girl clung to me even more seductively and, for a moment, I thought of Gwen in the tent at Ogmore.While Geraldo announced the next number she did not break away but blankly stared up at me, her face close enough to mine so that I could smell the warm sweet tincture of gin on her breath. She was, I guessed, even younger than I had originally supposed. No make-up could adequately disguise that totally immature, unlined, doll-like face.

I tried again. 'What do you do?' I asked.

'Do?' she responded, and laughed as if I had asked a foolish question.

The balding man looked up. He had overheard our unimportant brief dialogue.

'I'm an aviator, kiddo,' she said. 'Aren't I an aviator, John?' she said louder to the balding man.

'She's Queen of the May, sonny,' the man said. 'She's a war veteran and all she wants is silk stockings.'

'Yes,' she said, gently pressing with her two hands the back of my neck, 'I'm Queen of the May,' and hugged me, as we danced, even closer. It happened just after the music stopped. Scandalously, unmistakably, somewhere behind the partition of the bar, a woman screamed. A dreadful, elongated scream. I felt chilled hearing the shock of that single inquisitionary scream that went on and on, then ceased suddenly. The girl tried to close up to me once more, to dance, as if nothing had happened. Geraldo played 'Stardust'.

'What was that?' I asked.

'Have another cuppa tea,' the shoddy balding man called. 'Or dance.'

'There was a scream,' I said.

'Betty likes this tune, doncha Betty? You like "Stardust".'

'I like dancing,' said the girl. 'I really like it.'

She spoke with passionate sincerity – as if she liked no other thing, nothing else in the whole wide tittupy world.

'Dance,' the balding man growled at me threateningly.

'Do you like Gracie Fields?' the girl asked pointlessly.

I broke away, returned to my table and the girl rejoined her partner who resumed reading the newspaper. I should have questioned the match-striking bartender. Something had happened behind that partition. One would have heard a scream like that in a Gestapo cell. I half expected to hear another one but only the dance music blared on and the balding man shouted out above the music, 'New austerity plan to be announced from Downing Street, hey.' He put down the newspaper and addressed me, 'Christ, where are our fruits of victory, hey?'

Soon after, the tall lorry driver reappeared, mumbled something to the barman, then grudgingly nodded to me indicating that we were to go. I rose, looked towards the girl. She had her left index finger in her open mouth as if she were probing an aching tooth. I followed the driver out of the bar into the silence of the yard and the waiting lorry.

'That's an odd place,' I said but was once again ignored.

Strangely, I did not feel menaced by him any longer; but it was good to be outside, under the sempiternal stars of the night. As the lorry moved off, a dog nearby began barking again.

At Cowbridge people were coming out of the pubs. The traffic lights at the end of the long street were red. The lorry stationary, the taciturn driver brought both of his hands to his face. At first I thought nothing of it, but when the lights changed and he continued to be motionless with his head still lowered into his hands, I once again became alarmed.

'The lights are green,' I said. It was as if he hadn't heard me. 'You O.K.?' I asked.

Fortunately the lights stayed green a long time and when a car overtook us he eventually lifted his face from his hands, sat upright, sombre, and eased the lorry forward. In no time at all we left the lamps of Cowbridge behind us and became isolated in the country dark, the lorry's headlights conspicuous. Was he just exhausted? I did not know for how long and how far he had driven the lorry that day. Or had he, for a moment, as I suspected, cried tearlessly, hiding his face in his hands?

In the darkness of the cabin I could not help imagining all manner of things about him. Probably he had not long been demobbed. Maybe, at that particular moment, in Cowbridge, with the traffic lights signalling an admonitory red, he had been reminded of something malign, some evil bloody incident? And what about that scream in that grubby stopping place, a scream I would remember all my life?

I recalled a picture I had seen in an artbook of Gwen's entitled 'The Scream'. It portrayed a woman, her huge right hand covering her right ear and her huge left hand covering her left ear, suggesting she did not wish to hear anything at all, no news of the world, nothing, neither searing truth nor complacent lie, and least of all her own scream. She held her hands over her ears in a posture of

117

inconsolable sorrow and shocked depression. Her eyes were depicted as two circles with a big dot near the middle of each of them, and her mouth was open, tortured, open so wide, beyond anatomical possibility, as she screamed on and on forever. And no one knew for sure, not even the artist himself, why she was screaming. Oh yes, it was possible to offer explanations, provide stories, notions metaphysical or mundane. But, finally, the precise aetiology of her scream, like so much else, was unknowable.

The headlights picked out the ivy-clad walls and the thatched roofs of houses in the village of Bonvilston. I recognised them. Some summers back when I was a sixth-former, I had worked, like others in my class, on a farm nearby, stooking hay, picking potatoes, fooling around with the Land Girls.

'During the war there was a plague of rats here at Bonvilston,' I told the lorry driver.

'Yeh?'

Soon after, we rumbled into the brief but friendly lights of St Nicholas and I began to feel the promise of freedom as we approached my hometown – like one about to be released, if not from a prison, at least from a binding relationship. We descended steep Tumble-Down-Dick and on through the featureless streets of Ely, past its occasional landmarks, the crematorium and the evil smelling Ely paperworks until we reached Cardiff proper. I was lucky. At Victoria Park I could see that the trams and buses were still running.

'I'll be going down St Mary's Street to the docks,' the lorry driver said.

So by the Castle he dropped me off. 'Thanks,' I said.

Madagascar

As the train slid slowly from the shadows and morning echoes of Paddington, the brunette opposite peered out of the window so that I was able to look at her without impudence. She wore her dark, curly hair almost as short as a boy's and this hairstyle must have been partly responsible for my first, false, through-the-corridor-glass impression of fresh, sweet youth. She was elegantly dressed, too much so for my taste, too formal, too artificially turned out. Uninvitingly so, I thought: the sort of woman who accompanied suited business men at expensive restaurants and who, in winter, might well wear a fur coat. But she was chewing gum, that was the odd thing. Women elegantly groomed do not usually chew gum. She was a duchess, I decided, who chewed gum.

The train gathered speed past century-old, soot-smoked walls and fungus-rotting houses, some of which had cardboard fixed in their windows instead of glass. The war had been over for five years but still occasional houses revealed their blitz dereliction ever more blatantly: their interior privacy exposed to reveal drab, wallpapered bedrooms in cross-section; and staircases climbing up to nowhere.

It was going to be a long, boring journey. I wished that I had taken out the *New Statesman* or the poetry magazine I had bought at Zwemmer's before I had settled my case on the luggage rack. I should have kept them accessible up there in the string bag which contained my wrapped-up meat and butter rations that I was taking home to Cardiff. In that crowded, non-smoking compartment, I decided I would wait until we had passed Reading before conspicuously rising to my feet and going through the necessary exhibition of lugging down the case, opening it up, taking out the periodicals, shutting it and arranging it once more on the rack.

For no evident reason the train, melancholy, whistled, as if it knew time was passing and it felt compelled to record a placid, hopeless, routine complaint – *transit hora sine mora*. Every journey in a train from the station of the past to the station of the future had a dream quality about it, a dream rusting away behind into amnesia as the train sped forward. I gazed beyond the edge of my neighbour's *Daily Telegraph*, through the window at a ploughed-up field full of scattered seagulls, then, the other side of a long hedge, at a grassy meadow full of standing cows, some of which ran away from the scare of the train. The curly-headed duchess, still chewing gum, opened up a paperback so that now everybody in the doped carriage, except myself, was preoccupied in alternative worlds, reading.

As a student, I had travelled this way so many times before with my little grass-green return ticket: Paddington, Reading, Swindon, Newport, Cardiff – only this time it was different. I was returning to Cardiff as a newly-qualified doctor to undertake my first job, a three-weeks locum for my Uncle Max who had booked a holiday for himself in the South of France. In late July he had telephoned me at my digs in London. 'Would you do me a favour?' he had asked me. 'The locum I'd arranged – well, I've been let down anyhow.' I had hesitated for several reasons, not least because I felt strongly about the justice of our having a National Health Service and Uncle Max, having opted out, only took on private patients. He had misunderstood my hesitation. 'The going rate is fifteen pounds a week. What do you say?'

Three weeks, I had thought. Forty-five pounds. With that money I could pay off my debts and, at a later date, take a holiday myself.

'You'd want me to do your rounds, apart from taking surgeries,' I prevaricated. 'I haven't got a car.'

'I've spoken to your father. He'll lend you his. You know they've just derationed petrol. Look,' he continued, 'you won't be too busy in August anyhow. It'll be good experience for you.'

'I was thinking of going away myself. After the exams and everything, I could do with stretching out on a beach.'

'Leave it till September,' Uncle Max urged.

And that's exactly what I had schemed to do, eventually. I had arranged to go with my art historian friend, Nick Tremayne, in his car to Italy in September, after my three-week stint in Cardiff. Before that excursion, though, it would be strange to see patients without supervisory advice and without the backing of hospital resources. 'The first time.' That's how it had been continually these latter years: the first time in the formaldehyde stench of the Anatomy Room; the first time in the alarm of Casualty; the first, wide-eyed attendance in the Operating Theatre; first childbirth, first death, first post mortem – first everything I thought as the train, passing over a bridge, altered its previously predictable rhythm into an irregular brief clatter on the track.

We were almost at Swindon when the train slowed down before coming to a jerky full-stop. It waited, mindlessly, in silence, between some nameless parcelled fields. I took the opportunity to move into the corridor and light up a cigarette. The train did not move. It had apparently conked out and I opened the corridor window, pulling on its thick leather strap. When I put my head out of the window I saw the curve of the train. Ghosts of steam rose from the couplings between the carriages. I was more than half way through my cigarette, the train still unaccountably stationary, when I became aware of a commotion inside the compartment, the other side of the glass. The curly-headed woman appeared stricken, her hand over the right side of her face. I slid back the compartment door to hear her saying desperately, 'It's blood, it's blood.'

The man who had been reading *The Daily Telegraph* said, 'It's coming from there.' Another passenger, obviously an old age pensioner, repeated, 'Aye, it's up by there.' I looked up at the rack.

'Oh, my God,' I said. 'I'm sorry, gosh. Oh my God. It's my meat ration.'

'What?'

'The meat. I'm awfully sorry. What a thing... the parcel's leaking.'

'It's not my blood?' the woman said absurdly, no longer chewing gum.

'No,' I said, 'it's meat, just meat.'

I reached for the string bag. The man next to me kindly allowed me several pages of his *Daily Telegraph* to rewrap my parcel. As I was doing so the pensioner's grey-haired wife announced, 'Chicken is two an' elevenpence a pound now.'

'It's not chicken,' said her husband, 'it's meat.'

'For the third time this month they've increased the price of chicken by twopence a pound,' she insisted.

'It's meat, not chicken, Doris.'

'Beef,' I said, glancing towards the duchess whose curly head, however, was bent as she scrutinised her Vogue dress for beef bloodstains.

A train whooshed by in the opposite direction making our

carriage momentarily shiver and soon we began to move forward again past a glimpse of rusted rails and, in the distance, bright fireweed. 'I really am very sorry,' I said. 'So sorry.' Unsmiling, she nodded absolution.

Only one house in Cardiff has a blue plaque on it. Ivor Novello had lived there. My uncle's surgery was but a few houses away. When I arrived, Uncle already had his luggage in the hall. He was ready to leave for his holiday. First, he had to instruct me in his own routines. Beatrice was in attendance. She was a distant relative, an extremely efficient, unmarried, friendly, middle-aged woman who acted as housekeeper, book-keeper, cook, receptionist, and who had known my uncle since she was a little girl.

'Beattie will advise you about everything,' Uncle said.

Meanwhile, realising that as a newly qualified doctor I would be only too aware of my inadequacies, he kept assuring me 'Not to worry'. Though I think he betrayed his concern when he sighed, 'The way you're dressed, the way you look, like a medical student rather than a doctor.' My own doubts about my proficiency became more acute when I learned that he dispensed medicines himself and expected me to do so also. 'Here,' he announced, opening the door in the surgery of a large cupboard as big as an old-fashioned pantry, 'is my little dispensary.'

A row of huge jars containing different levels of coloured fluids stared down at me, intimidating me, interviewing me. I had never dispensed medicines in my life: it had not been part of my medical education. To write out prescriptions would be a novel enough experience for me. Then I recalled that my uncle had been trained as a chemist before he became a doctor.

'Don't worry. 'S'easy anyhow,' said Uncle Max. 'You'll find labels on the jars. Look.'

Sure enough, the giant jar of red medicine was marked *For Nervous Complaints*. 'Phenobarbitone,' said Uncle, 'and that jar over there... Bromides.' The one containing a grey, flocculent mixture was marked *For Stomachs;* the brown fluid *For Coughs*.

'I think you gave me some of that evil-tasting brown stuff when I was a kid,' I said.

'The worse the medicine tastes the more the patient believes it'll do him good,' responded Uncle. 'It works, you know.'

'With the help of God,' I said.

'And here's the white aspirin,' Uncle Max continued, pointing to another huge bottle on a lower shelf. ' And there's the pink aspirin for more sophisticated patients – arthritics, most of whom feel they should have something better than aspirin. Over there, look, the tonics.'

'You con them,' I said.

'For their own sakes,' my uncle replied without a quiver. 'All the jars are labelled and, as you'll see, every label has the dose written on it anyhow – a teaspoonful or tablespoon three times a day or whatever. No Latin obscurantism here. 'Course you'll have to write out prescriptions for antibiotics and the newer drugs. Mind you, see up there. Plenty of samples from the pharmaceutical firms to try out.'

'You know those lines of Pope, Uncle?'

'The Pope?'

'No, Alexander Pope.

Be not the first by whom the new are tried
Nor yet the last to lay the old aside.'

Uncle Max glanced at his wristwatch. 'You still writing poetry?' he asked. 'I read your book. Couldn't understand a word of it.' He smiled. 'Your father will say you haven't much time for nonsense like that now you're qualified.' He shrugged. 'You can stay here, if you like, anyhow, above the shop.'

'No, no thanks,' I said. 'There's a familiar bed round the corner in Cathedral Road. Mam and Dad are expecting me. I've even got my meat ration to take home.'

Uncle Max nodded. 'Anyhow, Beattie will look after you while you're here.' Then he was off for his holiday in St Tropez and I sat alone in his consulting room, very important, turning over the pages of the current *British Medical Journal* until the telephone rang and I picked up the receiver to hear a voice anxiously ask, 'Doctor?'.

That evening I took my first surgery, wrote out certificates, gave a final penicillin injection to a sailor from the docks who had picked up gonorrhoea, prescribed sedatives, the pink and white aspirin, and tonics for those whose symptoms seemed nebulous, not corresponding to any textbook description of organic illness. And that was it. There had been no crisis, nothing so far I couldn't handle. And yet most of the time I felt a fraud, as if I were impersonating someone else.

I gazed round the silent surgery; at the stethoscope on my desk along with the sphygmomanometer and the big tuning fork to test reflexes; at the bookcase behind the desk full with its medical journals and out-of-date medical textbooks; at the weighing machine and the sunlamp in the corner; the rack of test-tubes on the windowsill near the Bunsen-burner; and at the small, polished table next to the dispensary door on which Beattie, no doubt, had placed a vase of tall, bold, brilliant red gladioli with their green ensiform leaves. Secrets had been uttered in this room beyond my knowing and would, for certain, be uttered again in the future.

In the hall, I shouted out to Beattie, 'I'm off.' She came down the stairs as I collected my suitcase and the string bag with my rations in it.

Beattie said, 'It's unlikely that I'll need to trouble you, see, with any night calls. I'll only phone you, like, if it's a dire necessity.'

'You're Uncle Max's sentry,' I joked.

'Yes,' she said, seemingly pleased with that description.

The next day, after morning surgery, Beattie served me a light lunch and said, 'You're doin' great.' Twenty-four hours later she was giving me lunch and encouraging me with the same formula; 'You're doin' great.' She used that expression as often as Uncle repeated the word 'anyhow'. Meanwhile I was wondering where were the sub-acute degeneration cases? Where the woman suffering from thyrotoxicosis? Where the young man with Hodgkin's Disease?

At Westminster Hospital they had taught me, 'Common things occur most commonly', meaning certain things and symptoms, say, of an anaemia, pointed to an iron deficiency rather than the anaemia that is a sequel to lead poisoning. Now, though, if I prescribed an iron tonic it was not for a common iron deficiency anaemia but something altogether more common still – a functional tiredness. Taking the bottle of medicine from the pantry I would say firmly, like a hypnotist, 'This will do you good', and feel once more like a phony. Not that patients expected me to approach them too scientifically.

When I requested an ex-miner to take off his shirt so that I could examine his chest with a stethoscope, his previous experience of doctors made him accuse me, 'Most doctors 'ave the knack of listenin' to my chest without strippin'.' When I insisted that he strip to the waist, he said, 'Duw, you're from 'arley Street, are 'u?'

To be sure, before the week was out, I did encounter some patients with the definite illnesses that my medical education had prepared me for. I felt the small triumphant sense of true accomplishment when I immunised children against diphtheria, treated one patient with an asthmatic attack, another with heart failure, and gave morphine to an incurable cancer case. Almost always, young as I was, such patients treated me with exaggerated respect. Perhaps something primitive in them, deep down, led them half to fancy that there were secrets in this world that some men were privy to, secrets antecedent to all recorded history, that in more recent ages had been translated into Greek and Latin from the hieroglyphics of a lost language. Some patients seemed to believe that doctors, even young ones, had these mantic secrets in their possession – and if they knew that this was not so when they were healthy, they thought otherwise when stressfully ill. Then, longing for a wizard, the patient consulted his surrogate, the doctor who, instead of a wand and a charm, bore a stethoscope and a prescription.

It was on Friday evening, after my rounds, when I was thinking to myself how I must never become pompous like some doctors – because of the way certain patients set you up on a temporary pedestal – that I learnt of Gloria Talbot's phone call. Gloria Talbot, the elegant, gum-chewing, curly-headed woman whom I had met on the train. Before we had arrived in Cardiff I had discovered her name. The compartment had become chatty and the meat-dripping episode something of a shared personal joke. It appeared that Gloria Talbot's father had died last winter and his partner, a Mr David Pugh who had recently married, had invited her to stay in the Pughs' new home in Cardiff's up-the-hill suburb of Cyncoed. For my part, when mildly probed, I did not resist boasting that I was a doctor about to take on a locum for my uncle.

'As a matter of fact,' Gloria had said, mumbling, 'David... David Pugh isn't well.'

My pensioner friend, Doris, said, 'I allers listen to the Radio

Doctor.' And her husband told Gloria, 'When you're in Cardiff you should go and see Caerphilly Castle now it's floodlit. It's unbelievable.'

Friendly though it all was I did not expect the paths of those in the train to cross mine again. But now here was Beattie's message on the desk-pad: *A Miss Gloria Talbott phoned. She says she's not a patient but would you telephone Cardiff 394711.*

As I lifted my eyes from the desk I saw through the window a large bird; not a seagull, landing on the roof of the house across the road. I rose, moving towards the window, but it flew off again. According to medieval legend, a prophetic white bird visited the sick, the Caladrius. It was believed that if the bird looked at the patient he or she would recover; if it looked away, the patient would die.

The Kardomah, in Queen Street, as usual on Saturday mornings, was crowded. I looked across the faint grey-blue tobacco haze to the other tables. At one time, years earlier, when I was a medical student beginning my studies, taking my first MB at the Welsh National School of Medicine before I continued my education in London, I visited the Kardomah regularly and knew many of its denizens. Now I knew nobody. I felt as if something had been taken away – a gift once offered but now withdrawn irrevocably.

As I reclined in one of the maroon, imitation-leather chairs waiting for Gloria Talbot, I sipped my cup of coffee and listened to half the dialogue of the two women at the next table – literally half because the younger one was awesomely deaf. Her companion moved her lips in a slow, exaggerated, grotesque way and, despite the drama of her mouth's movements, no sound issued forth. The deaf woman lip-read, then answered in a curiously nasal and much too loud voice, not realising that despite the high decibel of the crowded café her voice could be heard several tables away. 'Ken's mad to go to Korea,' she pronounced. The other woman burlesqued her lips again before the deaf woman shouted, 'It's not our war.'

When Gloria arrived she discarded a bright canary-coloured mackintosh and untied a green, transparent scarf from her hair. As we talked over our coffee I wondered if we also could be overheard for Gloria, too, spoke in a loud, confident voice. Anyway it soon became evident that she had telephoned me not because of the colour of my eyes but because she wanted help. Not for herself but for Susan Pugh.

This was my morning off. I did not particularly want to talk about medical matters but here, irritatingly, was my first and last duchess who, as it were, put me back into the surgery.

'You remember I told you that my father's partner, David Pugh, had only recently married?'

'Mmm'

'Well, soon after they returned from their honeymoon he was ill – with a collapsed lung. They admitted him to a clinic called St Winifred's. He's better now. But instead of coming home from the clinic, he booked into the Angel Hotel and he won't budge.'

Gloria's face had become alert with the interest of what she was telling me. As one of the consultants at Westminster Hospital was fond of saying, 'To talk of diseases is a sort of Arabian Nights entertainment'. Especially for those, I thought, not in the medical profession.

'What does his doctor say?' I asked mechanically.

'He says David's better. Physically he's OK now. It's not a medical problem, the doctor says. *Jesus*. Sue's in a state. David won't see anybody. I rang David and he told me to keep out of it. His voice was different. Threatening. I've never heard him talk like that. My father always said David was a very mild man – for a businessman very scholarly and mild. But really, on the phone! I don't know what to do.'

I gazed past Gloria's curly black hair at the big window of the Kardomah that had become alive with a wriggling pattern of raindrops and rivulets. The deaf woman nearby shrilled 'All the old crocks are on the road again now petrol's derationed. We got stuck at Cowbridge.'

Gloria Talbot put her hand on my sleeve. 'I have to go back to London on Monday and Sue... she cries. She's very young.'

'Young?'

'Middle twenties.'

'Like me,' I grinned. 'Not so young.'

'Right,' said Gloria, her forehead furrowing. 'But David's forty-something. He shouldn't have got married. He's an old bachelor really.'

I couldn't interfere in this. The Pughs had their own doctor. It would be unethical for me to trespass; besides how could I accomplish anything? Then the bombshell: Gloria asserted I could be of help not only because I was a doctor, but also because of my book of poems. 'I told Sue I'd met you on the train and she showed me a book of poems by you. David writes poetry too, so Sue thought you were just the person to...'

In December, 1948, Hutchinson had published my first book of poems in an edition of five hundred copies. It was distributed worldwide, according to Hutchinson. They had outlets in Australia, New Zealand, Canada, India, Ceylon, Rhodesia, South Africa, Nigeria, the Gold Coast, Sierra Leone and the USA. Sir Stafford Cripps, our 'Iron Chancellor', had declared that the prime goal for Britain was 'higher productivity' and more 'export for dollars'. So there they were; busy busy, with all their might, flogging five hundred copies of my five shilling book in all kinds of foreign nooks, up hill and down dale, to the four corners of the world, saving the United Kingdom – which included Wales, Glamorgan, Cardiff, Cyncoed – from financial ruin. Was it any wonder that, apart from a few friends and family, I had never met anyone before who had actually bought and read my poems?

I had waxed eloquently in this ironic vein in order, I suppose, to elicit a smile from Gloria Talbot. I received no such signal and it was then that I privately decided that she had no sense of humour!

'David and Sue are fans,' said Gloria earnestly. 'I must get to read your book too.'

'I don't see how I can help,' I repeated.

'Look,' Gloria said flirtatiously. 'Look, come up to Cyncoed and have Sunday lunch with us tomorrow. You'll like Sue.'

'Well,' I said, 'I really don't think...'

'Please.' She hesitated. 'I hardly know Sue really. I came down because Susan's in a panic and has no friends in Cardiff. None at all. But since David won't see me, since his doctor says he's O.K. what can I do? What the hell can I do? I don't know what to do. What can anybody do?'

I had seen relatives of patients in hospital disintegrating, wildly insisting that the doctors do something when nothing more could be done. Few people can accept that there are certain iniquities that cannot be done away with, solved. At best I had learnt that the intolerable can be made just tolerable, no more. As for the rest, well the rest is a sympathetic, small smile on the face of a doctor and a hand gentle on a shoulder.

'I do think you may be able to help. I mean David may see you. He knows your poems.'

The two women at the next table had risen to their feet, were preparing to leave. The deaf woman was opening and shutting and shaking her umbrella so that very briefly I heard, as it were, a bird's wing fluttering. I thought, I don't want to get involved but how can I say 'No'? As the proverb related, 'When the pitcher falls on the stone, the pitcher shatters. When the stone falls on the pitcher, the pitcher shatters.' I was flattered that the Pughs liked my book, unnecessarily and absurdly grateful that they had even read it, but I guessed that David and Susan Pugh spelt T,R,O,U,B,L,E.

After a late breakfast, I glanced at the headlines of the Sunday newspaper and my mother said, 'What a summer we've had. Dreadful.' My father, still in his dressing gown, lit up his first cigarette of the day, then exploded smoke. That first puff had set him off on his usual morning bronchitic episode of coughing.

'Give it up, Dad,' I said.

'The first fag... clears... the tubes,' he breathlessly rationalised before sizzling off again into a second, alarming paroxysm of coughing.

'He really should give it up,' I repeated to my mother.

'You... give... it up,' he gasped dyspnoeically, 'or you'll end... up... like me.

My mother moved to the window as if she could not bear to see his respiratory distress. 'It's a wash-out,' Mother said. 'You're lucky you're going to sunny Italy, son, in a couple of weeks.'

Yes, it was raining yet again all over Cardiff, over all the higgledy-piggledy rooftops and chimney pots, over the desolate, soggy, cindered car parks, over the pub-closed, chapel-open scratched streets of Plasnewydd, Splott, Gabalfa and Penylan. Slow, steady, summer rain over my hometown, my native city of arcades, the thin rain falling noiselessly into the swollen River Taff and pricking small circles on the surface of Roath Park Lake.

'One day I'd like to go to Italy,' my mother said.

She had never been abroad. The only time my father had been

abroad was in the First World War, as a soldier in France. They had never been further for a holiday than Torquay.

'Will you want the car this morning?' my father asked. 'I thought of droppin' in on your Uncle Eddie.'

'Not unless there's an emergency and Beattie phones,' I said. 'But I could use the car lunchtime. I have to go to Cyncoed.'

'You'll be in for lunch, won't you, son?' said my mother.

'No, I'm sorry. I should have told you, Mother.'

'You can come with me and see Uncle Eddie, if you like,' said my father. 'Your Aunt Hetty was saying she hadn't seen you this year. And your Uncle Bertie will probably be there too.'

My father wanted to show me off to his brothers, I knew that. He was inordinately proud that he had a son a doctor. He wanted me, I think, to relate stories about patients I'd seen, the nature of their maladies, how Hero Me dragged them back into the light from Death's darkened door.

'You want to show off your prize specimen,' I teased him.

'Show you off,' he said, eyes lighting up. 'You're scruffy as ever. You need a haircut. Why should I show off a block 'ead like you? That saying – the apple never falls far from the tree. Ridiculous!'

Then he had another bout of coughing and my mother loudly chimed in that he should not go out with his wheezy chest on a wet day like this and as for that twister, Uncle Eddie, and that maniac, Uncle Bertie, well, if your father was so inclined, so keen, such a mutt, so daft, as to boast about me, he could damn well, good night, send them each post-haste, instead, a copy of that tidy medical scroll that I'd received which declared I was qualified to Practise Medicine, Surgery and Midwifery. Duw!

My mother cleared away the breakfast things noisily and my father, looking at me, raised his eyebrows conspiratorially before he retired into his bedroom to dress. I returned to the newspaper and read about the polio epidemic in the Isle of Wight; how Princess Elizabeth had given birth to a little girl; how the war was faring in Korea; how it was likely that Attlee would extend conscription from eighteen months to two years; and how British hens, cock-a-doodle-do, so patriotic, laid bigger eggs than they had done for years.

I put down the newspaper when I heard the distant sound of a violin. My father, who had never had violin lessons but who had a

130

good ear, rarely took down his violin nowadays, as he used to do when I was a boy. Now, though, in the bedroom he was playing, 'Daisy, Daisy', slowly, plangently. There is something about the small sound of music from a distant room. It doesn't matter whether it is great symphonic music or simply a tune on a comb. It holds you spellbound for a moment before one door opening and another closing. And my mother, hearing the melody, came in from the kitchen wiping her hands, her apron about her waist. I sat on the sofa with the newspaper on my lap and she sang softly, her face remarkable with pleasure:

Daisy, Daisy,
Give me your answer do.
I'm half crazy
All for the love of you.

★

The sun, the light of the upper world, struggled through at last and the streets and pavements were already half-dry as I drove my father's car up the hill to the relatively new district of Cyncoed. When I was a schoolboy I used to think Cyncoed very posh. My friend of those early wartime days, Keith Thomas, had once said, 'You have to be King Midas to live up there, mun', and I knew what he meant though I did not know then who King Midas was.

Cyncoed is Welsh for White Wood. Presumably at one time the land had been thickly wooded – perhaps with silver birch? Now, high up there, beyond the Observatory, miles north of Cardiff's centre, the countryside that once was uninhabited, no doubt sublime and terrible, had been tamed, cultivated. Soaring tall trees there were still: birch and elm, beech and ash, but safe, comfortable houses stood between them, big detached houses. I noticed how their slate rooftops were still wet with rain, shining in the sunlight, reflecting the smudges of chimney pots.

I discovered the Pughs' house soon enough and drove the car through its wide-open, white-painted double gates into their short gravel drive. Through the windscreen I glimpsed, at the back of the house, beyond some shrubs, a segment of an empty tennis court. I parked the car under a tree and before I walked over the crunchy gravel I heard the drip of residual raindrops from branches and leaves falling on the car's metal roof. The air smelt of damp undergrowth but the sun was warm, still August-warm.

It was Susan Pugh who opened the front door, who smiled me into the remarkably bare hall. If asked now what my first impression was of Susan Pugh, I would answer, 'Blue'. Not the 'blue' of depression or lamentation. On the contrary, whatever her marital problems she seemed cheerful. No, I mean the colour blue. She wore a very blue dress, a blue Alice band over her light brown hair and on the lobes of her ears, conspicuously blue earrings – all matching the steady gaze of her strikingly blue eyes. It is said that Zeuxis in painting an image of Helen of Troy, that embodiment of pure beauty, chose perfect features from different models. He certainly could have chosen the large, clear, oddly slanting blue eyes of Susan Pugh.

'You found the house quite easily, I hope,' she said, as I followed her doubtfully into what must have been the breakfast room. The hallway we passed through had been uncarpeted and one room that happened to have the door open also revealed its emptiness, owning neither carpet nor visible furniture. Susan Pugh must have guessed my thoughts because she said, 'We only moved in a month ago and what with David immediately having a spontaneous pneumothorax we haven't got things properly organised.' Her accent was mildly Australian. 'Well, you know, Gloria told you. But this room's O.K.' And then she mumbled, 'And the bedroom, one bedroom.'

On the windowsill I spotted a photograph next to a square-shaped clock. 'You're a twin,' I said. Susan Pugh nodded. 'Yes. Valerie is in Australia with the rest of my family. Can I offer you a whisky? That's all I have. David's particular poison.'

As she fixed me a drink I picked up the photograph. I couldn't tell which was Susan, which her sister. They were both sitting on a sofa, both smiling widely, looking up vulnerably with their slanting large eyes at the photographer. They had their arms about each other's shoulders like good comrades. Obviously they got on with each other, unlike those famous biblical twins, Jacob and Esau, who, according to legend, argued over their birthright even before they emerged from the womb. No photograph of David Pugh evident, I noted. Not one wedding photograph either. 'There you are,' said Susan.

132

'Thank you.'

Incongruously, on a trolley, a ginger cat rested. It sat half asleep, eyes half-closed, in a cat-Nirvana, in a state not of active pleasure but of no pain, no tension, no anxiety.

'That's David's cat,' Susan explained. 'She's not used to her surroundings yet.'

'Doesn't seem stressed,' I said.

'She's a bit mad,' Susan said. 'When I get out of my morning bath, when I let the water out, that cat jumps in and tries to drink up the dregs of the water I've bathed in.'

'No cat hath greater love,' I said. 'Where's Gloria?'

Susan Pugh looked alarmed. 'She went this morning, back to London,' she said. 'Surely you got the message?'

Startled, I shook my head. For the first time I noticed that the table had been set for two people, not three. I suppose I should have been annoyed with Gloria Talbot. She had manoeuvred for me to visit Cyncoed, but she was already elsewhere, alighting perhaps at this very moment at Paddington. Why?

It seemed she had learnt that her consort – 'Consort' was the unexpected, old-fashioned word that Susan Pugh used – had returned, unscheduled, to London and she, Gloria, in profound thraldom, had hurried to be with him. She had left a message with Beattie. This apology I had not yet received. I hadn't thought about whether Gloria had a regular boyfriend or not. True, I had noticed she wore no ring on her finger but I'd never had Gloria Talbot in mind as a possible real diversion or target. Susan Pugh was another matter – or could have been, had circumstances been otherwise. On first sight I found her sexually alluring. But Susan Pugh was married, recently married.

She told me how she had met David Pugh when he had been in Western Australia on a business trip soon after his partner had died, but she said little about her present predicament. I learnt only how, on the very day they returned from their honeymoon, David Pugh had experienced a right spontaneous pneumothorax.

'Such bad luck,' Susan said. 'The doctor told me that he had a little blister on the outside of his right lung that suddenly leaked air, and like a bicycle tyre it deflated. Poor David – he was so white, so short of breath. I didn't know what to do. I was told a spontaneous pneumothorax can occur for no known reason, that the blister would self-heal in a matter of weeks and then the lung would re-expand, back to normal. And that's what happened. Only when he was better, he didn't come home.'

The textbooks did indicate a mysterious aetiology but the few cases I had seen in hospital always had stress triggers. Was a honeymoon one such for some? I had heard all about honeymoon cystitis, but a honeymoon pneumothorax?

But Susan was continuing. 'He won't talk to me, won't see me. And there are things to be seen to, about this house, about a hundred things.'

I nodded, but I told myself again: I'm not her doctor. I mustn't even show off by talking about my experiences of spontaneous pneumothoraces.

'You must be hungry,' she said. 'Lunch will be ready in a jiffy.' She went into the kitchen and returned holding a saucepan. 'I'm a vegetarian,' she pronounced. 'I hope you don't mind.'

Over lunch she talked about David Pugh's love of poetry, how she had been charmed by him when he quoted the verses of an Australian poet to her. Have you heard of John Manifold?' she asked me. I hadn't. Quietly, smiling, she recited off by heart:

> My dark-headed Kätchen, my spit-kitten darling
> You stick in my mind like an arrow of barley
> You stick in my mind like a burr on a bear
> And you drive me distracted by not being here.

She stopped. 'Shall I go on?'

'Please,' I said.

She continued without embarrassment in a way that underlined for me that this was no English person – but a direct Australian. Or maybe it was simply the slight flavour of her accent.

> I think of you singing when dullards are talking
> I think of you fighting when fools are provoking;
> To think of you now makes me faint on my feet
> And you tear me to pieces by being so sweet.

134

The heart in my chest like a colt in a noose
Goes plunging and straining but it's no bloody use;
It's no bloody use, but you stick in my mind
And you tear me to pieces by being so kind.

As she recited it was as if a switch had been touched. Her very face brightened. 'It is a charming poem,' I said. 'But you're not dark-headed.'

'And I'm not called Kätchen,' she laughed.

Later, after we had cleared the dishes together, she suggested that we should have a game of tennis. I'm sure she hadn't planned it, she merely looked out of the window and impulsively cried, 'Do you play tennis?'

'Yes.'

'I think the court will have dried out,' she said.

'I haven't any tennis stuff.'

But David Pugh's daps fitted me, more or less, and Susan changed into very short shorts so that my heart went plunging like a colt in a noose, and it did so again whenever she bent down to pick up the tennis balls near the net. The President of the Royal College of Medicine once remarked on the beautiful vision of young women unclothed to the waist, visions given to artists and doctors in the course of their work. As I served I had a vision of Susan Pugh playing tennis topless with me.

When we returned to the house she halted, turned, confronted me with her blue eyes, intense. 'It's so good of you,' she said, 'to offer to help me.' I happened to glance at the step that led up to the kitchen door. David Pugh's cat sat there, front feet together, sedate, ladylike. It knew. Accusatory, unblinking, in a trance, it appeared to stare right through me to the accumulating soots of my puritan soul.

I opened the door of the waiting room. No more patients. Wednesday morning had been the least busy so far. And there were no rounds on Wednesday afternoon. So I would go, I decided, to the mid-week evening game at Ninian Park. Cardiff were playing Manchester City. Perhaps Susan Pugh would consent to keep me company? 'No no,' I thought, 'to hell with that.'

I went back into the surgery and picked up the cup of coffee that Beattie had brought in for me earlier. The coffee was cold but I sipped it nevertheless and glanced at one of the leaflets on the desk. I couldn't, shouldn't telephone Susan. Besides, she would ask if I had been to the Angel Hotel. She would be direct. She didn't seem ever to beat about the bush. She didn't seem to own the reserve of the women I had known in London. She called me by my first name as if I had known her for years – like Americans do, like the friendly Welsh for that matter. She appeared to be without guile – unlike Gloria Talbot.

So many leaflets. So many bombardments from the pharmaceutical companies advertising the advantages of this or that product, for this or that symptom or condition. They had an air of authority about them. I looked away from the leaflet. The telephone waited there on the desk, beckoning me to dial that Cyncoed number. I thought of the line from that poem she uttered: 'And you drive me distracted by not being here'. After our game of tennis she had offered me a cooling orange drink and told me how David Pugh had sent her money to return to Australia – fare money and extra. 'I can't go back,' she had said. 'We're married. Things may not have gone very well between us but I care for him. Doesn't he realise I care for him? We cut our honeymoon short but... he needs time. He's been a bachelor for so long. I will give him time. What happens in the bedroom is not everything, is it?'

It's a helluva lot, I thought. I read the leaflet again. It carried an injunction common to many similar advertisements: *This product is almost free of undesirable side effects*. It would have been good, I thought, if I could have had an affair with Susan without undesirable side effects! But that was impossible even if she had similar desires, which as far as I knew she had not. I looked up from the leaflet which listed the contraindications for prescribing the advertised drug, thus giving the rest of the copy a spurious authenticity.

I would go to watch the football game on my own. I shouldn't follow my impulse to invite her to come with me. She was impulsive. She must be impulsive to have married a man she hardly knew, a much older man too. She could not have known David Pugh well in Australia. A month? Six weeks? Christ, she was not cautious. She was someone given to saying, 'Yes, yes', rather than, 'No'.

Strange, when the telephone clamoured as I sat there, I felt sure it would be Susan but a man's voice asked, 'Doctor?'

136

'Yes.'

'Oh.'

'Yes.'

'I'm a bit worried,' he said. 'This is Stephen Knight, Doctor. My wife says I should ring you.'

Mr Knight hesitated. It was as if he were ashamed to confess something. At last, he said simply, 'The water I'm passing is green-coloured. Definitely green.'

I hadn't a clue why that should be but I reassured him and invited him to come and see me in the surgery next morning. Afterwards I extracted *Symptoms and Signs in Clinical Medicine* from Uncle Max's bookcase. On page 141 I read: 'Abnormal constituents may produce a complete change in the colour of the urine. Bile gives it a green or green-yellowish appearance; blood a red or reddish-brown colour. The possibility of excreted drugs modifying the colour of urine should also be borne in mind, especially such common ones as rhubarb which gives an orange colour and methylene blue (frequently contained in proprietary pills) which gives a green colour.'

I closed the book, replaced it in the bookcase, I stood there restless, a little bored. When I succumbed and dialled the Pughs' house Susan, as I expected, soon asked me if I had seen her husband.

'Not yet,' I replied, and at once regretted saying 'Not yet.' For that qualification implied that I would do so soon.

In the car, as we reached the district of Canton, Susan made a consulting-room confession. At the breakfast table, the morning after their wedding night, David Pugh had referred to the voodoo lily, an exotic plant that at times poured forth a ghastly odour to attract carrion flies. 'You see,' he had explained, 'its odour is akin to dead meat. It fools the flies. They are attracted into its female-pollination chamber. If these carrion flies have visited another voodoo lily previously then the flower is fertilised.' Susan paused. 'I'm afraid I – well I threw the milk I was drinking at him. He stood up and walked out of the room. But it was a pathological thing for him to say. I know I easily go off the handle but... '

At this I dared to ask, 'Hadn't you been with him before the

137

wedding night?' At once I realised I had asked her less out of concern than simply because of prurient curiosity. I knew she had turned away from me though I looked straight ahead at the road. 'In Australia – only once,' she said softly. 'I should have realised then. But it was the first time. And the first time you don't always expect a bull's eye, do you?'

We had come among a lot of cars now and had to queue up at the traffic lights. We were getting near the ground. 'David's such a sensitive man about some things. He's really learned, knows all sorts of unlikely things. But when it comes to the feelings of a woman he has no idea at all.'

'Most men haven't,' I said, obliged to respond somehow but realising that what I had said sounded smug – as if I wasn't like most men.

'You're right. Absolutely right,' she said vehemently.

Susan's moods altered quickly, unaccountably. A minute later it was as if she had disclosed nothing intimate to me at all. 'Look, look,' she cried excitedly.

A man on the nearby pavement, accompanied by several others, was dressed in fancy clothes, all blue and white, the Cardiff City colours. Seeing how Susan was staring at him, he lifted his improbable clown's hat in salute. She unwisely waved and, all triggers released, he and the others wolf-whistled and one danced near to our slow-moving car, making childish party faces at her. I do not think Susan was aware what an intensely sensual being she appeared to men. As we drove nearer to Ninian Park we encountered more and more people converging on the ground, men mainly, all walking purposefully in the same direction.

In a run-down side street, in the nostalgia of evening summer-sunlight, I parked the car and soon we were marching with the widening crowds past the programme-seller with an auctioneer's voice – 'programme, programme, getcher programme' – past the character selling differently coloured rosettes. There were policemen on foot and policemen on horses and amidst all the whirl of movement some pedestrians were gathered before an unhygienic-looking van whose owner was purveying sizzling sausages and onions.

Within the stadium a uniformed band played martial airs. There must have been some thirty thousand people at this Division 2

138

game. Behind the goalposts, in the heavy darkness high up beneath the sloping roof, spectators struck matches to light cigarettes and pipes so that small brilliant lights kept appearing in different places, over and over, flaring up here, then there, before vanishing into oblivion. A bulky Samson of a man near us, altogether too big for the wooden partition of the bench he was sitting on, lit up his pipe and his coughed-out smoke, acrid, drifted our way unpleasantly.

'Who are those people behind the touchlines?' asked Susan.

They were the war-wounded, cripples in their wheelchairs. After the First World War, casualties were privileged to be placed there. By 1939 most of these veterans had disappeared, like the lights from struck matches, into the long dark. But after the last war the concession was renewed and new survivors of bombshells, limbs shattered, reappeared to sit in their little motors behind the touch-lines, near the corner-flags.

Susan had never been to a football match before. I tried to explain the differences between soccer and hockey. I pointed out the skills of Ken Hollyman, one of the Cardiff City players; explained why Grant was offside, why the crowd were shouting at the ref. But what she admired most were the acrobatic leaps of the green-jerseyed Manchester City goalkeeper, Bert Trautmann, an ex-prisoner of war. At half-time I left her momentarily to queue up for two plastic cups of sweet tea. When I returned I saw she was in conversation with someone and her face looked frantic.

Before I descended the gangway to row K where we were sitting, the man who had engaged Susan in conversation moved away. She sat down, her left hand to her mouth. 'Anything wrong?' I asked after I had squeezed past bony knees.

'Let's go,' she said. 'Please.'

'What's the matter?'

'Please. I have to go.'

The players were coming out from the tunnel in their coloured jerseys, throwing their long shadows on the turf as we rose to quit the stadium. 'I'm so sorry,' she said. I knew I would have an explanation but not till we were outside in Sloper Road. I could hear the crowd within Ninian Park shouting, a mass voice oohing and aahing, rising and falling, while the last sunlight of the day gleamed on the squadrons of car roofs in the open, deserted carpark.

'That man you saw me talking to. He's an Australian. He's from

Perth. I don't know what he's doing over here.'

We walked under the bridge, the streets almost empty now, towards the parked car. 'He thought I was Val,' she said. 'He thought I was Valerie.'

That was not an explanation. To be mistaken for a twin sister was no reason to be so desperately exercised. It wasn't until we were in the car that she said very quietly, 'David's crazy. He too says I'm Valerie. Me, I'm Valerie, he says! He says we switched. Can you imagine?' Her slanting blue eyes searched my face as if she waited for me to comment. She continued, 'You know David went ahead of me, back to South Wales to fix up the wedding arrangements and the new house. Then he sent for me. Only he reckons – at least he pretends to believe – that it wasn't me who came. Not me, but my sister. For God's sake, what a thing to make up!'

I didn't know what to say. I didn't say anything. It occurred to me how little I knew of her. She seemed such a spontaneous open person but patently there were shadows, depths, secrets, histories unavailable to me.

'Drive me home, please,' she said quietly.

'I thought we'd have a bite to eat at the Windsor. In the docks. It's er, good food. Best place in Cardiff.'

'Sorry,' she said. 'I want to go home. I'm so sorry, I've spoilt your evening. May I go home? Do you mind?' Then bitterly, 'I call it home.'

We were both silent in the car until we drove up Penylan Hill. Then, as the lamp-posts all lit up simultaneously, making the twilight darker, she said determinedly, 'I'm going to speak to David on the phone. I've got to speak to him. And I want you to listen. I've got to have it out. Would you mind very much listening?'

Once more, in the breakfast room I stood near the door feeling-superfluous really, an awkward eavesdropper as she dialled the Angel Hotel and asked for 'Mr David Pugh, please.' I noticed, in the corner, a saucer of milk, the milk barely whiter than the saucer. The cat was asleep on a chair. Susan said tentatively, 'David?' She was cradling the phone to her ear, her pretty face grave as if she were listening to music. I should not have been there; this was a private act. 'David, this is Susan. Darling, I must...' There was a disheartening click. 'He's cut me off again,' she said, wounded. 'As soon as he, right away, when he hears me, as soon as he hears my

140

voice...' She put the receiver down and turned her back on me.

I was slow to realise that she had begun to cry.

'Susan?' I asked.

At first it was a controlled sobbing but when I spoke her name again the sobs became totally uninhibited, a totally reckless sobbing so that her body shook. I felt I was observing her through the wrong end of a telescope. There are some small distances that can still seem far. When I moved towards her she tried to hide her face from me. I glimpsed, briefly, naked despair before she brought both her hands half-clenched to hide her face.

'Please,' I said. 'Susan, please.'

I touched her gently on the shoulder but she gestured as if she wanted me to go away, to get the hell out of there. There was nothing in the room but her unrestrained weeping.

'I'll go and see him,' I said. 'Susan, listen to me. Please.'

Later, when she calmed down, before I left Cyncoed, I learnt a little more about Susan. Having witnessed her cry – she seemed so ashamed to have been observed weeping – I now had sanction to hear more about herself. 'Ever since I left home,' she said, 'it's all been so bloody unreal.'

Not that Susan's routine back in Perth sounded inspiring to me. She had no sooner taken a degree in English, like her twin, at the University of Western Australia, than her mother had suffered a stroke and she, not Valerie, had been the one designated to look after her. 'Valerie had only a week earlier gone off to Sydney,' she explained, 'having landed a job with ABC radio. She's done very well, very well. And I'm pleased for her.'

'You've never minded that?'

'No. Val and I were always – we still are – very close. You know,' she continued, 'you're special when you're a twin. You're a star. But only when you're together, you know? On your own you're simply like everyone else, not special at all, not a star. I think that's why we always used to stick together in company. Ever since I've had to go it alone I feel, well, half a person, know what I mean? Mum never encouraged us to be separate. We always were dressed the same, given the same presents on our birthday and at Christmas. We went to the same school, did our homework together, shared the same bedroom, told each other our secrets...'

'It was your mother who became ill?' I said.

'Yes,' she said. 'She's recovered a great deal from the stroke now, but she still needs some help.'

She walked over and cuddled the cat. 'I'm sorry' she said. 'I'm sorry. First of all I spoilt your football game and now I've been boring you.'

After supper Mother said, 'It's a shame you've got to go out this time of night to see a patient.'

'It's not that late,' said my father.

'It's not a patient,' I said. ' A friend of a friend – a businessman who owns a factory.'

'There's nice,' said my mother without thinking. 'But this time of night?'

'He's a businessman who writes poetry,' I said.

'Gawd,' said Dad.

Susan had told me that David Pugh's factory manufactured machines which produced artificial lace: point net machines and warp net, whatever those were. 'Your grandmother loved lace,' mother said. 'She had lovely lace things. Brussels lace and Honiton. Maltese lace too. Made entirely by needle and thread. Shawls too.'

'An ornament only looks beautiful on a beautiful person,' my father stated.

'Welsh flannel is good,' my mother said irrelevantly. And then repeated what she had told me a thousand times, 'I used to nurse you, son, in a shawl, Welsh fashion, when you were a baby .'

'Still a baby, he is,' said my father. 'It's a wonder you don't mash his bananas for 'im still.'

My mother saw me to the front door as if I were a stranger in the house or as if I were about to embark on a long journey across wild seas or barren deserts, not just to the Angel Hotel, hardly a civilised mile away. From the porch she peered over the front hedge down the wide avenue of the tree-lined, lamplit Cathedral Road. 'Anyway, it's a beautiful summer night for a change,' she remarked. 'It's really warm.'

At the top of Cathedral Road I turned left and drove the car over the bridge that spanned the River Taff before parking in Westgate Street – a street that had only recently become respectable and no longer haunted by prostitutes.

The bespectacled man at reception telephoned to let David Pugh know I was in the foyer. I half expected to be turned away but I was told without fuss the number of David Pugh's room. 'Please go up, sir. Fourth floor. The lift's over there.'

On the fourth floor, almost opposite the lift cage, waiting at an open door, stood a gingery, unshaven, middle-aged man about my own height. 'Gloria,' he said, 'Gloria Talbot told me you might look me up.' He spoke thickly as if he needed to clear his throat. He swayed a little as I followed him into a pleasant double room and when I saw an almost empty bottle of whisky on the varnished ledge next to one of the single beds, I realised he had been drinking heavily. 'Codswallop,' he said for no evident reason.

The curtains of the room had not been drawn so that I faced a long dark window over Westgate Street. I knew that in daylight I would have been able to see down below beyond Westgate Street the Glamorgan cricket pitch of Cardiff Arms Park and a glimpse, too, of the River Taff.

'Shall I shut the window?' he asked. 'It's a warm night. Very warm night.'

'It's fine,' I said.

'I've read your stuff,' he continued, 'ever since, well ever since I came across a poem of yours in *Poetry Quarterly*. I learnt you were from Cardiff too. Two poets, hey, two poets in one small city. Bound to meet, right, sooner or later?'

I hadn't come to talk about poetry. I had one mission only in mind: to persuade him to see his wife, so that, civilised, they could talk things over together, face to face. It was what Susan wanted. Not such a big thing to ask.

'Me, you and Dylan,' David Pugh was saying inanely, maudlin.

Yes, all I had to do was to be a catalyst, to be a matchmaker between husband and wife. 'There's another glass in the bathroom,' David Pugh said, about to open a door. 'But not much of this left.' He indicated the whisky bottle. 'I'll send down for another.'

'No no,' I said. 'Thank you. I'm not staying. I just wanted to have a word with you about Susan.'

Without entering the bathroom he closed the door that he had just partly opened, turning round to confront me. His receding hair was the same colour as his marmalade cat, and his eyes, watery, were blue but not like the blue of Susan's at all. He obviously had not shaved for a couple of days. The skin of his face was rough and reddish, his neck short, his chest broad, his stomach paunch announcing middle age. Hardly an ideal tennis partner for Susan Pugh, I thought. What had she seen in him to have married him so quickly? Physically he was no great shakes.

'You want to talk about Susan?' he said quietly.

'Yes.'

'I don't want to talk about Susan,' he said, a little louder.

He sat down heavily in a chair near the window and poured himself the rest of the whisky before looking at me with un-disguised hostility. Suddenly, startling me, he shouted, 'I don't want to talk about Susan to you. What business is it of yours? You're not my doctor.'

'I haven't come as a doctor,' I said uncertainly, realising that perhaps I shouldn't have been so direct. I should have taken a drink with him, been politic, talked poetry a little, even asked him about artificial lace, before referring to Susan. 'I've come because... well, because... as a friend. I mean... '

'Friend?' he said, his eyes softening, his posture relaxing. 'Oh, haw, Jesus, friend.'

'Susan says you think she's not Susan but her sister,' I said. 'You don't think that really, do you?'

He drank the whisky and said, 'I'm still getting occasional pains in my chest.'

I wasn't sure whether he was ignoring my question deliberately or simply hadn't heard me. I paused. Cautiously I said, 'Your doctor will tell you that it's on the cards to experience occasional niggling pains after a spontaneous pneumothorax. There's nothing to worry about. Those niggles will go away, become less frequent as time passes. But I was asking you about Susan.'

'Susan? You mean Valerie. You think I can't tell who I married and who I didn't?' He stared at me intently, his face thrust forward aggressively, stared at me without blinking, eyes now narrowing suspiciously, as if I were an enemy. 'The woman I fell in love with in Australia isn't the one in my house, *my* house in Cyncoed.'

'They may look alike but I'm – '

'But nothing,' said David Pugh loudly. 'Codswallop. It's not just the fact that they look alike. Though there are differences even there.' He stood up. 'I'll tell you something sir, I don't want you to repeat.'

144

I was taken aback that he called me 'sir'. He picked up the whisky bottle but realising it was empty he put it down again. 'I'll tell you, yes. You're a doctor. You can keep a secret.'

'I'm not here as a doctor.'

'But you can keep a secret.'

'Yes, I suppose...'

'Madagascar,' he said.

'What?'

'Madagascar. You know what Madagascar looks like?'

'It's an island,' I said, 'near the south-east coast of Africa.'

'Brilliant,' he said sarcastically. 'You know its shape?'

'Yes. More or less. I can visualise it.'

'A birthmark,' he mumbled. 'A pretty birthmark like the contours of Madagascar.'

He placed his right hand over his eyebrows and let his chin drop on his chest. He sat there motionless, his hand over his eyebrows, over his eyes, over his nose and said nothing more. I waited, aware for the first time of an occasional car passing in Westgate Street far below.

'You're saying,' I said 'that one of the twins has a birthmark shaped something like the island of Madagascar that the other doesn't have?'

His head still down, behind the barrier of his hand, in a sepulchral voice, he mumbled again, 'Clever boy. You've got it in one.' Again I waited but the silence within the room became intolerable. He sat there and finally removed his hand. His eyes were closed. He sat with his eyes closed, shutting me out and I remembered Susan crying. This man was crying too, in his own way, without uttering, mouth closed, eyes closed. Again I felt myself to be an intruder .

'I'd better go.'

'Don't go,' he said, stifled, his eyes still shut.

I searched in my pocket for my cigarettes and lit up. And waited. At last he opened his eyes. 'I was thinking,' he said in a melancholy but sober voice, 'I was thinking how most Australians have never seen the interior of Australia, the other side of the bush country, never seen it, not once. But they know it's there, that unseen wilderness.'

'Would you see Susan, speak to her face to face? Settle things?'

'See Valerie? What's the point? No. No no no.'

The 'No' was emphatic. I rose and moved to the door. 'When you go,' he called, 'as soon as you go, I'm going to throw myself out of that window.'

'What?'

'You don't believe me,' he said in a very calm voice. 'The moment you go I'll jump out there.'

'C'mon,' I said, not knowing what to say. 'Look – '

He suddenly lobbed the empty whisky bottle accurately through the open window. It must have dropped four floors through the dark and shattered on the pavement below. I did not hear it smash. He went back to the chair and sat down, seemingly exhausted. I glanced out of the window. The pavement under the lamplight fortunately appeared empty.

'On her left buttock,' he said, 'that woman in Cyncoed has a birthmark shaped like Madagascar. Susan never had one like that. I know, I know. So it must be Valerie. It has to be Valerie. Besides her character is different. Other things... '

'You're just imagining it all,' I said reflexly. 'Look, if you really believe what you're saying, challenge Susan.'

'Valerie, not Susan.'

'Valerie then. You must see her. It's not fair to her.'

'Not fair to *her*!'

'She doesn't know what to do.'

'What I told you is a secret,' David Pugh said. 'You won't repeat what I said about that woman in Cyncoed.'

'You've been sending her money to return to Australia. That's not good enough. There are things to be seen to. Now.' I heard my own voice, I sounded like a shrill headmaster.

'You don't believe me,' he complained. 'You think I'm making up a tale like the aborigines tell one another.'

'You've got it all wrong. You haven't been too well and – '

'And I've got it all wrong. That's what you think?'

'Isn't it possible?'

'I know it sounds unlikely,' he said reasonably, 'but unlikely things happen you know. If I tuned into Radio Baluchi from that bedside radio there and listened to, I dunno, some prof. maybe discussing in English the mysterious Khan of Khelat, would you say there's no such radio station?'

'I don't know what you're talking about.'

'You would. I can tell. You're sceptical about improbabilities. Like so many, I suppose. I tell you the good twin's been swapped, that I've been cheated, swindled, bloody hell I've been swindled and Christ, you come here sanctimoniously saying I've got it wrong. Christ, you're telling me.'

He walked over to the bed and picked up a book lying on the eiderdown. He took a spectacle case out of his pocket, put on his glasses and opened the book as if I wasn't there.

'Can I tell Susan that if she phones again you will at least speak to her. That's not much to ask.'

He continued reading as if he hadn't heard me and when, eventually, he did look up he seemed surprised I was still there.

'You can go,' David Pugh said imperiously, as if dismissing a servant.

I hesitated. 'Why don't you go?' he said more softly. 'Don't worry... I won't, no I won't throw myself through that window. I don't hate myself that much.'

I felt sorry for him. Patently, the man was ill. 'Go,' he said, 'the way you're looking at me. As if I'm in a zoo. I'm not, I'm certainly not to be visited as if I were a giant iguana or an elephant tortoise from the Galapagos.'

I left. I knew what I had to do. I had to discuss matters with David Pugh's doctor. He wasn't my patient but he needed help, probably psychiatric help, imagining as he did that his wife had been swapped for some scheming look-alike. His behaviour in the hotel room was not just bizarre; it was surely symptomatic of one unhinged: his drinking, his placid depressive voice that would now and then build up into a rage, his throwing of the empty bottle through the window – a surrogate suicide – and the way, finally, he had picked up that book in a hypnoid state as if I wasn't there before, like some haughty general, he commanded me to go.

As I drove the car back down Cathedral Road I wished I had asked him why he believed the twins had been swapped. What, I should have asked him, did he think was in it for them? What motive? It didn't matter. Tomorrow evening I would find out the name of David Pugh's doctor from Susan and make an appointment to see him. I would insist he visited his patient. I would tell my plan to Susan. I was looking forward to seeing her though I had no great news to impart. For a moment I visualised Susan undressed, not

147

playing tennis this time, but standing still with her back to me, the small map of Madagascar clearly visible on her left buttock.

Brrr brrr Brrr brrr. Blankly I replaced the receiver silencing its repetitious signal. Once more, no reply. I collected Uncle Max's traditional doctor's bag containing the emergency medical accoutrements, stuffed the stethoscope into my pocket, picked up the heavy sphygmomanometer and quit the surgery. I would try to telephone Susan again after seeing the last patient of my Friday afternoon rounds. I would phone from a public telephone box to alert her that I was on my way. 'Put the kettle on,' I'd say.

It was just after four o'clock when I came out of the house in Marlborough Road. The elementary school, the red-bricked building that I'd attended when I was so high, was located nearby. It had been damaged during the war, bombed, but it hardly looked different now. Up the road I spotted a red telephone booth. I passed the gates of the school's playground. I used to come whooping out of them shouting, 'Swap you for a blood alley', or 'Fight you for your honour'. For a moment, I recalled a certain classroom, its smell of chalk, its powdered pre-war ink. I could see on the blackboard, in Mr Griffith's tidy hand, a multiplication table.

When I opened the telephone door there was a smell of stale urine. Quickly I dialled the Cyncoed number but, disappointed, eventually had to press button B to get the coins back. Where was Susan?

I walked back to the car, again passing the playground. In my imagination I could hear the piping voices of my former classmates singing, 'Let the prayer re-echo, God bless the Prince of Wales'. Then, though, mistakenly I believed that awful patriotic lyric to be, 'Let the prairie echo, God bless the Prince of Wales', and used to wonder vaguely if the shivering grass prairie could be found the other side of Caerphilly Mountain.

Before I reached the car I decided that I would simply drive up to Cyncoed, knock on the door, ring the bell. It would be nice to arrive bearing a small gift, a box of chocolates perhaps. So I made a small detour to the shops that I knew were near Waterloo Gardens.

The flower and plant shop was surely new? I had not remembered a flower shop. I was not in the habit of buying flowers. My

148

machismo image of myself did not encompass the carrying of a bunch of troubadour flowers. Meekly, I chose the red gladioli, like the ones Beattie had placed in the surgery. I laid them down awkwardly on the passenger seat next to me and steered the car up the hill to Cyncoed. I was looking forward to seeing Susan, to giving her the flowers, to telling her the news that would interest her, to being with her. But when I arrived the white gate was shut, all the windows closed, the front door an unfriendly barrier that would not open to my ringing of the bell. I saw a note in an empty milk bottle on the step to the right of the door. I picked it up. It read peremptorily: *No Milk Today*.

When I returned to Cathedral Road to scrounge tea from my mother, I took in the bunch of gladioli and offered it to her. She kissed me on the cheek and said happily, 'How thoughtful of you, son, how sweet.'

I knew my responding smile was like that of a man who had just been defeated at a card game and that even my posture was not upright like a palm tree. Worse, my mother made such a fuss about those tall flowers as she arranged them in a vase. It was as if I had brought her blue and purple clothing from the bazaars of the Orient, silver plates from Tarshish, gold from Uphaz.

I learned from Susan that she had stayed in London with Gloria Talbot on Friday night. Thursday evening, about the time I was visiting the Angel Hotel, Gloria had telephoned to say she had tickets for Christopher Fry's *The Lady's Not for Burning*. Gloria Talbot had been persuasive. 'Do come, Sue,' she had said. 'It'll make a change for you. Stay here for the night.' So Susan went and returned late on Saturday. It had been her first time in London. Now it was her first time in Porthcawl.

We strolled, Susan and I, beside the strenuous sea. As so often in Porthcawl, it was a windy day. We had escaped from the Sunday crowds by walking the other side of Rest Bay. 'We should've gone to Ogmore,' I'd said. 'It wouldn't be so crowded there.' But Susan had wanted to visit Porthcawl. Apparently, David Pugh had spoken of the place often enough. He had been in the habit of playing golf there with his partner, the late Mr Talbot.

I had told her about my visit to the Angel Hotel. I did not tell

149

her, though, about David Pugh's threatened suicide. When I remarked on his obsession with the Madagascar birthmark she had merely shaken her head back and fore, back and fore, unsmiling, in puzzlement. Beyond the Miners' Holiday Home she abruptly bent down to some brambles and plucked a blackberry. Most of the berries were a nasty red colour, the colour of inflammation, but a few had ripened and it was one of these she brought up to my lips. I opened my lips and in slow motion she popped it in, half teasing me. I then bent down, selected the juiciest blackberry visible before placing it with care between her invitingly parted lips. She took my hand and we stared at the sea with its high spray leaping over the rocks and beyond, through the windy sunlight, at a large coal dredger inching its way towards Swansea from the Gower Coast.

When we turned back to the Rest Bay and the Common with its occasional shelters, I suggested we should walk over to the funfair. 'We could go on the Ghost Train, the Figure of Eight, the Kingdom of Evil or the Big Wheel.'

'How about some tea somewhere instead?' said Susan.

In the distance I could see the striped deckchairs on the prom, the empty ones billowing in the breeze. Opposite was the Seabank Hotel. We could get tea there.

'It's a bit respectable,' I warned Susan. 'The sort of place where my mother likes to meet her cronies.'

Most of the tables in the tearoom were occupied but one of them, near the high vertical windows that overlooked the promenade, had just been vacated. As we settled in our chairs I could see across the road the horizontal wires that carried the different coloured electric bulbs which would come actively alive after dark as long as the summer season lasted. And above them, in the distance, clouds were hurrying over as if they had some terrible but urgent appointment.

The middle-aged waitress, dressed in black and white like some maid in one of Noël Coward's comedies, advanced, pad in hand. 'Set tea for two, love?'

After she had gone Susan took from her handbag a piece of paper, wrote on it, then handed it back to me. 'David's doctor,' she explained. 'Dr Huw Jenkins. That's his phone number and address.'

'It's only a walk away from my mother's place,' I replied. I'll make an appointment with him tomorrow if I can.'

Susan gazed around her. 'I expected Wales to be so different from this. There are places in Australia exactly like this.'

'Could be worse,' I said. 'Someone could be singing a lie to a harp.'

Her big blue, slanting, serious eyes looked straight into mine. 'David promised me so much,' she said. 'Not that I expected a queen's golden crown, you know. I'd have settled for a funny paper hat.'

While the waitress was serving us the set tea I believed I saw the man I had glimpsed at the football match, the one who had upset Susan. He took a chair at a distant table. Susan had her back to him and he had not seen her. He was alone. I was tempted for a moment to say, 'There's the fellow who took you for Valerie,' but I sensed that such information would merely agitate her. There were several occupied tables between us so there was a chance they would not observe each other.

'Strange that David should talk about a birthmark shaped like Madagascar,' said Susan. 'I remember him talking once about the Mirany,'

'The what?'

'The Mirany – a dance, an old dance the Madagascar women performed when their men went into battle. They'd let down their hair and dance and dance and dance for the sake of their warrior men. The dance was supposed to protect their husbands and sons.'

'What's that got to do with a birthmark?'

'Nothing,' Susan said. 'But what a funny thing for him to say. To say that I've a birthmark shaped like Madagascar. I haven't. I haven't!'

Susan poured out the tea. 'Would you dance the Mirany for me?' I ventured.

'Nope,' she smiled.

I reached for one of the utility cakes with its artifical cream. 'I suppose when you were young you, as identical twins, must have played all kinds of practical tricks on people.'

'Sure, sometimes we'd speak in unison,' Susan said. 'That used to blow people's minds. Sometimes I'd say I was Val. Sometimes she'd say she was me. We'd confuse people. I don't find that funny anymore.'

151

I glanced over her shoulder at the distant profile of one who surely had been confused.

'It wasn't always sweetness and light between us,' Susan said.

'There were times when I thought of Valerie as Public Enemy Number One, Two and Three. But whenever there was resistance from somebody else we'd join up like glue. You know about Tweedledum and Tweedledee?'

'Mmm?'

'Tweedledum and Tweedledee
Agreed to have a battle.
'Cos Tweedledum said Tweedledee
Had spoiled his nice new rattle.
Just then flew down a monstrous crow
As big as a tar barrel.
It frightened both the heroes so
They quite forgot their quarrel.'

When we rose to leave and made our way across the tearoom I was startled to see that I had made a curious mistake. The solitary man at the table raised his head as we passed him. It was somebody else. It wasn't the man I had seen at the football match buttonholing Susan. In fact, the resemblance, as far as I could recall, was quite superficial. It disturbed me that I had been so wrong. I felt unsettled in a way I couldn't define. And for no sensible reason for the first time it occurred to me, supposing this Susan I was accompanying out of the Seabank Hotel was, as her husband claimed, not Susan at all. An impostor? Absurd, absurd.

We walked silently past the shelters that neighboured Porthcawl Pavilion. They exuded a whiff that reminded me of the odour inside the telephone box near Marlborough Road Elementary School. A wan cry of seagulls drew us across the road to lean on the promenade railings and watch again the sea spray climbing high over the rocks and over the protecting wall. It dampened our faces. For a moment Susan cuddled close, taking my arm, and she said provocatively, 'I do like you, you know.'

We lingered too long at Porthcawl. If we had been less tardy, more decisive, we could have avoided the hordes of cars all simultaneously turning their bonnets homewards. Slowly, one behind the other, like an immense funeral procession, they reached for the A48 roundabout. The nameless melancholy at the certain conclusion of a happy day! Before we reached Cowbridge, the cars coming from the opposite direction had their lights on and, in the horizontal mirror above and to my left, I glimpsed the flamingo bruises of sunset.

'When I was a schoolboy I used to feel a sense of emptiness and panic on Sunday evenings after a day beside the sea,' I said to Susan. 'Going home to an empty firegrate and homework for Monday not even begun. The impermanence of things.'

It was quite dark when we descended the curve of the hill, Tumble-Down-Dick, towards the lights of Cardiff below. Soon we would be near the city centre. We could, on the way to Cyncoed, pass the Angel Hotel.

'Look,' I said, 'you could confront him right away. I know the number of his room. I'll come with you if you wish. We could cross the foyer into the lift, whizz up and simply knock on his door. He'd open it... and there you are.'

She did not respond at once. When she did so her voice was tight and shrill. 'So simple, isn't it? It sounds so simple to you. You haven't a clue, you just haven't got a clue.'

I feared she might cry again. My tactless suggestion had dissolved all munificent smiles. She looked away as if I had mentioned something utterly odious. I had spoilt things, our togetherness.There would be no blackberrying tonight. When I stopped outside her house she did not relent, did not ask me in, offer me a light supper, a drink. She hardly procrastinated. Undeterred, I turned to kiss her on the lips – a goodnight kiss that signalled 'Hello'; but at the last second she turned her head so that I was offered her cheek instead. All the same she knew what I was about, for now, troubled, more hesitant, she opened the door of the car. It was too late: our happy day had ended as if with an obituary.

'I'm not going into that hotel like a commando,' she explained. 'I mean I want him to speak to me voluntarily. I don't want a scene, a huge scene. I want him to be reasonable. Otherwise it will be worse – everything will get worse, don't you understand? Please see his doctor for me. Please.'

I watched her open the white gate. She held up her hand in mild salute. She looked very slim and vulnerable. I drove back to Cathedral Road, back to a Sunday evening and a familiar room, feeling that the weekend's homework had not yet been done.

The last patient of the Monday evening surgery looked familiar. It was the sailor whom I had treated two weeks earlier when I had first arrived. He'd had, I recalled, a dose of gonorrhoea. 'More trouble?' I asked.

'No,' he said.

'No?'

'I thought I'd like one more jab to make sure.'

I shuffled through the notes and as I did so I heard again distant thunder. All through my surgery there had been far rumbles as if a storm were breaking somewhere. I found, at last, his brief case-history. Uncle Max had written that the sailor had been 'exposed' and had wanted a course of penicillin. But though the single exposure had been three weeks earlier, the sailor had never had any signs of gonorrhoea. Nevertheless, my uncle had been persuaded to give him the injections. And had been paid for it, what's more, at a guinea a time. He should have been reassured, I felt, observed possibly, but sent away without being given the antibiotic. That was the temptation with private medicine: to overtreat the patient and to be paid for it. Strangely, I had not thought twice about it that first evening surgery of two weeks ago.

Ah, I had been a flustered, unquestioning novitiate then!

'You've absolutely no problem now?' I asked the sailor.

'None.'

'Have you been with anybody since that first exposure?'

'No.'

'Not since I saw you last?'

'No, no.'

'Absolutely sure?'

'Definitely .'

Then you don't need another injection.'

The sailor fumbled in his civilian clothes and brought out a purse. He extracted a pound note and a shilling which he put on my desk as if it were the counter of a shop.

'I want another jab,' he insisted.

'Are you sailing soon?' I asked.

'No. I've a shore job now.'

'Down the docks?'

'Yes.'

'Well,' I said reassuringly, 'if you had any problems below in the

154

past they're over now. I'll examine you if you wish but...'

Afterwards I emphasised that he had no cause at all to be anxious. He waited, mute, and again there was audible thunder as if Beattie upstairs had moved some heavy furniture. At last he declared, 'I just want to be hundred per cent sure.'

'But you can be sure. You've had enough penicillin.'

'One more jab, please, Doctor.'

I sat behind the desk again, thinking it would be ridiculous to give anybody a penicillin injection simply because of a phobia. To continue giving him jabs would be to compound the possible original error.

'Where's the other doctor?' said the sailor, obviously having no confidence in me. 'I'd like to see the older doctor.'

'He won't be back till the end of this week. He's on holiday.'

I recalled that time when I had been a student attending psychiatric outpatients. How the consultant psychiatrist intended to give some electroconvulsive therapy to a depressed patient as, indeed, he had done weeks earlier. But when the patient entered it was evident he was hypomanic, in no need of further ECT. He spoke loudly, full of bright bonhomie, and lay down on the couch saying, 'This really helps'. The psychiatrist merely pretended to pass a current through the head of the patient who, however, left the hospital a happy and satisfied man. Similarly, I now filled the syringe with sterile water so that I could inject it into his thigh. The sailor, relieved, thanked me and departed from the surgery believing more penicillin was circulating in his body, fighting non-existent cocci.

The front door closed. I walked back into the hall and suddenly there was a huge slam of thunder – as if the gods were displeased with my act of deceit. As recently as June the examiners at Queen's Square in London had offered me a glass of sherry while I signed the document that incorporated the Hippocratic oath: I will follow that system of regimen which, according to my ability and judgement, I consider for the benefit of my patients and abstain from whatever is deleterious and mischievous. I will give no deadly medicine to anyone if asked... With purity and holiness I will pass my life and practise my Art... Into whatever house I enter I will abstain from any corrupt act, above all, from seduction...'

When I opened the door Beattie looked up from a newspaper.

155

'What's a girl's name or old coin?' she asked.

'I don't know,' I said.

'Four letters,' she said.

Again the sky banged and crunched and crumpled. Soon lightning dramatised the room. It had begun to rain, to rain with a heavy, serious noise.

'This morning I left a message for Dr Huw Jenkins to ring me. He wasn't available. So if he rings tonight, will you give him my mother's number?'

Beattie nodded. 'Dr Huw? Right? – he's an odd bod.' She put down the newspaper. 'Don't like this weather,' she continued. All the rain we've had could make the Taff flood again. You remember when Billy the Seal swam out of the pond in Victoria Park down Queen Street?'

'I do,' I said. 'But when Billy died, did you know they did a post mortem and found old Billy had ovaries?'

I drove the car down the length of Cathedral Road through the pattering, perpendicular lines of rain. It was raining, as they say sometimes in Wales, 'witches and walking sticks'.

The hall smelt of stale sweet biscuits. Mrs Jenkins directed me into their front room. Though it was getting dark she did not switch on the light. 'He won't be a minute,' she promised me. The front room obviously served also as Dr Jenkins' tidy waiting room. I sat on one of the amber-coloured, velvet reproduction chairs close to a small, polished table on which shiny periodicals were stacked – *Vogue* and *Punch* and *The Illustrated London News*. The room was dominated by the particularly loud tick of a big, elaborately ornamented clock on the mantelpiece. Symmetrically, on each side of the mantelpiece, the same size, identically framed, paintings of rustic scenes inertly confronted any human occupant sitting on the long, amber sofa opposite. It was a cheerless room, somehow made more gloomy because of an unlit gas fire.

'Well, well, well,' pronounced short, flabby Huw Jenkins as he pushed forward the door. He waited for a moment, as if expecting applause as he came on stage, before resuming, 'You're Max's nephew I understand, right? Well, well.'

He had zinc hair but black eyebrows over darting eyes and a pronounced nose. As he spoke he kept washing his dry hands. 'You went to see a patient of mine at the Angel, I gather. He told me you went to see him.'

'You've seen David Pugh then, lately?'

'Yes, yes, yes.' He laughed. 'Now there's a case for you, isn't it?'

'I went at his wife's request,' I said limply. 'To talk over non-medical matters.'

I did not wish him to think that I, unethically, was homing in on his territory. He lowered himself into a chair and seemed even smaller sitting down.

'Poor girl, aye. Disaster. Best for her to go back to Australia. That's what I advised her. Go back to Australia, I said. Go hell for leather, that's what I said. You see, no hope there. When it comes to women, David's a castrated monkey. Well, well, can I offer you a sherry?'

Before I could reply he asked after my Uncle Max. 'Will you eventually take over his practice?' he said.

'I don't think so,' I replied. 'Look, all Susan Pugh wishes to do is to discuss matters rationally with her husband. Face to face. She feels you could persuade him to do that.'

'Well, I only met her once, you know. A pretty slut. But I can't get involved there. No, no, no. She wants a lawyer, I reckon, not a doctor. I've known David for years. As I told her, she hasn't a hope in hell.'

I don't know why I felt so aggressive. I wished he would switch on the light, I wished he would stop washing his hands, I wished the penetrating tick of the clock would soften. 'You told her David was fit,' I said. 'She doesn't even know that you're still visiting him. I didn't know either.'

'Why should you know?' He stretched his face forward pugilistically. Then he relaxed. 'Well, well, Max's nephew. Rudy and Kate's boy, right? She was a pretty woman, your mother. Very pretty woman.'

He rose and stood with his back to the unlit gas fire. 'You want my opinion? Dai Pugh needs time. Not because of his pneumothorax. No, he's over that. But he's still in mourning.'

'Mourning?'

He lowered his voice as if he were going to utter a scandalous secret. 'He's in mourning for Bill Talbot – his partner. He loved Bill, you know. The love that passeth understanding, you follow

157

me? Well, mourning is a kind of illness, isn't it, and David likes his drop. He was tipsy at the funeral. The priest embarked, aye, on the usual sanctimonious twaddle about Bill Talbot's qualities when David hits him, hits him, see, on the mouth. My God, that was something. Well, well.' He washed his hands again. 'He should have gone into mourning for his lost love and cancelled the Australian trip, right? He shouldn't have beetled off to the other side of the globe and got involved with a girl to the extent of marrying her. Nemesis. Nemesis. He's a bit depressed, but–'

'More than depressed,' I interrupted. 'Suicidal.'

'No, no,' said Dr Jenkins. He laughed. 'No, no, if that's what's worrying you. No, no, he'll be all right. As soon as that girl hoofs it back home he'll be OK.'

'He's quite sick now.'

'It'll blow over. That girl must have schemed to get him. He's filthy rich, you know. Yes, yes, filthy rich.'

'Did David Pugh tell you he believes she's Valerie, the twin sister?'

I explained how David Pugh was deluded. In the growing darkness of that front room, I dared to suggest to this somewhat eccentric, experienced old doctor that Pugh was unbalanced and needed psychiatric help. Dr Jenkins, as I spoke, searched in his pocket, took out a spectacle case, extracted the spectacles and after putting them on, moved to the door to switch on the electric light. It was as if he'd seen through the lenses how dark it was in that room. But he did not take much notice of what I said.

'Twins are funny,' he declared. 'I've had a case, here, in Cardiff, where one has dominated the other, absolutely dominated him. Then this domineering one died – motorbike accident on the Western Avenue, motorbikes are bloody dangerous – anyway afterwards, the other, the gentle twin, not only becomes a bullyboy but has become, literally, twice his size. After his brother died he ate and ate until he's the weight of both of them put together now. What do you think of that, Professor?'

'David Pugh reckons one twin has a birthmark on her buttock and the other hasn't,' I persisted. 'That's why he says Susan is Valerie. Of course, she hasn't got such a birthmark. It's a crazy notion. I mean crazy in a clinical sense.'

'Well, well, well, if you ask me,' retorted Huw Jenkins crudely, 'it's Bill Talbot who probably had a birthmark on his bum, ha ha ha.'

'You know David Pugh very well?' I said.

'Yes, I know him.'

'If you, as his doctor, think he's sound in mind you could try to persuade him to see his wife, face to face, and thrash things out. That's what she wants.'

'She wants dough, that's what she wants, the bitch.'

There was no point in losing my temper. There was nothing I could do here. I rose from the chair, preparing to leave.

'You want my advice?' continued Dr Jenkins. 'You're newly qualified so let me give you some advice. Don't rush into things. Things sort themselves out eventually. Don't be ... hectic. Don't hurry. Be like a policeman called to stop a fight. He goes adagio, adagio, knowing that otherwise he'll get the force of their blows. Not only patients but doctors have to be patient. Slowly, slowly, my boy .'

Washing his hands he led me into the hall. 'Those original Siamese twins – born the beginning of the last century some time, now there was a case. Chang and Eng joined by a band of tissue from here to here.' He signified from his lower chest to the umbilicus. 'Married sisters and fathered twenty-two kids between 'em. Doesn't that make the mind boggle? Ha ha ha. More than sixty years they lived,' he said, stopping before the front door. 'One day Eng woke up to find his twin dead. Think of that experience, eh? Joined up to a dead man. A couple of hours later he was dead himself of course. Well, well.'

He opened the door and smiled. 'Give my best to Max.'

I waited all Thursday evening for a call from Susan. None came. I had told her of my meeting with Dr Jenkins and suggested we should meet. 'I'm leaving for London on Saturday,' I had reminded her. Uncle Max would be back Friday night so I would have only two more evenings in Cardiff. 'After surgery tonight, perhaps we could do a flick and–' But she had put me off. 'I'll ring you,' she said in a wretched, stifled voice, obviously depressed by my failure with Huw Jenkins. It was too late for her to contact me now. Already my mother was preparing to go to bed. 'Goodnight, son. Don't be long, Rudy.'

My father leant forward in his chair, pointing the poker at the empty firegrate. Perhaps out of habit. At the first sign of autumn a fire would be burning there, or rather the failing remnants of one this time of night, and he would poke at it to make it burn more quickly, to tame it beyond doubt, before following my mother into their bedroom. Now he just played idly with the poker, staring at the firegrate while musing, 'Duw, it don't seem like three weeks since you came.'

Soon my locum stint would be over, yet my planned holiday in Italy seemed unreal, a fantasy, a long time ahead.

'You'll be glad to get your car back,' I said.

'Aye. I bet you've very near buggered the gears by now,' he agreed.

My father's criticisms, though habitual, were rarely sincere. If I showed him a small literary magazine where a reviewer or critic had praised my poetry, he would teasingly explode, 'That feller's soft in the 'ead.' And the last couple of weeks he had repeatedly remarked, 'Poor Max. By the time he returns I bet he'll have very near no patients left.' Now, though, he spoke without chastening banter. 'You could do worse than put up a brass plate by 'ere in Cardiff,' he persuaded me. 'The name's known. Reputation will bring you many patients.' I think he had a vision of all those people tapping their sticks and crutches on the road to Lourdes about-turning and making for Cardiff where I would delay their entrance into Death's Empire. But it wasn't a question of staying in or leaving Cardiff. I did not want to experience a lifetime's consolations and desolations of General Practice.

'I expec' you've learnt a lot these last few weeks,' continued my father.

I knew so little. Doctors know so little. Like Dr Mesmer of old, doctors should wear a magician's purple cloak not a scientist's white clinical one. A mere three weeks in General Practice confirmed that view for me. Disease was so often a matter of abnormal function rather than damaged structure – the aetiology too frequently unknown, the diagnosis a question mark, the treatment symptomatic, the prognosis uncertain.

'So many riddles, wrapped in mysteries, inside enigmas,' I said, quoting one of the consultants who had taught me at Westminster Hospital.

"Ow do you mean?'

'Everything's so perplexing, Dad. Not least human behaviour – and as a doctor, most of the time I have to exude an air of total confidence. So often I feel myself to be a fraud. And only as useful as those ancient priests who treated patients by chanting, "O Fever, with thy Brother Consumption, with thy Sister Cough, go to the people below."'

My father looked worried. 'You're soft,' he said. 'The trouble with you –' Before he could criticise me further the telephone sounded. At this late hour it would not be Susan. I knew even before I reached the phone that I would hear Beattie's voice calling me away from my parents' congenial house into the night.

'It's not eleven yet,' said Beattie. 'An' I judge it to be urgent.'

I left my father before the empty firegrate, leaning forward, poker in his hand, as I gathered my equipment and Uncle Max's emergency bag. For a moment I wondered if I would be able to cope. I felt in my pocket to make sure I had the front door key.

'Don't wait up, Dad,' I said.

When I was a small boy, on saying 'goodbye' he would lift me up to his face. I would breathe in the aroma of tobacco smoke and become aware of the skin of his face as rough as sandpaper. Now he just raised his head and said, 'Take it easy.' We were both men after all.

As I went for the car, I was aware how the small summer wind from open fields, cool from grass, had invaded the city. If a nightingale sang somewhere out there I did not hear it, but the daytime urban noise, like a machine turned down, had so shrunk that the City Hall clock striking the hour was clearly audible. Before I turned on the ignition of the car it had struck its melancholy note eleven times.

It had been a week since my first night call. Then I had sallied forth at dawn with my nostrums, later to summon an ambulance because of what I judged to be an abdominal emergency. In the event, the patient had been kept under observation before being discharged. Presumably I had been wrong. Now what would I encounter? The dinginess of pain? Or the grim horsemen riding away even as I arrived too late?

Without confidence, I drove to a house in Richmond Road, crossing the bridge over the River Taff that flowed blackly, secretly below, then passing by the Castle walls opposite the Angel Hotel with its lit windows. I did not see, flying through the air, a body from the fourth floor.

'As soon as she knew you were on your way, Doctor,' said Mr Lewis, 'it stopped as suddenly as it had started. I'm sorry now I brought you out this time of night.'

'She's had an attack before?'

'Just once, Doctor. Your uncle pressed something in the neck. Like magic, it stopped. That was over a year ago.'

Pamela Lewis was on leave from the ATS. She should already have been back with her unit; worse, she had suddenly felt rapid flutterings in her chest and neck and had been very short of breath. Soon she was prostrate and her parents, despite her previous episode, had thought she might be having a fatal heart attack.

Mr Lewis led me into a room with too much furniture in it. Pamela Lewis was lying dressed, not in uniform, on the sofa with her shoes on. From the brief history I could offer a diagnosis: paroxysmal tachycardia. I knew young people were more likely to experience it than those in later life. Without warning the heart would suddenly beat two or three times its normal rate and this wild galloping would continue for a matter of minutes, or even days, before ceasing abruptly. I had read about these paroxysmal episodes in textbooks but had never actually witnessed an attack. It could be stopped usually by a simple trick: by steady pressure of the thumb at a certain point in the neck, or by pressing the eyeballs, or even by simply ordering the patient to hold his or her breath for as long as possible.

I sat down beside the young woman with her pasty, uncooked face and smiled, taking her wrist to feel her pulse. She did not smile back. I knew paroxysmal tachycardia did not usually signal an abnormal heart but I had to make sure.

'You haven't been taking any medicine, drugs?' I asked as I continued to feel the inside of her wrist.

She shook her head. The father and mother drew closer so that I felt too observed. I could not distinguish her pulse. I needed, therefore, to listen to her heart with a stethoscope. I asked for her blouse and brassiere to be removed.

It seemed an age before her white breast was exposed. I lifted up

162

her full left breast to place the stethoscope over the area where I would expect the apex of the heart to be. Then I counted the beats but Mr Lewis said, distracting me, 'I thought she was a gonner, Doctor.' I lost count and had to start again. Her heartbeat was still rapid, but not out of control, and was regular. Reassurance, heavy, confident reassurance was all that she needed.

'She'll be O.K.,' I pronounced. 'Her heart's fine. A good strong heart. Fine. All's well.'

'Will you write a letter to her M.O.?' asked Mr Lewis. 'They can be sticky, them doctors in the army. She can stay here, surely, for the weekend?'

'I'll see she gets home comforts, Doctor,' chimed in Mrs Lewis.

I caught their daughter's anxious stare. She seemed too exhausted even to button up her blouse.

'Yes,' I said. 'I'll write a note. Have you notepaper and an envelope, please?'

I suspected that her absence from the unit without leave had been the starting gun which had made her heart bound forth and then bolt. As I waited for Mrs Lewis to fetch the notepaper, Mr Lewis drew me confidentially to one side. 'Her M.O. is a great puddin' of pigshit,' he told me sincerely.

I looked about the room. So many photographs. On the sideboard, on the mantelpiece, framed on the walls. One was of a man next to a flagpole on the tower of a castle. Earlier in August the National Eisteddfod had been at Caerphilly and I had read how the Union Jack on the tower of the Castle had been torn down and burnt by a small group of Welsh Nationalists.

'Yes,' said Mr Lewis. 'I was there.'

'Very dramatic shot,' I said. 'You took all these photographs?'

'It's my hobby,' Mr Lewis said.

'It's all he thinks about, photos,' Mrs Lewis said as she returned to the room.

'I'm all eye, really,' agreed Mr Lewis.

I sat at the table and wrote to Pamela Lewis's medical officer, and as I did so I heard her mother say, 'Do up your blouse, dear.'

Mr Lewis led me through the hall, all the time thanking me and apologising for bringing me out so late. Suddenly he said, 'I'd like to give you that photo of Caerphilly Castle.' I did not want anything. No doubt Beattie would send Mr Lewis a bill eventually.

Why didn't he have the sense to register with a National Health doctor? 'Thank you, anyway,' I said. But he wished to be delivered from the sin of gratitude in a more personal way: at the front door he again took me into his confidence. 'The two-thirty, tomorrow,' he whispered urgently, 'Pope's Oak, Doctor. That's one Gordon Richards will win. Definitely.'

'Right,' I said. 'Pope's Oak.'

'For sure,' he said, 'as my name's Alf Lewis, it will win.'

He did not shut the door until I reached the gate. Alone now I felt strangely elated. I had done nothing except listen to a girl's heartbeat, reassure her and write a note, yet I felt triumphantly alert. I certainly did not feel sleepy. I decided to wind down by driving the car into the country, drive it anywhere fast, through the reversing darkness of hedges until I had calmed and was ready to return to Cathedral Road.

I did not initially consider steering the car up towards Cyncoed but it was where the car wanted to go. I knew it would be risky. I hardly wished to be involved in legal complications and one did not have to be a prophet to guess that the Pughs could one day be in court, involved in divorce proceedings. But I was beginning to rehearse in my mind erotic possibilities if I knocked at this midnight hour on Susan's door. It would have to be a one-off. And would I be welcome?

I turned a corner too fast as in imagination I confirmed heuristically that Susan owned no Madagascar birthmark! 'It's no bloody use, it's no bloody use but you stick in my mind, like a burr on a bear...' How did it go? How did that poem go? 'Go go go,' said the bird.

At the top of Penylan Hill I had made a solemn decision. It would be like the throw of a dice. Yes, I would let fate decide. If I discovered the house to be utterly dark I would simply drive on. But if one, one single lucky electric bulb shone in her house, upstairs or downstairs, in the hall, in the breakfast room, or in the bedroom, then I would park the car, dare to open the gate and summon Susan to the front door. I would say, 'I've been out this way to see a patient and, passing by, saw from a light in your house that you were still up.'

And she, perhaps, a knockout in her night things, would respond softly, stepping back into the hall invitingly, 'What kept you so long?'

Excited, I saw a light was on so I did park the car and I did open the gate. Alas, I did not summon her to the door. For as my feet crunched over the driveway the front door opened, seemingly of its own accord. The bleached light, segmented, beamed forward into the dark like an interdiction and I heard a man's voice say, 'C'mon, c'mon you little ball of fire. C'mon.' Whoever it was then called out, 'The damned cat won't budge,' and I heard Susan call back, 'She's got to go out.' I listened clandestinely to a brief, continuing inconsequential dialogue. At last, a man appeared darkly in the doorway and pushed the cat bodily outside. He muttered, 'Go an' pee, go on, you little judy " before he closed the door and the shaft of light disappeared. The man, whoever he was, had said little but what little he had said revealed he was an Australian. It certainly was no David Pugh in there. Who then, who? Whoever he was, I wished him Thersites' long list of ailments.

I had come here once, enthusiastically, bearing flowers but Susan had been absent. Then I had felt a blank disappointment, I had felt jarred. But this was something else, this was something more. I stood, abandoned, in that dark front garden feeling bruised, cut. I ached with unsatisfied concupiscence and became almost angry when I saw, first, the light at eye-level vanish and, moments later, another light precipitately flood the front bedroom. Like a voyeur I observed Susan come to the windows and blind the glass with curtains, leaving me even more emphatically cut off among the graphite foliage and trees. I felt completely estranged, a ghost experiencing a ghost's resentment about those alive and happy, a ghost's self-pity at a death imprisonment.

It was a moonless night. I gazed up beyond the slanting silhouette of the roof of the house at the wide expanse of sky, at star beyond star, at stars bright and stars faint, at those apparently near and those infinitely far, until I felt myself to be so small, so very small, irrelevant, ridiculous. Even as I peered upwards a star, unhinged, fell meaninglessly; it tumbled blazing across the sky till it vanished.

Resigned, I was about to give up, return down the gravel drive, when something brushed against my feet. It was the cat. She rubbed herself against the bottom of my trousers. I bent down to pick her up. I stroked the cat and, as if to underline an irony, the light in the bedroom went out and all the house and all its windows became private, forbidden.

As I waited outside Cardiff Station, beneath the clock, I suddenly realised that if Susan didn't appear within the next five minutes I would not see her again, ever. She had telephoned me at the surgery but two hours earlier while I was having my final discussion with Uncle Max. I was reporting to him what I had done and what needed to be done. 'Beattie says you've done great, anyhow,' Uncle Max had said. Then Susan telephoned me. Uncle, looking very suntanned, stood only a few yards from the desk where I sat as I told her that I would be catching the two o'clock train to London. She insisted that she would come to the station to see me off 'because I may have returned to Australia by the time you come back from your holiday'. But she had not appeared yet and soon I would have to turn, enter the station, cross the barrier and climb the stone steps to the platform.

It had been awkward talking things over with Susan while my Uncle stood next to me. She had lied, 'I've been wanting to be on my own, to see no one, these last few days, to think things over, think things out without distraction. That's why I haven't been in touch, you understand? And I've decided to go home, to let the lawyers get busy. It's all I can do. I've done my best. As my father used to say – you can't do better than your best. It's one big bloody mistake I made, that's all. I'm sorry to have involved you... You've been very sweet...'

'When I put the phone down Uncle asked, 'Not a patient?'

And I had replied, 'No, not a patient.'

Close to the taxi-rank two women and a small boy watched a juggler performing who, that Saturday afternoon, seemed unlikely to find much money collecting in his pavement cap. He must have been a novice. He kept dropping one of the three large wooden skittles. When he erred and the skittle hit the pavement, he would solemnly pick it up and begin his act again. At first I thought he was dropping the skittle deliberately to provoke laughter. But this was not so. His concentration was immense but his three skittles flung up into the air went spinning too briefly before one fell and he had to dart forward to retrieve it.

When I left the front of the station the two women had already abandoned him so that his remaining audience comprised one small, staring, scowling boy. I passed through the barrier, sad that

166

Susan had not appeared. Had she been delayed? Was she sitting right now, upstairs in some bus, somewhere between Cyncoed and Cardiff station? Or had she changed her mind and, ruthlessly, not set out as promised? And did it matter? There were many questions I might have dared to ask, had she arrived. Had I done so would I have received truthful answers? Besides, what business was it of mine? I had no claims on her.

The train was steaming into the platform and I knew that my life that was so rapidly changing would change again. Three weeks out of a lifetime – what would I clearly recall later? The whisky bottle falling out of sight through the Angel Hotel window? The exchange of blackberries at Porthcawl with a blue-eyed, brown-haired, slender Australian girl? The incompetent juggler outside Cardiff Station? So much that was random and so much that was indecipherable, like the secret of an unknown colour.

I stood at the carriage window in case Susan breathlessly appeared on the platform. She did not. The whistle blew, the guard waved his flag, and the whole of my three-week sojourn receded at fifty miles an hour. Much, no doubt, would be soon forgotten, occasions and conversations, like so much water that has fallen on sand; and the voices remembered, in or outside the surgery, no more real than those dead ones that still sing on scratched gramophone records.

Focus 1953: Near Moscow

Do not speak of the feats of statesmen; count rather the number of people they have had killed.

A long black Packard with greenish-tinged, bullet-proof windows, its curtains sufficiently drawn to hide its back seat occupant, sped hushed over the thin snow on this particular road away from Moscow. The uniformed chauffeur once again glanced in the mirror and saw his awesome passenger, Lavrenty Pavlovich Beria, First Deputy Premier, Minister of Internal Affairs and Chief of State Security, remove his rimless spectacles and breathe on the lenses before cleaning them with his handkerchief.

The headlights lit up, on either side of the road, piled, packed snow and adjacently, the woods of pine and birch. When the limousine reached the first high brick wall the guard dogs barked alertly. After the Packard passed through the guarded second wall, the lights in the windows of Stalin's dacha became visible. Within, the Leader and Teacher of the Workers of the World, Father of All Soviet Peoples, The Greatest Military Leader of All Time, True Genius of the Sciences, Best Friend of All Children, Faithful Comrade-in-Arms of Lenin, The Greatest Man that ever lived on this Earth, Murderer of innumerable millions, was dying.

Beria recalled how only three years earlier, on the Mountain Eagle's seventieth birthday, he had, at that remarkable party, wished him 'A Life of One Hundred Years in Health, Happiness and Prosperity'; and how pleased Stalin had been when he had cleverly, theatrically, arranged a slide of his master's face to be hugely projected onto a cloud over the Kremlin to amaze the idolatrous dense crowd in Red Square. Well, now it seemed as if the demigod was done for. No more would he, Lavrenty Beria, Hero of the Socialist Workers, Marshal of the Soviet Union, who had been decorated with five Orders of Lenin, an Order First Class of Suverov, two Orders of the Red Banner and seven medals of the Soviet Union, have to fulfil every filthy assignment given him by the Great Stalin. Never again would he need to fawn and grovel before him, flatter him insatiably and inform on potential personal enemies.

The car came to a halt and the chauffeur alighted smartly to open the door for the one whom he had overheard say, quite recently, 'Give me somebody for twenty-four hours and I'll make him confess he's the King of England.' People said of this Georgian, Beria, that he led a modest, obscure personal life, that he was 'a man without a history'; others, from Georgia, whispered that once upon a time twins inhabited Beria's body, but over the years the good twin had been devoured by the evil one. The chauffeur knew something of Beria's fearful needs. Another chauffeur who had disappeared from the M.T. section had told how he had been ordered to take reluctant, virginal schoolgirls from the gates of the Fyodor Dostoevsky High School in Moscow to Beria's secret dacha.

'I don't expect to be too long,' ordered Beria. 'Be ready to pick me up.'

When an individual dies, those near him or her may behave in an unpredictable manner. Afterwards, as a result, some are sternly criticised: 'You know what he did?'; 'You know what she said?' Everybody, on such emotional occasions, must surely be allowed licence to behave as they will, without censure, however outrageous their comments, gestures, acts – even Beria, Chief Executioner and Master of Concentration Camps, Death's pimp.

Beria entered the large room where Stalin, seemingly unconscious and breathing with obvious difficulty, lay on the sofa on which he usually slept. Apart from the doctors, Malenkov, Khrushchev and Bulganin were in vigilant attendance. Khrushchev was weeping. As Beria came closer to the sofa he smelt the odd odour of sour milk. Soon after, Stalin's daughter, unsmiling and pale, came into the sorrowful room.

Stalin had suffered a cerebral haemorrhage, a paralysing stroke and the doctors, in their old fashioned way, had been applying leeches to the dying man's neck. Ironically, only a few months earlier the Kremlin physicians, among them Professor Vladimir Vinogradov, had been arrested and jailed, having been accused of criminal connections with International Jewish Organisations and American Intelligence. At least the doctors in this room, whatever their qualifications, were not Jews.

An hour later, when it seemed to be the end, Stalin opened his eyes. He raised his left arm and pointed at something not there. He stared with concentrated insane rage at those whose heads had bent towards him. Involuntarily Beria fell to his knees. He could not look upon the cyanosed, pockmarked face of his fellow Georgian. In genuine lament he took hold of Stalin's hand and kissed it and kissed it. He suddenly recalled the death of his own father, Pavel Beria, who had died when he was only a boy of twelve. He remembered his mother swaying and sobbing, his father's dead hands clutching a crucifix to his chest, his father's eyes closed.

When Beria let Stalin's hand go it was wet with tears. The hand dropped without vigour. Once again, the tyrant's breathing became obstructed, stertorous. Beria stood up. His own chest felt tight. He, himself, felt difficulty in breathing. He had to cough. As he stood there over his 'great mentor', thick sputum came into his mouth. When he coughed again, this time explosively, it seemed as if he had deliberately spat on Stalin's bluish-tinged face. He could see Khrushchev staring at him, amazed. His thick spittle lay, unmistakably, on Stalin's large moustache. Nobody wiped it off. He wanted to explain that he had not meant to spit on Stalin. But why should he explain anything to these filth? Probably they were plotting against him already. He would outsmart them. One by one. He would piss on them, one by one. He, alone, would save Russia, become the Great New Father of All The People. He would solve the food problem by returning to pre-Stalinist agricultural policies; he would rely less on heavy industry and allow some private enterprise; he would bid for better relations with the West, he would...

Stalin stopped breathing. One of the doctors beckoned a giant of a man to step forward and give the dictator artificial respiration. The giant with the weightlifter's shoulders pummelled a dead body. Stalin had become a sinister cadaver. Those around the sofa stared at each other as the giant continued to pummel a lifeless dummy. Beria turned on his heel and, barely acknowledging the others, quit the death chamber for the cold, fresh March air outside. Dry-eyed he called for his limousine.

As the chauffeur held back the door Beria paused. 'Your wristwatch,' he said.

'My wristwatch?' repeated the chauffeur, surprised.

'It's on your right wrist.'

170

'Yes, sir,' said the chauffeur, trembling.

'When you drove me here it was on your left wrist.'

'I usually wear it on my left wrist.'

'Why did you switch over?'

'I washed my hands, sir.'

'But you put it back on your right wrist. Why?'

The chauffeur did not answer. He did not know why he had put it back on his right wrist. He thought of his colleague who had made remarks about Beria and who had disappeared.

'With respect, sir, I don't know.'

Beria climbed into the back seat. The chauffeur closed the door and hurried to the driving-seat. Driving back to Moscow he again glanced in the mirror. His passenger was gnawing at some sausage and swigging at a vodka bottle. The chauffeur could not guess that Beria was not thinking of him or his wristwatch but was already composing in his head a funeral speech. 'Stalin, the Great Companion in Arms and the Brilliant Continuator of Lenin's work, is no more. Now, once again, we must increase our vigilance. The enemies of the Soviet Union hope that our loss will lead to disorder in our ranks. These calculations will come to naught. Those who are blind will see our Party has closed its ranks in unity, in brotherly unity. Eternal Glory for our beloved dear Leader and Teacher – the Great Stalin.'

PART THREE

OGMORE ELEGIES

My Father's Red Indian

Look at a good map of South Wales and you'll see Ogmore-by-Sea plainly marked. It is half-way between Swansea and Cardiff, on the coast, of course, facing the small hills of Somerset that I can now observe hazily, fifteen miles away, across the grey, twitching, Saturday evening sea of the Bristol Channel. Not quite a village, not quite a resort, it is a place where sheep outnumber seagulls, where seagulls outnumber dogs, where dogs outnumber its human denizens.

My father loved Ogmore. He regularly drove the car down the A48 so that he could fish where the river, trying to rid itself of all the Welsh rain from the inland mountains, pours itself ceaselessly into the sea. 'I'll catch a salmon bass today,' my father would say optimistically in those far, long-ago days before the war when I was a small boy flying low over that Ogmore beach with my arms outstretched, or kicking a pebble into the rocks and shouting 'Goal!' or just playing with my yo-yo and whispering, 'Knock, knock, who's there?' while the sea-wind replied threateningly, 'Me, the bogeyman, me, Adolf Hitler, and I'll make you and little Audrey cry and cry and cry.'

I love Ogmore as much as my father did. That's why, since I've been in South Wales a week now, staying with my mother at her Cathedral Road flat in Cardiff, I drove out here on my own today. I like the open acres of sheep-cropped turf that spread upwards from the rocks to the bluish ribbon road where the post office is and the petrol pump and the small Sea Lawns Hotel. I like the green ferns, the gorse in yolk-yellow flower that smells of Barmouth biscuits, and the old grey stone walls flecked with mustard lichen. I like the tons and tons of sweet air, and the extra air between the fleeing clouds and the blue. I like the dramatic, slow, chemically coloured sunsets – unpaintable, unbeatable – and those lights of Porthcawl across the bay that in an hour or so will suddenly appear, so many shivering distant dots as darkness deepens. I like even those scattered bungalows over there that scale the slopes of

Ogmore-by-Sea, hideous as they are with their tidy lawns and hydrangea bushes and their neat, little, surrounding red-brick walls. Bungalows called Sea Breeze or Cap Dai or Balmoral or Cartref.

Just after tea I overheard a lady, a stranger to me, who lived in one of the bungalows, say in the post office, 'Jack Evans, 'e ought to be put away, I'm tellin' you, stark ravin', stark ravin', duw.'

Jack Evans, I thought, I wonder if it's the same Jack Evans? He would be an old man now.

A common enough name in Wales. I did not like to question this lady who wore a green scarf tied about her head and who said nothing more about Jack Evans. 'Ta-ta,' she called as she closed the door that made a bell briefly, sadly, tinkle.

'South Wales Echo, please,' I said, and carrying the newspaper I walked down towards the sea, towards a dog barking.

After the war, when I was a student, my father continued regularly to visit Ogmore-by-Sea. But the river had become polluted, the Bristol Channel more of a sewer, and he caught no more salmon bass, no more of those little flat dabs either, that my mother liked so much. Even the skate, with their horrible human lips, had vanished. Nothing lived in that sea except an occasional conger eel and the urine-coloured seaweed. Still my father stood there with his rod, all day, uselessly, until sunset when his silent silhouette listened to the crashing, deranged rhythms of the sea.

'Stark ravin', stark ravin',' the woman had said in the post office. And didn't my mother think Dad stark ravin' as he stood in his footprints throwing a line of hooks and raw pink ragworms into the barren waves?

'Might as well fish in the dirty bathwater upstairs,' my mother grumbled.

'But I'm not the only one,' father growled one day defensively. 'Since two weeks now another fella comes to fish near me. We'll catch something one of these days.'

'Who's this other crazy fisherman?' my mother asked.

'Name of Jack Evans,' my father replied. Then he hesitated and with his left thumb and index finger pulled at his lower lip. He was obviously going to announce something important. But he mumbled something. I didn't hear what he said that made my mother laugh.

She laughed, stopped, laughed again, and choking cheerfully

gasped, 'That's a good one, ha ha.'

My father, uneasy because of her response, ignored me when I asked, 'What did you say, Dad?'

My mother, chuckling, tried to wipe tears from her eyes. 'Your father says, ha ha ha, that this Jack Evans is ha ha ha ha ha ha, oh dear, oh dear.'

'What?' I asked, irritated.

'Ha ha ha,' my mother continued, 'a *Red Indian*, ha ha ha.'

'He is too,' shouted my father, angry now. 'For heaven's sake, stop laughing. His mother was an American Indian, his father Welsh. What's funny about that?'

My father picked up a newspaper but didn't put on his glasses. He just stared at the paper and said, 'He's a Welsh Red Indian. When his mother died, Jack was sixteen, so his father brought him back to Bridgend which is where the Evans family comes from.'

'We're Welsh Jews,' I said to my mother. 'So why should we laugh at Welsh Indians?'

'You and your old fishing stories,' my mother said dismissively and disappeared into the kitchen.

My father put down the newspaper. 'He's a very interesting man is Jack Evans,' my father said, pensively, quietly.

Next time my father went fishing by the river mouth at Ogmore maybe I would go with him and meet Jack Evans, interesting Welsh Red Indian. My father drove the twenty-odd miles to Ogmore most weekends but somehow I never found time to go with him. There was a film to see, a party to go to, or I just wasted time playing poker in the students' union. So I did not meet Jack Evans. My father, though, became more and more expert in the culture and history of the American Indian.

'Oh, aye,' said my father. 'We do 'ave some very hinteresting conversations, me and Jack.'

'No fish, though,' I said.

'Had a definite bite yesterday,' said my father.

My father was not a religious man, not a philosophical man either, but standing there, by the side of the sea with Jack Evans, both men silent for the most part I should think, they must have thought thoughts, dreamed dreams that all men do who confront the man-absent seascape for hours and hours. My father never spoke a word of praise about the altering light in the water and the changing skies but he did occasionally stammer out some of his newfound Jack Evans knowledge, and when he did so my mother gazed at him with unaccustomed, suspicious eyes as if he were unwell, or as if he had brought home, uncharacteristically, a bunch of flowers.

'D'ye know,' he told us, 'the American Indians are a bit like Jews? They 'ave no priest between man and his Creator, see.'

'No mediator, no intercessor?' I asked.

'Exactly,' my father continued. 'And like Jews, would you believe it, they don't kneel to pray. They stand up erect, aye.'

'So what?' my mother said, disturbed.

'They don't try and convert people either – like Jews, see. An' they have a sort of barmitzvah, a sort of confirmation, when they're thirteen.'

'I don't like Jack Evans,' my mother suddenly declared as if she had decided he was a savage. 'What does he want?'

But I was curious to learn more about the Red Indian confirmation ceremony and so I asked my father to tell us more about it. It seemed, according to Jack Evans anyway, that after a purifying vapour bath the thirteen-year-old Red Indian would climb the highest point in the vicinity. Wishing to stand before God in all humility the youth would strip and stand naked and motionless and silent on tip of hill, or top of mountain, exposed to the wind and the sun. For two days and one night, for two sunrises and two sunsets, the naked boy would stand erect watching all the stars coming out and all the stars disappearing.

'Good night,' said my mother. 'What an ordeal for a young boy.'

We sat in the room, none of us speaking for a while. Then my mother said, 'I bet that Jack Evans could do with a vapour bath. Bet he smells and could do with some Lifebuoy soap under his armpits.'

My father looked up, pained. 'I'd like to meet Jack Evans,' I said quietly. 'I'll come to Ogmore with you next weekend, Dad.'

'All right,' my father said. 'I've told 'im you write poetry. He was very interested to hear that. Soft in the head I told him you were. But I 'spec' he'll be glad to meet you.'

'Fishing by there in Ogmore, both of them,' my mother said. 'Blockheads.'

The next weekend I sat in the back of my father's Morris Minor next to his fishing tackle, next to the worm bait in an old tobacco tin. My mother, at the last moment, decided to come too. 'Just for the ride,' she explained. Like me, though, I'm sure she was curious to meet my father's own Red Indian. On the other hand, my mother always took delight in travelling in a car. Always she sat next to the driver's seat, the window on her side open a little, however chill a wind screeched in to freeze the other back-seat, protesting passengers.

'Just an inch,' she would plead. And content to be driven, to rest from her house chores, ten miles outside the town she'd sit there regal, giving my father directions or humming happily the gone music-hall songs that have faded into nostalgia.

As we came down Crack Hill to leave the A48 for Ogmore her hum became louder and soon words, wrong words, replaced the hum. 'I know she loves me, because she says so, because she says so, she is the Lily of Caerphilly, she is the Lily – Watch the sheep,' she suddenly shouted. The hedges and green fields raced back- wards and there, ahead of us in the bending road, forty yellow eyes stared at us. Afterwards, when father accelerated again, my mother asked in a voice too loud, 'He doesn't wear feathers an' things, does he?'

'For heaven's sake,' my father said. 'Don't be tactless. Don't ask him damn soft things like that.'

'Good night,' my mother replied. 'I won't speak to the man at all.'

She pulled out some Mintoes from her handbag, gave me one and unwrapped another to push it into my father's mouth as he stared steadily ahead at the road. Through the window now the landscape had changed. Down there in the valley, beyond turf and farms, the river snaked its way this side of the high sand dunes and then, abruptly, as we climbed an incline the open sea fanned out, the dazzle on the sea, the creamy edge of it all visible below us as it curved elliptically on the beach from the promontory of Porthcawl all the way round Happy Valley towards Ogmore and the mouth of the river. Such a deception that sea. So beautiful to look upon but so empty of fish. Even the seagulls of Ogmore looked thin, famished, not like those who feasted on these shores before the war.

'Can't see anyone fishing down there,' I said to my father.

'Tide's coming in,' he replied. 'Jack'll be by presently.'

179

Jack Evans seemed in no hurry. My father fished alone and my mother and I waited until we became tired of waiting. We went for a turfy walk and when we returned we found my father on his own still, casting his line into the incoming sea. We decided to go for tea in the Sea Lawns Hotel and we left my father the flask and sandwiches. When we came back again, still Jack Evans was absent. There was just the derelict wind and, out there, a distant coal tramp steamer edging its way on the silver dazzle towards Cardiff.

'Brr,' my mother said. 'It's an arctic wind. We'll wait in the car. Don't be long.'

We did not meet Jack Evans that day and the next weekend it was raining monotonously. Besides, I wanted to see Henry Fonda in a film called *Strange Incident*.

'Duw, you want to see a cowboy film,' my father mocked me, 'when you could come with me an' meet a real live Red Indian.'

'It's raining, Dad,' I said.

'He'll be down there this week, sure as eggs,' my father said.

So father drove that Saturday to Ogmore alone and that night when he returned he gave me a note. ''Ere,' he said. 'Jack Evans 'as written this out for you. He said sorry to 'ave missed you last week. But you might like this Red Indian poem of his. Read it out loud to your mother. It's short, go on.'

I opened up the piece of paper. I have never seen such big handwriting – bigger than a child's. You up there, I read to myself and then I read it out loud for my mother sat there inquisitively. 'It's about a falling star,' I said.

> You up there
> you who sewed to the black garment
> of endless night
> all those shining button-stars
> how your big fingers
> must have been cold.
>
> For the buttons do not hold
> some are loose
> some fall off.
> Look how one drops now
> down and in towards us
> and out of sight.

My mother nodded. 'Very nice,' she said. My father seemed triumphant. 'Even I understand that, son – it's about a shooting star – now why can't you write clear stuff like that instead of those modern poems you produce?'

'That's how Red Indians think,' my mother interrupted him. 'They don't understand about shooting stars. I mean they don't know the scientific explanation. They think God's fingers were just numb with cold. Fancy. Good night.'

I stared down at the handwriting. Nobody genuinely wrote like that, I thought. And then it occurred to me: Jack Evans didn't exist. My father had made him up. Why not? Some people wrote novels, others plays, or worked at poems like me. So why shouldn't my father have invented a character? And yet? How would my father have got hold of that poem or all those facts about Red Indian religion? My father was no scholar. Somebody with erudition had talked to him... so why not Jack Evans? All the same I looked at my father suspiciously.

I'll come with you to Ogmore again one of these days,' I said.

I did too. About once a month I accompanied my father on his fishing trips. But I never met Jack Evans.

'Funny,' said my father, 'how he never makes it when you or your mother come.'

'He's got Red Indian second sight,' I muttered.

I remember it was 21 June, the longest day of the year, when I ambled into Cardiff Central Library and saw in the spacious reference room my own father studiously reading a book – something he never did at home. At once I guessed the book was about American Indian culture. Now I was certain he had invented Jack Evans, that his recently acquired knowledge about American Indian history and religion and poetry had been culled from books – not from any real, gossiping individual. My father sat, the other side of the room, at a long black table, bent over a book, unaware that his son was watching him. And I felt guilty standing there, finding out his secret. I felt furtive and quickly left the reference room lest he should look up.

My own father... crazy! Fooling us like that. As I ran down the steps of the library, disturbed, I do not know why I wanted to cry. My own father whom I loved, who was a bit eccentric, yes – but I'd thought not this crazy – living in a fantasy world, having a fantasy companion fishing with him in the sea that contained no fish. Hell, I thought, good grief! I decided not to say anything to my mother.

That night after a silent supper my father brought a piece of paper out of his pocket. 'I went to the library today,' he announced. 'I wanted to find a Red Indian poem for Jack. They were very helpful. The girl in the library let me 'ave a look at a book called *Literature of the American Indian*. Very hinteresting. I found this in it. It's an Eskimo poem, really. I'm not sure whether it's the same thing as a Red Indian one.'

He handed me the piece of paper and I felt relieved. I wanted to laugh. So my father hadn't made up Jack Evans. Now I felt ashamed that I had ever thought he had. I stared at my father's handwriting that was simple but small, mercifully small.

'Read it out, son,' said my mother.

'It's called "The Song of the Bad Boy",' I said.

My father stared at me bright-eyed, his mouth a little open. My mother smoothed back her hair. They were waiting so I read it out loud, 'The Song of the Bad Boy'.

'I am going to run away from home, *hayah*
In a great big boat, *hayah*
To hunt for a sweet little girl, *hayah*
I shall get her some beads, *hayah*
The kind that look like boiled ones, *hayah*
Then after a while, *hayah*
I shall come back home, *hayah*
I shall call all my relations together, *hayah*
And I shall give them all a thrashing, *hayah*
I shall marry two girls at once, *hayah*
One of the sweet little darlings, *hayah*
I shall dress in spotted seal-skins, *hayah*
And the other dear little pet, *hayah*
Shall wear skins of the hooded seal only, *hayah*.'

My mother laughed when I finished and said, 'The little demon.' And my father said, 'What does *hayah* mean?' I didn't know. Did it mean anything? Did it mean Hooray?

'You can ask Jack Evans!' said my mother.

He never did though. Jack Evans never turned up in Ogmore again. Regularly my father went fishing, regularly he stood near the river's mouth on his own. First he assumed that Jack Evans was ill. He did not know exactly where he lived. In Bridgend, probably. In some ways, my father admitted, Jack Evans was a mystery man. 'An' I can't look him up in any damned phone book,' Dad said. 'There are so many Evanses about.'

Gradually, catching nothing except seaweed week after week, and having no companion, my father became discouraged. Only in the best blue weather would he drive the car to Ogmore and even then he would rarely go fishing. His chest already had begun to play him up. He would sit in the car and cough and cough, gasping for breath, while my mother muttered anxiously, 'Good night, I do wish you'd give up smoking.'

The next year he did give up smoking. He gave up everything. The one Sunday we did go to Ogmore he did not even take his fishing tackle with him. He sat for hours silently, then almost shouted, 'They spoilt it, they ruined it. Oh the fools, the fools!' And he stared morosely at the polluted sea.

The years have not made me forget the timbre of his voice, nor the righteousness of his anger. I strolled over the turfy hillocks above the rocks and stared at the wronged sea. I remembered my mother, now an old widow in her Cardiff flat, still saying, 'Good night', and I continued walking towards the sea and the sunset. I wondered if there would be any fishermen this Saturday evening down by the mouth of the river. Because of the woman with the green scarf in the post office I half expected Jack Evans to be fishing there – an ancient grey-haired man not quite right in the head, standing where my father stood, wearing Wellingtons like my father did, as the smallest waves collapsed near his feet. 'Stark ravin', stark ravin'.

I quickened my pace as the strong sea-wind moistened my eyes. There was not going to be much of a sunset. A few seagulls floated like paper towards the flat rocks on my left. Soon I would be beyond the small sand dunes on my right and the grey wall and the last bungalows. Then the river mouth would be visible. Indeed, three minutes later I saw the river below me and, in the distance, one solitary man holding a bending rod. I wanted to run. I scrambled over the rocks, shuffled over pebbles until my feet became silent on sand. As I approached the fisherman, I saw that he was, alas, quite young and I felt stupid as I walked towards him, still carrying my *South Wales Echo*.

He had seen me and I veered away a little but the stranger called, 'Got the football results?'

I glanced momentarily at the newspaper in my hand. 'No,' I said. 'I got this paper earlier. Too early.'

The fisherman nodded and I asked, hesitating, 'Any fish in these seas?'

Perhaps the wind carried my words the wrong way for he replied, 'Costs 'ell of a lot these days, mun. The price of bait, duw, shocking.'

'Do you ever catch fish here?' I asked again, louder.

'They caught a cod down by there near the flat rocks last week,' he replied. 'I'm 'oping for a salmon bass meself.'

He probably lived in Ogmore-by-Sea. Perhaps he would know about the Jack Evans 'who ought to be put away'.

'Jack Evans?' he replied. 'No.'

I nodded and was about to turn back when he surprised me with, 'You don't mean Mac Evans by any chance?'

I wanted to laugh. I was looking for a Welsh Red lndian not a Welsh Scotsman!

'No, no,' said my new-found fisherman friend. 'Max Evans, mun. We just call him Mac for short.'

'Is Mac... Max Evans a bit... er... crazy?'

His hands tightened on his rod so that his knuckles whitened and he laughed. Suddenly he stopped laughing. 'By Christ,' he said. And solemn, he paused again as if to tell me of some disaster. 'You should see Mac on a motorbike,' he continued.

I grinned, half turned and raised my hand. He smiled back. I walked away up the crunching pebbles, over the rocks, onto the turf. Way at the top, on the road, the lamp-posts jerked on and Ogmore-by-Sea immediately became darker. Lights came on, too, in the post office and the Sea Lawns Hotel, and as I walked up the slope the moon in the sky became more and more bright.

Focus 1968 : London

Very late on Sunday night the doctor on duty leaned over and with a wet sponge wiped the congealed blood from the white young face of Edwin Ramsay. The X-ray had revealed a fractured skull. Ramsay, a theological student, was but the first victim of the Grosvenor Square confrontation to be admitted to Casualty.

Earlier that October day, visitors coming out of the National Gallery were startled to see a huge demonstration forming in Trafalgar Square. Near the platform, under the soaring column for Nelson's statue, crowds had gathered. Some held banners aloft: WILSON CONDEMN BOMBING OF VIETNAM. HALT   U.S. AGGRESSION and LONG LIVE HO CHI MINH. A disemboddied voice, tinny, echoing and fuzzed, uttered, 'Awakened humanity... Might of the Pentagon... Suffering... Napalm...Torment...' while the fountains' silver shreds of water collapsed ceaselessly into the huge copper-sulphate stained basins. The other side of the Square, the red London buses passed by like a slow carnival. Suddenly, the frugal autumn sunlight lifted beyond the clouds, making gauze of the fountains and spotlighting details of the crowd: the men holding children on their shoulders, the students, the isolated groups of families, the solitary men puffing pipes.

As the pigeons wheeled overhead, no electrifying Sermon on the Mount was preached through the loudspeakers that Sunday afternoon, but the crowd discerned, through the clichés and the stale layers of hesitant political speech and jargon, another language, one more magisterial, one seldom spoken. Among those moved by the vocabulary of protest against the ravages of Vietnapalm was the idealistic student, Edwin Ramsay. At three-thirty p.m. a message from Bertrand Russell was relayed over the loudspeakers; then, after a thin patter of clapping the loudspeakers were switched off and the usual sounds of Trafalgar Square resumed their dominion: the traffic hum, the threshing fountains, the occasional padded flapping of pigeons' wings.

Soon the crowd, amoeba-like, formed a pseudopodium, meta-morphosed into a long procession, shepherded by policemen who stopped the traffic, who restarted it, who stopped the people marching, then restarted them. Money boxes were shaken like castanets at those spectators passive on the pavement or on the steps of the National Gallery. One man, detached from everybody else, called out without ardour, 'Three shillings. Thoughts of Mao. Three shillings.' Now came a score of people under orange banners, shouting as they marched, 'Yanks out! Yanks out out out out out!' The policemen held them up, allowed the traffic through, before letting them proceed, their hoarse cry of 'Yanks out out out out', fading in the distance. Suddenly, incongruously, a van appeared with a placard on which was written, 'The Lord Jesus Christ is Returning'.

The sun slid down behind the buildings, a dazzle of silver and orange on the highest office windows. Still the procession filed past through the Square, group after group, interminably, with their identity banners: THE CAMBRIDGE LABOUR PARTY, THE UNION OF LIBERAL STUDENTS, THE IRISH WORKERS GROUP – all waving slogans such as STOP YANKEE BUTCHERS NOW and VIETNAM FOR THE VIETNAMESE. An estimated quarter of a million people were marching to the U.S. Embassy in Grosvenor Square.

The previous March, the first huge London rally protesting against U.S. military involvement in the Vietnam war had resulted in a riot. So this time the television crews waited expectantly, their cameras ready. As darkness inhabited London the arc lights were turned on the crowds at Grosvenor Square who sang, 'We shall not be moved. We shall overcome.' In neighbouring streets, out of sight, secret squadrons of enormous vans containing additional riot policemen were waiting for their hour. It was late before the crowd began to disperse. Only the most passionate and persistent protes-tors, among them students like Edwin Ramsay, remained outside the Embassy. There had been little violence so the TV crews dismantled their equipment. The arc lights were put out.

The camera teams were on their way home when the back doors of the huge vans were opened and the riot police disembarked, allowed off their leashes. They surged forwards with their riot equipment, as rehearsed, into the furtive darkness of Grosvenor Square, their truncheons eagerly ready.

An Old Friend

After we had taken out a mortgage on Green Hollows at Ogmore-by-Sea, whenever possible, Joan and I would drive out of London, down the M4, to breathe in the clean, fresh, Ogmore air. It was good to get away from my job at the Chest Clinic and visit the place I loved best on this earth. Now and then, en route, we would pick up my aged mother from her Cathedral Road flat in Cardiff so that she could stay the weekend with us; and sometimes one of my daughters, Keren or Susanna, or my son David, with or without their friends, would accompany us. Then Green Hollows would be loud and crowded; otherwise it seemed spacious and quiet.

That June evening when Wyn Phillips first called on us, only my wife, my mother and I were there. I had been in Cardiff to record a *Dial a Poem* earlier and, back at Ogmore, I told my mother that if she wished to hear me read it, all she had to do was dial a certain Cardiff number. She stood in the hall, the telephone receiver next to her ear, while I dialled the numerals for her. 'I haven't heard you read your poetry for twenty years,' she complained. I leaned towards her and the telephone receiver to ensure that the correct dialling tone sounded. I heard a click, a woman briefly introducing me and then my own voice reading a poem. My mother (in 1975 she was eighty-five years old) stood very still, listening, concentrating. Then she bellowed into the phone, 'Speak up, son.'

Later, while Joan prepared the evening meal I took my mother out into the garden. It was still warm enough for her to sit in a deckchair on the terrace and turn her face towards the far sea where people lingered on the beaches and a few – specks from this distance – braved the new darkness in the arriving waves.

Meanwhile, because the grass was overgrown, I pushed the mower laboriously forward, then with greater ease pulled the machine towards me. Every few minutes the spray of green stuff and daisies ceased, for the blades would choke, the wheels lock. Where I had been working, the lawn was a lighter green than elsewhere. I had managed to make the mower function more continuously when I happened to gaze up towards the terrace. My mother had struggled to rise from the deckchair, her stockings were wrinkled and she looked beyond me in apparent dismay. I turned to see a stranger coming towards me. Because of the metal whirring of the lawn mower I had not heard the wooden gate's click or footsteps munching the gravel drive.

'Wyn Phillips,' the stranger introduced himself. 'You remember, we were at school together. At St Illtyd's.'

I remembered a Wyn Phillips – when boys we had both played for St Illtyd's cricket team: but this cadaverously thin individual resembled no youth I had known. Besides, Wyn Phillips and I must have been roughly the same age whereas this man was old.

'Wyn Phillips?' I hesitated.

'I've lived in the Far East for years but now I've a bungalow down the road. I've had to retire, you see, because of my health.'

His voice was soft, unassertive. He spoke as if in enemy territory. With the years, physically, it would seem, there had been less a development than a shocking metamorphosis.

'Gosh,' he said, with sudden warmth, 'do you remember, Dan, the time you and I managed to sink that rowing boat in Roath Park Lake? We'd drunk too much. We became U-boat commanders!'

I had no recollection of such an incident. My mother continued to stand up, staring at Wyn Phillips with a peculiar, anxious intensity. I edged towards the terrace. 'This is an old friend of mine,' I said to my mother. 'Wyn Phillips, whom I haven't seen for years.'

'You've left the gate open,' said my mother, scolding our visitor. 'You'll let the sheep in.'

'Of course,' said Wyn, smiling at the old lady and turning towards the gate. 'The sheep in Ogmore get in everywhere.'

'They'd eat the nice flowers here,' my mother said. 'The devils.'

Our garden, which spread out in front of Green Hollows – mostly to one side of the short drive and below the terrace – thanks to Joan's industry looked handsome. I would not have minded the sheep attacking the grass but not those white and red roses, the peonies, the blue anchusa – or even the bruised purple-red valerian that, weed-like, sprang up everywhere and which we called by the local name, devil's dung.

After he closed the gate no flowers captured Wyn Phillips' attention. He stood beneath a tree, sighing, 'Good heavens, good heavens.'

I pulled a leaf from one of the branches and passed it to my unaccountably agitated visitor. 'It smells like a dispensary,' I said.

'Do you know the name of this tree?' he asked.

'No,' I said. 'I've often wondered.'

He lifted the leaf to his nostrils, unsmiling. He sniffed it again and again as if it were important that he should identify its medicinal odour, his eyes closed as if he were at a concert and listening to profound music. He opened his eyes, troubled. 'I've smelt that smell before,' he pronounced, 'but I can't recall where. I'll keep this.' He put the leaf in his pocket. 'I have a friend who used to work at Kew Gardens. When he comes to Ogmore next I'll get him to identify it. I'm sure it's a rare tree for this country. An Oriental tree.'

'My daughter-in-law's wonderful with the garden,' my mother beamed.

I examined our tree with fresh interest. 'Not every man has an Oriental tree in his garden,' I said.

'I can do better than that,' Wyn Phillips countered. 'I have an Asian wife. You must meet her.'

'When I was a girl,' said my mother pointlessly, 'and I lived in Bridgend, we used to come to Ogmore in a pony and trap.'

Autumn and Winter

In subsequent visits to Ogmore-by-Sea I did not see much of our neighbour Wyn Phillips, though his bungalow was only a few minutes' walk downhill towards the river mouth. I was busy: our children and their friends had joined us; or I had to visit my mother in Cardiff; or I had an article to write, a book to review, a deadline to meet; or a football match to go to. Besides, Wyn Phillips and I had different interests. Old he may have looked, but he had a mind like a questing adolescent: he delighted in talking about abstractions, about the Meaning of Life and Death. Perhaps it was because he had been so ill. It seemed he had suffered a polyarteritis which, the doctors had told him, 'had fortunately become arrested'.

Once he solemnly remarked to me in the Craig – the nearest pub to Green Hollows – trying to initiate a soulful debate, 'I think you know yourself, Dan. But I don't. I don't know who I am.' And this before he had even sipped at his first pint of beer! Wyn was not given to making small talk or being light about things. And despite my occasional probings he hardly referred to his life in the Far East or even to his wife, though he did reveal that she liked reading poetry. 'Malay poetry,' he added.

I am not certain that he pursued such earnest existentialist questions with other people so remorselessly. I sensed that because I was a doctor and wrote poetry he half believed I knew the secret of things, was all-wise. Talking to Wyn, because of his overestimation of me, I often felt inadequate.

One late morning, during the Christmas period, Wyn Phillips telephoned. 'Come over for a pre-lunch drink,' he urged me. 'I have important news for you.'

'Joan's in Bridgend, shopping,' I said.

'Leave a note for her – ask her to join us later.'

I left Joan a note. *At Wyn Phillips' for a drink. He invites you to join us. 12.18 p.m.. Love, D.* Then I ventured into the cold, misty day, passing my Oriental tree, now leafless, of course. As I proceeded down Craig-yr-eos Road I heard the foghorns sounding from Nash Point. I could not see where sea and sky joined because of the smudging mist. When I reached the turf and turned towards the estuary I kept to the path next to the stone wall until the new-built houses and bungalows loomed into sight. Here the sound of the sea seemed louder, a continuous background noise.

These new structures had been built on sand. Farther up, where we were, it was rock, solid rock. The meaning of the Welsh word *craig* was *rock*. Craig-yr-eos Road – 'Rock-of-the-nightingale'. How many decades, on their unstable base, would these new homes last? Yet what a view they all had on a clear day, despite the tarmac that had been laid down for cars to park on; despite too the coastguard's low stone building with its red flag which even in this mist looked like a public urinal commanded by a communist. Beyond the river mouth, now, I could see indistinctly the sand dunes – the second highest in Europe.

When I was a boy those sand dunes had been requisitioned for an army shooting range. Now, though – probably even in this weather – all kinds of isolated, strange people walked their hidden ways, or jogged through them. Joan and I sometimes went walking there in the milder seasons. And we had been startled by young men running through in single file, utterly silent because of the soft sand, between the narrow valleys of the dunes. It was like meeting joggers in a desert.

In the Phillips' front room I heard again the distant foghorns sorrowfully hooting. 'It's an eerie sound,' Mrs Phillips remarked. Soon after, she scuttled away saying she had lunch to prepare and left me holding a glass of sherry. At once, Wyn launched into a Big Theme: 'So many things are changing here in Wales,' he declared. 'A man is what he is partly because of his surroundings, right? But they're putting up new buildings, tearing down old ones, building new bridges, new roads, so that the old familiar places become bloody well unrecognizable.'

'You can say that about Ogmore,' I said.

'When things alter so much,' said Wyn with sincerity, 'don't we feel assaulted deep within us? We become anxious. That explains nationalism?'

'How do you mean?'

'Don't we need to redefine ourselves since so much is crumbling away, or being added to without our permission? For a start, it forces us to define our nationality. I have to say, for a start, that I'm Welsh.'

I must have looked at the bottom of my glass – for Wyn, as if prompted, brought over the bottle of sherry. 'Well, I'm learning Welsh as a matter of fact. Still, I didn't bring you over to tell you that. It's news I have about your tree.'

His friend from Kew Gardens had stayed with them in Ogmore, and they had walked over to Green Hollows.

'It's a Korean tree,' Wyn said triumphantly. 'An *Evodia danieli*. From Korea.'

'*Danieli*,' I said. 'That sounds apt.'

'I told you it was a rare Oriental tree,' said Wyn. 'Here, let's drink to it.'

But then he began to cough and cough and cough so that he could hardly catch his breath. His wife came in, worried. He sat down on the sofa, wheezing and gasping, while I took the glass from his hand and said gently, 'You'll be all right, Wyn. Breathe in and out, slowly. That's right.'

191

On Sunday my youngsters luxuriated in having a lie-in. So did my mother that particular morning. The sweet Ogmore air of May must have knocked them out. Joan came in from the garden asking, 'Would you mind going up to the farm to get me a dozen eggs?'

The Powell farm was but a mile's walk – it straddled the road this side of Southerndown. I put the *Observer* to one side and elected to go the indirect way, along the turf near the seashore, then to climb upwards, steeply, to the high road. At the bottom of Craig- yr-eos Road, though, instead of going towards Southerndown I turned towards the river mouth. I decided to call on Wyn Phillips briefly, just to say hello, just to see if he was O.K.. Other friends earlier that month and in April, had visited Green Hollows. I had boasted as, one by one, they passed under the *Evodia danieli*, 'This is a rare tree, do you know? From Korea. Have a whiff of one of its leaves.' And each, in turn, had looked thoughtful, suitably impressed.

But Wyn had not been into our garden this spring, since the leaves had budded. Suddenly I felt a sense of dread, a feeling of utter emptiness, purposelessness, blackness, depression. My mother would have remarked, 'Someone walked over your grave'. And I wondered whether I would find Wyn critically ill. A minute later there he was, as if summoned, coming towards me looking so much fitter than he had appeared to be in the winter.

'Yes,' he said, 'I'm fine. I've put on weight.'

'I'm just off to the Powell farm for eggs.'

'You're going the wrong way.'

He offered to accompany me on my errand. Despite the uninter-rupted sunlight there were so few people about that they all greeted us with a 'Good morning, lovely morning'. A few people walked their dogs doggedly, a few on the rocks fished for fish patiently, and we stopped from time to time to gaze across to the seagulls flying level with the cliffs of Southerndown or to observe nearer, below us, for we were higher now, the reflected sun on the wrinkled, silver-paper sea.

Before we climbed towards the farm, Wyn turned forward a few yards to the edge of the cliff as if he had spotted something extra-ordinary. 'My God,' he said, putting his hand on my arm, 'they're screwing.'

I looked down obliquely between the rocks. Far below, on an

apron of pebbles, a young man and woman copulated. Both were clothed above the waist, both bare below it. It occurred to me that they would have been more comfortable in the sand dunes, hidden by the sharp rush and marram grass. I turned away.

Wyn said loudly, 'Hang on. It's interesting!' They would not have heard him because of the sighing sea.

'C'mon, Wyn,' I said.

But he continued to watch them unashamedly while I began to climb slowly towards the farm. 'It's a Sunday morning service,' he called to me.

He caught me up soon after, saying accusingly, 'You're a puritan.'

'You're a voyeur,' I responded, irritated.

Wyn Phillips suddenly became enraged. I did not mean to quarrel with him. He had observed in Green Hollows that we owned some binoculars. Right? Why? I told him truthfully that they had been a gift from my sister years ago, that I rarely used them. But I had used them? Yes, I had used them. And why had I used them? To look at the coast of Somerset, at Tusker Rock, at the ships out at sea sometimes when I was bored. Or towards the promontory of Porthcawl or Happy Valley beyond the dunes. Or to catch a seagull in motion, or to... 'And what if you saw two neighbours copulating, you'd put the binoculars down, would you, you'd put them down if you were on your own and no one knew that you, peeping Dan, were watching, right?'

'Don't be childish, Wyn,' I said.

He stood still, a little out of breath. 'It's too much for me to climb up to the farm,' he said quietly. 'I'm going back.'

'Wait for me,' I said. 'I won't be a tick. Sit here for a bit.'

'No. I'm going back.'

I nodded. He started to move down between the fresh yellow-flowered gorse towards the cliffs again, then halted to call vehemently, 'You should know yourself. You don't know yourself. I was wrong about you.'

Summer

The summer of the drought. The reservoirs empty. I was unable to leave sweltering London. One Saturday in early July, working in the

193

library, I thought with resentment, 'How ridiculous not to be at Ogmore in weather like this.' Before leaving the reference room I noticed a book on the open shelves called *Living Trees of the World.*

Soon I was reading, under '*Evodia*', 'The most familiar kinds have large deciduous pinnate aromatic leaves, broad clusters and dry fruit capsules which open to reveal glossy black seeds.' I paused. Aromatic the leaves of our tree were, yes, but it had never developed fruit capsules. In Korea, no doubt, it would have done, but in Wales the tree declined. I read on: '*Evodia danieli...* of Korea and northern China, about twenty-five feet tall.' Ours reached to only half that size. A young, still-growing *Evodia danieli* perhaps? Or stunted, because not growing in its natural habitat? I quit the library.

At the end of the month we did manage to snatch one weekend in Ogmore. The whole family joined us. We bathed in the sea that was as warm as the Mediterranean. There had even been fires in the bracken: large patches black as tar were surrounded by scorched ferns and gorse. Once, after a swim, after coming through the wooden gate I looked up intently at our *Evodia danieli* and spotted green capsules. 'Look,' I said excitedly to Joan, 'this non-Welsh weather has made our tree sprout fruit.' It had never done so before. I pulled down a couple of green capsules. 'Open them up,' I continued, 'and we'll see the glossy black seeds.'

Joan could not open it with her fingers. 'I don't think it is a fruit, she said. 'It's like a nut, an unripe nut.'

'Our Korean tree's gone nuts,' said our son, David.

'A nut?' I said, surprised.

'Sunstroke,' said David.

In the kitchen David cut across it with a knife. Hearing voices, my mother who had been asleep joined us, stood near David, watching him. 'Gosh, he's a clever boy,' my mother said, happily.

Cut, it resembled a cross section of a very small brain.

'It's a walnut,' Joan said. 'It's not an *Evodia danieli*, it's a walnut tree.'

'I've always liked walnuts,' my mother declared. 'When you were so high, son, remember how on my birthday you bought me some nutcrackers from Woolworth's? In those days every item was sixpence.'

My own son was laughing – the uninhibited laughter of a seventeen-year-old. How absurd! Wyn's friend, that expert, had got it wrong. 'Maybe it's an Oriental walnut tree, Dad,' David said, as if to console me.

'This is definitely a walnut,' Joan said, thinking prose.

'Who told you it wasn't a walnut tree?' my mother asked me.

I told her. She had met Wyn Phillips a year ago. 'Remember, Mother?'

She did not remember. 'Is he a Yiddisher boy?' she asked.

During August, American friends stayed with us – Mack Rosenthal and his wife Vicky. Bank holiday weekend, we drove to Ogmore. In the car Mack told us how he was writing another critical book – on Yeats, among others. As we approached the Severn Bridge Mack railed against the 'non-poetic' treatment of Yeats by so many learned academics.

'I don't want to read another essay on Yeats,' I said truthfully.

Mack did not hear me. He was in full flight! 'Hibernophiliac critics, Maud-Gonneomaniac critics, critics who plunge into the chthonic mysteries, critics who begin books entitled *Yeats* by quoting Dr Johnson and conclude by quoting Dr Buber, critics... '

'Where are we now?' interrupted Vicky as I slowed, preparing to pay the toll to cross the Severn Bridge.

A Welsh poet had pointed out that the toll money was craftily collected on the *English* side of the bridge.

'The Welsh ground down again,' I informed the Rosenthals.

'Will we be in Wales when we cross the bridge?' Vicky asked.

I looked forward to showing Ogmore off to Mack and Vicky 'that gong-tormented sea', the altering light on the estuary, the stepping stones across the river near the ruins of Ogmore Castle.

'Have you friends in Ogmore?' asked Vicky.

'Not close friends,' I said.

'There's Wyn Phillips,' said Joan.

'Wyn has no sense of humour. I wonder what he'll say about the walnuts.'

When we arrived at Ogmore we gladly tumbled out of the dry warmth of the car. The Rosenthals, perfect guests, made suitable noises about the splendour of the sea views.

'How about an ice cream?' I suggested.

At Hardee's store they sold Thayer's ice cream. 'It's Welsh, it's creamy,' I boasted, as if I manufactured the stuff myself.

'Wow ,' said Mack. 'I like ice cream in all its depth and variety. It is often uncomplicated in appearance but its taste may promote underlying reaches of associations. I say all this, of course, icily.'

'I'd sure like to taste a Welsh ice cream,' said Vicky, a little worried in case Mack was offending me.

'Life without ice cream,' continued Mack, 'would, I believe, be very much less worth living.'

'Oh, c'mon, Mack,' Vicky said louder. 'I really would like an ice cream.'

I set out for Hardee's while the others sorted themselves out after the journey and unpacked. But I did not bring any ice cream back to Green Hollows that afternoon. I had no sooner closed our front wooden gate than Mrs Phillips appeared down the narrow Craig-yr-eos Road. I smiled. 'How's Wyn?' I asked.

She smiled and paused. 'He's dead,' she replied. She continued to smile so that for a moment I thought that I had misheard her. 'He died a month ago,' she said.

'When I saw him in May,' I said stupidly, 'he looked so much better. He'd put on weight.'

'The steroids,' Mrs Phillips explained.

I struggled to discover appropriate words. Mrs Phillips stood there disconcertingly smiling. Her husband had died a month ago, so perhaps she had no more public crying to do. 'Wyn left a letter for you,' she said. 'Will you come down with me now?'

'Of course.'

Why had she not posted it to me? And what had Wyn written about to me? I remembered our last meeting: how I had climbed to the Powell farm for eggs while he called out, scandalously condemning me, 'You don't know yourself.'

'It's hard to believe Wyn's gone,' Mrs Phillips said, her mirthless smile no longer enduring.

A mile or two out to sea, black Tusker Rock was visible and, beyond it, a coal tug slowly moved eastward towards Cardiff, small, caught in no binoculars. The turf above the rocks was strangely discoloured – straw-coloured because of the long absence of rain. We turned there and soon the squat, desolate coastguard's building came into view. Uncharacteristically, the car park was full. I had never seen it so crowded, sunlight glinting on rooftop after rooftop.

'I'm so very sorry,' I said quietly.

When we reached her bungalow the sign startled me: 'FOR SALE' and curtly beneath it: 'PRIVATE CALLERS FORBIDDEN'.

'Where will you move to?' I asked.

'I'll go back to Singapore,' she said. 'My relations... I don't know why we came here in the first place. Wyn had no real roots here.'

When she gave me the envelope (quite a large envelope) I did not know whether to open it there and then. But Mrs Phillips seemed to have no curiosity about the letter and moved a little towards the door so that, rightly or wrongly, I imagined she wished me to go. We shook hands silently.

As I climbed Craig-yr-eos Road I opened the envelope. There was no letter inside it. Only a dried leaf with an unmistakable aromatic odour. The leaf which Wyn had thought to be an *Evodia danieli* – I had not had the opportunity to tell him about the walnuts – was brittle, friable. It was probably the leaf Wyn had put in his pocket a year earlier. I walked on to Green Hollows wondering, holding the leaf carefully in one hand, the envelope in the other.

The White Ship

Those who have a frail elderly parent alive, living apart from them, expect, sooner or later, to receive that black-edged telephone call which will relay the worst news, a message intoned, sepulchral and apologetic. That unhappy, unquiet summons would probably be delivered in the dead middle of the night. That was why when I woke up in the dark, curtained bedroom and heard the telephone's insistent clamour downstairs in the hall I immediately thought of my aged mother who dwelt some twenty-three miles away in her Cathedral Road flat at Cardiff. My wife beside me stirred, still in iceberg cecity, four-fifths asleep. I hurried from the bedroom; switched on landing lights and, with bare feet, quickly descended to the hall and the bleak telephone.

'Dr Abse?'

'Yes.'

'This is Gene Harvey.'

'Who?'

'Gene Harvey. You remember. I wrote to you last year from New York about coming to interview you for *The Soussia Review* when I returned to Bristol.'

'*The Soussia Review*?' I repeated automatically.

'Yes. I hope you remember. You were kind enough to give me your assent.'

I looked up from the telephone. My wife stood at the top of the stairs, her face a remarkable, textbook illustration of worry .

'It's four o'clock in the morning,' I said, half relieved, half irritated at this idiot American for frightening Joan and me out of our now expunged tranquillity.

'I know the time, I know the month, I know the year,' said Gene Harvey in unwarranted aggressive tones. 'It's gone half past four and I'm here. In Bridgend. I'm stuck here. There's no buses, no taxis, nothing. Nobody's about. I'm fed up.'

'You're fed up!'

'What's the matter?' asked my wife.

'I'm calling from a telephone booth near the bus station,' Gene

Harvey continued. 'I've had a mishap. And this place is *deserted*, a morgue, a damned ghost town. You have a car, I take it?'

I must have lost my temper because Joan intervened, suggesting I calmed down. I but vaguely remembered receiving a letter from someone in New York about a new literary magazine.

'I don't feel up to walking six miles to Ogmore-by-Sea,' Gene Harvey explained imperiously.

'You don't?' I said.

'No,' he said.

'I could cry for you,' I said.

He put the phone down. I held the ticking receiver. I was about to deliver a few explosive verbal salvoes but he had cut me off. I felt rather as if I had tried to open a door and the knob had come off in my hand. 'He cut me off,' I told Joan.

'I'm not surprised,' Joan scolded me. 'Whoever it was, you were rude.'

'*I* was rude! This idiot, bloody uncivilised American rings me up at half past four in the morning, asks me without a sorry or a please or anything to pick him up, a complete stranger, orders me, more or less, commands me to pick him up at Bridgend and when I quietly demur, when I courteously infer that I'm not too keen about that he hangs up on me.'

I felt roused, adrenally awake. I went into the kitchen. 'Do you want some tea?' I asked my wife.

I was holding the kettle under the cold water tap, listening to the changing sound of water falling on water on metal, when the telephone brainlessly clamoured again. At that hour of the morning an active phone somehow sounds louder than ever. This time Joan went into the hall to answer it. She is not only more diplomatic than I am, more even-tempered, but she is kinder too. To be frank, she is a ridiculously soft touch. So before she replaced the receiver she had agreed to pick up the poor, lost, helpless, unappealing Mr Gene Harvey and bring him back to our house, Green Hollows, at Ogmore-by-Sea. This meant, of course, that after a needless alter-cation between my wife and me, I would have to insist – after I had drunk my tea, after I had dressed – that I, no other, would reverse our car into Craig-yr-eos Road and nobly, gallantly, selflessly, drive the six and a quarter miles to Bridgend bus station.

And all this, I learnt from Joan, because this stupid American had met someone by the name of Gus Jones on the train who, somehow, had villainously persuaded him to visit a sleazy one-roomed Bridgend nightclub.

'So what did he say happened at this so-called nightclub?'

'A mishap,' Joan replied.

'What kind of mishap?'

'I don't know. He didn't say.'

I still felt angry as I sipped at the tea which had, I suddenly noticed, an odd chemical taste. I could not make up my mind whether the milk had gone sour in the sulky summer weather or whether the authorities had, secretly, in the middle of the night, doused the water supply with chlorides, fluorides and God knows what other carcinogenic or spleen-rotting, liver-rotting, brain-rotting chemicals.

'You know,' Joan said, just before I left the house, 'he didn't have an American accent.'

'That's right,' I said, 'you're right.'

I drove slowly, not out of spite – let the bugger wait – but because now, half an hour or so past cock-crow, the sun had lifted just above the eastern wooded hills and, with the sun, my spirits had lifted also. The first light swamped the greeny, ferny, undulating turf of Ogmore to glint on the chromium estuary below – like sun dazzle on a mirror. Beyond the mouth of the river, under some wheeling gulls, the open grey sea crawled in slow motion to visit its irregular altering, white, fussy edges along the curve of the bay. A scene then to delay anyone. The other side of the river, the sand dunes, the second highest in Europe, topped by sparse marram grass, seemed to be swimming with shadows.

Nobody was about. No one at all. No man, no woman, no child. I drove forward in second gear on the high road that followed the course of the river below. There I spied two very white static swans. Near the curb of the road, isolated gangs of sheep looked up momentarily at the oncoming car and, more surprisingly, a rabbit came into view. It was worth rising at dawn to see Ogmore like this, to breathe in the unused, spacious, gorse-tasting, summer air. I resolved to take a dawn walk some time. Well, maybe.

After I had passed the closed doors of the Pelican pub and the grey ruins of Ogmore Castle I accelerated until the river was no longer in sight and, in no time at all, I reached the outskirts of

200

Bridgend. Despite the now unambiguous daylight, the procession of lamp-posts, insomniacs all, were still on, sentries guarding the whole small town, though not a car, not a pedestrian was in sight. I, sweet-tempered, orderly citizen of Wales and the world, stopped the car when confronted by an unnecessary red traffic light. Afterwards, at 5.35 a.m. precisely, I turned the corner towards Bridgend's deserted bus station – not one bus in the bays – and ahead of me I observed a solitary, centre-half tall, portly man wearing an open-necked scarlet shirt and green billiard-cloth trousers. At his feet a large dilapidated suitcase. When I halted the car beside him he leaned down to the car's window, unsmiling, disgruntled, and delivered the world-shattering quote of the year: 'So you found me then.'

As I turned back towards Ogmore, Gene Harvey complained, 'This place is dead.' Almost at once an individual walked out from a side-street, close to the corner Indian restaurant – the town's hard-working burglar I presumed, on his way home at last.

Gene Harvey was, as Joan had perceived, English. He was an antiquarian bookseller and dealer in manuscripts whose head-quarters were in Bristol but he spent much time in the U.S.A. Oh no, he couldn't live permanently in the U.S.A. He was too attached to Bristol north, not to mention the country of his birth that also had engendered the comic genius of Chaucer, the genius of Shakespeare, the ineffable nobility of the King James Bible. 'Not forgetting the glory and the power of the Elizabethan age, *n'est-ce pas?*' he declaimed.

As we approached the ruins of Ogmore Castle I asked him about the mishap he had endured in Bridgend the previous evening and whether or not he had intended to contact me earlier, much earlier. He did not answer. Instead he commanded me to stop. He seemed amazed as if he had never seen the ruins of a castle before. He wished to examine it more closely. 'Background material for my interrogation of you,' he explained.

'The interview?' I said.

'No, no,' he said. 'I don't interview. I interrogate.'

As we left the car to clamber on the ruins he continued, 'I ask questions and you answer. Each time you don't evade my question you submit, *n'est-ce pas?* I confess I enjoy the feeling of dominion I have over the interviewee. I choose the questions – whatever comes to mind – anything I like, I ask in freedom and you respond in bondage. What's your particular perversion?'

'What?'

'What's the colour of your wound?'

'Why should I have a wound?' I said.

'All writers have,' he boomed. 'You're all walking invalids – even though you were until recently, I gather, a practising physician.'

I decided then, perhaps precipitately, that as soon as we reached Green Hollows I would get the interview over as soon as possible. Meanwhile I would play polite host whatever my inner seethings. So I told him about the ruins, acting the role of guide to a tourist: how beside this shallow river the Castle had been built in the twelfth century, how its lord and master had been the Norman knight, William de Londres, who had oppressed the local fierce Welsh.

'You can cross the river here on those ancient stepping stones to the thatched village of Merthyr Mawr. There's a superstition that it's bad luck to step over the stones unless you first spit into the river three times,' I told Gene Harvey.

He expressed no courteous interest in my contribution to the dialogue. Instead he responded, 'I'm hungry' – and then energetically chimed out in singing tones, 'Breakfast time.'

Back in the car he muttered, 'You writers all have stinking wounds like Philoctetes. Yes, like my friend Cal had - like John and Sylvia.'

I suppose you might say that as far as I was concerned it was approximately hate at first sight. Before breakfast was over I perceived that Gene Harvey was the last person in the world to act as an interviewer. He appeared to have little capacity to listen. He seemed stone-deaf when Joan or I volunteered even brief information or offered a précis of an opinion. He was an inveterate name-dropper and a teller of anecdotes. 'Sam,' he was saying, 'is fractured within; but he has a sense of humour.' He paused to butter more toast before continuing. 'Last April I was having a drink with him – I had some business in Paris. We were in a bar near the Champs Elysées and he had a few of his Irish acolytes around him – a couple of actors and a radio producer from Belfast who kept on saying. "What do you think of this play, Mr Beckett, and what do you think of that?" Anyway, I was telling Sam about my great admiration for Catherine the Great.'

'Catherine the Great?' asked Joan.

'Yes, my dear. You remember when Prince Potemkin accused her of keeping fifteen lovers on the lead simultaneously, X going out of one bedroom door while Y entered by another, she protested, "That's not true. I only entertain five lovers at any one period."'

Joan laughed politely.

'When I told Sam that story' he said, 'Sam took his glass of beer – he was drinking beer – and poured the beer over his head and uttered a libation, the words of which I quite forget except he concluded with, "Come star of the nether world". Then all the others round that table deliberately lifted their glasses high and poured the beer over their own heads.'

'Sounds great fun,' I said.

'Good old Sam,' remarked Gene Harvey. 'Do you think I could have another egg, my dear?'

'I read a story about Beckett in *The Guardian*,' Joan said, 'in which he poured beer over his own head.'

After breakfast, Mr Harvey asked if he might rest somewhere, as he had had hardly any sleep the previous night, and despite my dumb signallings, Joan suggested that he could use the spare bedroom upstairs. His face transparently brightened at this offer and I guessed that we had an uninvited guest on our hands who might well prolong his stay beyond my patience. As he lugged his large suitcase up the stairs behind Joan I was tempted to call out loud the injunction of the American poet, Marianne Moore: 'Superior people never make long visits'. Wonderfully, almost saint-like, though, I refrained. I stared at the clock that stared at me. It was not yet half-past seven. The early morning birds were wild outside. It was going to be a long, long day.

Who does not feel a twinge of remorse when confronted with an accumulation of unanswered letters? So, despite the glorious summer weather, I stayed indoors to deal with my neglected correspondence while Mr Gene Harvey slept upstairs and Joan laboured in the garden. Many months had passed since I had received that letter from New York requesting a *Soussia Review* interview. That was one note I would not discover among the pile of envelopes on my desk. I could not remember how I had responded. I had probably foolishly written, 'Yes. Let me know when you come this way.' Something like that. I had assumed, of course, that *The Soussia Review* was one of those fat American literary periodicals published from Soussia, wherever that was, not a periodical about to be launched in Bristol.

Before answering my correspondence I decided to look up Soussia in Larousse's *World Geography*. It was not listed. I reached higher in the bookcase. My father, soon after the First World War, bought a set of grey, handsomely bound encyclopedias from a travelling salesman. These encyclopedias, published by the defunct Gresham Publishing Company, now adorned my book-shelves at Ogmore-by-Sea. I took down Volume X, gold-lettered ROM-SWA and turned to page 284. Between *Souslik* (the name of rodent mammals belonging to the genus *Spermophilus* of the squirrel family) and *South*, Robert (British divine, born 1634, and most celebrated preacher of his day) there was no mention of Soussia. Nothing. I had drawn a blank. I returned to my desk and letter-writing.

By lunchtime I was ready to walk up to the post office having answered the most urgent of the letters. My wife, still in the garden, asked me to bring back a loaf of bread from the village shop. We would, when I returned, she explained, have a light lunch. 'Bread, cheese, tomatoes. And I'll make a salad, O.K.? And maybe, since we have a visitor, we'll open a bottle of wine...'

It was when I came out of the post office that I saw the white ship close, so close to the shore. It was the most beautiful ship that I had ever seen. I could imagine the vessel being launched for the first time, the workmen who had constructed her, proud of the conjugation of their small, individual craftsmanship, all watching from the banks of the river as she floated away – her superstructure white as a cloud in sunlight, breathlessly white, her white clipper bows, her two raked white funnels blasting out the new, old, melancholy birth-cries of all steamships. And the workmen cheering, cheering their own sacred workmanship, cheering at the sheer beauty of her as she passed them, free, no longer theirs, on the way to the sea.

I walked across the road to lean on the railings. These overlooked the declensions of dipping green turf, gorse bushes and ferns, all the sloping way down to the rocks and the pebbles and the sand and the sea. The ship rode high above the water, utterly clean in the sun-dazzle – white bridge, white poop, white forecastle, and two slanting, luxury white funnels. Never had there been, on this bit of sea, in all the scores of years that I had visited or lived in Ogmore, such a ship. If there was such a thing as a celestial vessel then this, surely, would be it!

I had never seen, either, a ship of this size moving inexorably towards the shore side of the dangerously wide area of Tusker Rock. The tide was fully in so that the huge roof of black, jagged Tusker Rock, less than a mile from the shore, was submerged, invisible. Did the Captain of that ship know what different depths he was steering through?

Further down the road I saw a neighbour of mine, Tony Dyson, with his dog. Tony was standing still, transfixed as I was, watching the white ship manoeuvre, hushed, even closer to the shore line. There had not been a wreck on Tusker since before the war.

In the old sailing-ship days, the people living along the coast made a partial living as wreckers. At night they used to tie lanterns on to the sheep that grazed on the turfy high cliffs in order to bamboozle the sailors and entice them to steer their sailing boats onto the jaws of waiting, hungry, Tusker Rock. Now I wanted to send up a rocket, a firework, to warn the Captain of the white ship of the real, near danger.

The ship had only a few people on deck. I could see them clearly as the vessel drew into Hardee's Bay – such a big ship to come so remarkably near. Gradually it followed the curve of the shore before the river's mouth, silently, silently. From where I stood I could not hear anything. The ship so white, so stately, moved across the dazzle of sunlight as in a dream. It turned when it had presumably cleared the secretive danger of the rocks below, it turned to steam towards the distant promontory of Porthcawl.

I looked down the road. Tony Dyson was disappearing into the distance, pulled by his dog. Still I delayed, holding the loaf of bread and leaning on the railings. I wanted to see whether the ship would pull into the quay at Porthcawl or simply float beyond the promontory out of sight, westward, out of existence. As it was, I absurdly felt that if I closed my eyes and then opened them again the celestial white ship would not be there. Slowly, slowly, it reached Porthcawl. In the far distance it now seemed small and Porthcawl's lighthouse on the promontory appeared to be no bigger than a thimble. The white ship drew up to the quay.

Gene Harvey did not reappear until early in the evening, and having drunk a cup of tea he suggested we begin the interrogation, *n'est-ce pas?* 'Afterwards,' he boomed, 'perhaps you will allow me to take you both out for dinner. Is there a good restaurant near here?'

'You'll have to watch out for the last train leaving Bridgend,' I said unkindly.

He immediately addressed Joan. 'It would be helpful, my dear, if I could stay the night here. Then I could leave first thing tomorrow morning.'

'Of course,' Joan said.

'It's settled then,' said Gene Harvey. 'Now, would you kindly book up a table for three, say for eight.'

All right,' I said to Joan. 'Give Frolics a shout. We haven't eaten at Southerndown for quite a while.'

'Frolics is one of the best restaurants round here,' Joan explained.

Gene Harvey took off his jacket, rolled up the sleeves of his scarlet shirt and placed a black apparatus with cassette on the table. Joan left us to it while Gene Harvey continued to talk at a hundred miles an hour about me being a Welsh Jew and wasn't that interesting or was I a Jewish Welshman but it didn't matter anyway for come to think of it, whatshisname James, the brother of Jesus, yes James, if he'd had his way, if Paul hadn't done such a good PR job, Christianity wouldn't have separated from its Jewish heritage, *n'est-ce pas*, and we'd all be Jews... '

'I wonder if we could have a drink, perhaps a whisky,' he suddenly interrupted himself, 'before we begin the, er, interrogation?'

I rose from the table and brought back a half-full whisky bottle and two glasses. I decided that since there was no way out I might as well submit to this interview and, at the same time, be tolerably sociable. I would indulge in the stoic virtue of imperturbability. It was not easy though. His peroration continued as if there had been no interruption. Religion, he averred, was idealism divorced from reality. 'Yes, I'm a pagan, my boy. I accept neither the Beatitudes of Jesus nor the Decalogue of Moses.'

He switched on the apparatus. 'Testing,' he roared. 'One two three four, test-ing.' Then he poured himself a very full glass of Scotch which he proceeded to sip neat. 'You know,' he said, 'I've known lots of poets here and in America – Delmore, Cal and John were friends of mine – but I never interrogated them. My field, you see, is fiction not poetry so I'm going to concentrate on asking you about your prose, O.K.?'

'O.K.,' I said. 'As a matter of fact I'm writing fiction at the moment.'

Gene Harvey ignored that and extracted a piece of paper from his pocket. 'You once remarked,' he said, 'that your ambition was to write poems which appear translucent but are in fact deceptive. Let me quote directly: "I would have a reader enter them, be deceived he could see through them like sea-water, and be puzzled when he cannot quite touch bottom." Now, when it comes to prose are you also interested in deceiving the reader?'

'Well...' I began.

'Hang on,' Gene Harvey said. 'Let me just see if this cassette is working.'

Afterwards, to my surprise, the interview proceeded more or less competently and without too many anecdotal divagations, though, at one point, I was puzzled by being asked a question about Coleridge. Harvey had soliloquised about how he had attended Robert Lowell's last public appearance in New York where Lowell had read in tandem with Allen (Ginsberg) and how a friend of Allen's, Gregory Corso of course, somewhat tipsy, had interrupted Cal while he was reading and how he, Gregory, deliciously admired one of Cal's lines, 'The paranoid inert gaze of Coleridge', but surely Coleridge wasn't paranoid, *n'est-ce pas* and, 'Are you a great admirer of Coleridge?'

When, an hour later, Gene Harvey switched off the machine, he seemed pleased with himself. He poured himself the last of the whisky and announced, 'With editing, I think I have enough material there, though I can't say you're easy to interrogate.'

It was my turn to ask questions. 'Why do you call your periodical *The Soussia Review*?' I asked.

'Years ago Wystan suggested the title to me.'

'Soussia ?' I persisted.

'Soussia was known as The City that Time Forgot,' explained Harvey solemnly. 'It was an ancient Hebrew city, thriving thousands of years ago on the edge of the Negev desert. It was a city never mentioned once in the scriptures, not once. Nobody knows the origin of its name or why its inhabitants mysteriously abandoned the city. But I have a theory.' He paused, waiting for me to ask him about his theory. I asked him. 'I think,' he said, lowering his voice as if to impart a secret, 'I think all the inhabitants of Soussia went mad.'

He pressed a button in the machine so that the cassette sprang out. 'I expect the majority of those who lived in Soussia were scribes of a sort, walking invalids, do you see?' He laughed.

'You know' I said, 'Dylan Thomas wanted to write a script about a town that went mad. That script eventually became "Under Milk Wood".'

'I know,' said Gene Harvey contemptuously. Then, surprise, surprise, it turned out that his father had been a friend of Dylan's. Swiftly he launched into several unfunny anecdotes about good old Dylan's wonderfully hilarious behaviour. It seemed that when he'd visited them he'd stolen Harvey Senior's shirts. 'Though I was only so high,' Gene Harvey said, 'Dylan passed on to me his Weltanschauung. When in doubt, fox 'em.'

At Frolics, the waitress left the bill on our table. Gene Harvey picked it up, glanced at it, then put it down again as if it were red-poker-hot. 'Oh, for heaven's sake,' he exploded, 'I've left my Barclaycard in my other jacket back in Ogmore. How stupid of me.' I had guessed that this would happen, something like this, the moment he generously, expansively, ordered a second expensive bottle of wine – insisted on it, in fact. 'Please allow me the privilege,' he had said gallantly.

While I paid the bill I heard him pronounce loudly, so that the other diners at Frolics could also hear him, 'It's half-past nine already. Did you chant, when you were a kid: What's the time? Half-past nine, Hang your bloomers on the line?'

'Yes,' replied Joan in a small voice.

'Dylan had a variation on that, a wonderfully filthy variation.'

On leaving Frolics for the car we encountered Tony Dyson and his wife walking their dog in the lucid starlit night. The air was cooler now, turf-sweet and fresh. We stopped briefly and discussed the white ship that we had seen earlier that day. Joan, who had just ceased gardening, had observed it from the terrace. 'I didn't see anybody on board,' she said.

'No,' agreed Tony.

'I think there were a few people on deck,' I affirmed, 'but it did have the feeling, didn't it, of being unmanned, of having sailed this way from the invisible world – on its way to some unknown island?,

'Magical,' said Tony, 'but, by Christ, it was dangerous coming this side of Tusker Rock. I suppose it was some sort of pleasure craft, a holiday ship, I mean. I wonder if it picked up any passengers at Porthcawl.'

Our conversation seemed to sober up my previously garrulous interrogator. He just listened uncharacteristically silent, while the Dyson's dog, stretched on his leash, intimately sniffed at him. The moon was so luminous our shadows were printed on the narrow-country road. It was such a pleasant summer night that I wished we had walked the mile or so to Frolics. A useless wish. We bid goodbye to the Dysons, Gene Harvey still oddly speechless, and opened the doors of our car.

We had driven for only a few minutes before the open sea came into sight, the black-backed sea with a wide band of thrilling moonlight traversing it, aimed at us. Soon we passed the Powells' farm and could see across the bay the lights of Porthcawl, and, out at sea, a signalling lighthouse flashed. The moon, high above the cliffs of distant Somerset, was round and full and preposterous.

'Stop the car,' Harvey suddenly shouted. 'Stop the car.'

I glanced to my left. In the half light, he looked, suddenly, wildly unwell. At the house, during the interview, he had finished off the bottle of whisky and, not much later, had drunk a bottle of wine, apart from eating a gargantuan meal. So maybe he felt sick? I halted the car on the edge of the road and he clambered out on to the turf and quickly walked some twenty yards down the slope.

'He's probably nauseous,' I said to Joan. 'You stay in the car.'

As I approached I could see he was gazing out to sea intently. 'There,' he said, 'do you see it?'

'What?'

'The white ship. In the moonlight. Is it real or is it a mockery?'

There was nothing to be seen, nothing at all but the moving moonlight on the darkness of the sea. Was he hallucinating, or drunk, or just assing around?

'It makes you believe in Eternity,' he said. Then angrily, 'It's all dissimulation, pretence, falsehood, deception. Like the stars. How many of those we see are still there?'

'What?'

'It's gone,' he said seriously. 'The ship has gone.'

'It was a trick of the moonlight,' I said. And I know I sounded unhelpfully complacent. 'Let's go back to the car.'

Back home, to our horror, he suddenly lay flat on the floor and would not speak a word. Joan, solicitous of course, kept asking if she could get him anything – or wouldn't it be better, more comfortable for him to rest upstairs in bed? He did not seem to hear her. It was as if he had gone through a hole in the air and existed in another world. He remained stretched out horizontal on the carpet, his eyes open, hardly blinking, staring at the ceiling as if he expected some vision to appear there, God's handwriting: Mene, Mene, Tekel, Upharsin.

I bent over and took his pulse. It was quite full, quite regular, not fast not slow, quite normal. Joan was trying to hand me a cushion to place under his head but, instead, I said loudly, firmly, as if I were speaking to a naughty, procrastinating child at bedtime, 'C'mon. Get up. It's time to go to bed.'

I was relieved to hear him speak. 'I feel... sometimes... that my body doesn't belong to me. Do you know what I mean?' He jackknifed to the sitting position, then in a desperately unhappy voice whispered, 'I feel fractured inside.'

'What?' asked Joan.

He stood up. 'I'm such a failure,' he said. 'But I saw that ship, believe me, please believe me. I saw it clearly, that pure ship in the moonlight.'

The room in which breakfast is taken should be quiet. It ought to be mandatory to speak, if one speaks at all, in hushed tones as in a bank or a library. But next morning, at breakfast, Eugene Harvey had assumed his ebullient mask again and boomed out opinions and anecdotes like a cannon firing. It was as if nothing untoward had happened the previous evening, as if the mask had not slipped a little to reveal the terror and emptiness in one unblinking exposed eye. He insisted on telling us, volume turned on full, all the literary gossip: which author was sleeping with whom, how much X received as an advance on his new novel, why Y left her literary agent, how a certain Faber poet had the morals of that Sultan whatshisname, *n'est-ce pas,* who loved to steal his guest's valuables and shed much blood.

'I bought,' he said, finishing off the orange juice that I had my eye on, 'a manuscript of a longish poem from him in 1978. I sold it to Texas. A year later he offered me an identical manuscript. He'd copied out his own original complete with additions, scratchings, deletions. Why, if I hadn't a reputation to consider, I could have sold that unique manuscript ten times over – to Texas, Indiana, Boston, Syracuse, everywhere.'

'I need to go into Bridgend this morning,' I said to Joan, 'so I'll give Gene a lift. Can I get you anything?'

'No hurry,' said Gene Harvey, spreading marmalade on his toast, 'no hurry at all.'

It was past ten before Eugene Harvey brought down his large suitcase into the hall. I wondered what he had in it. He was still wearing the same scarlet shirt, and the same ostentatious green trousers. 'Could I use your phone before I leave?' he asked.

I waited in the kitchen while he made his call. I don't know why I assumed he would be contacting someone close to him at Bristol. Though the kitchen door was closed, I could hear his voice, somewhat muffled, in the hall. 'Norman?' I heard him say. 'It's me, Gene Harvey. You remember. We met on that anti-Vietnam war march years ago. With Mitch and Cal. And more recently at ... What? Five o'clock in the morning? Oh. What? I wanted to... no, Gene Harvey. No, I wrote you about *The Soussia Review.* I hope... Oh hell.'

He had obviously been cut off. Whomever he had been telephoning had put the phone down. Five in the morning, he had said. God Almighty, he must have been phoning New York. He came into the kitchen carrying his suitcase. 'Some people on the phone,' he complained, 'they can't think properly. They become stupid when they can't talk to you face to face. You can meet people who are Einstein face to face, but on the phone they can't add up two and two.'

Joan appeared with a shopping list for me to take to Bridgend. Taking leave of her, Harvey solemnly kissed her hand. 'You have a wonderful wife,' he said to me, still holding my wife's wrist. 'I only had one love in my life. Alas, we were divorced years ago.'

It was another summer's day, a little hazy so that across the Channel the coasts of Somerset and Devon were not visible and even the promontory of Porthcawl seemed distant. An old Anson from R.A.F. St Athans buzzed high up in the layered blueness of the sky, its engine cutting off from time to time before it resumed its steadier drone. I did not dawdle though. We sped along until we encountered some sheep crossing the road. Then, as we waited, I spotted far down below on the river near the rising sandhills, the same two halcyon swans.

'Shall I drop you at the bus station in Bridgend?' I asked.

'That'll do.'

I do not know why I felt guilty about getting rid of Harvey. I owed him nothing. Yet he had a knack of making me feel defensive. He told me how fortunate I was to have a house, to have a wife, not to be alone in the world. Suddenly, for no evident reason, he embarked on a story about Anthony Burgess who, according to him, had undertaken a lecture tour in Japan.

Mischievously I said, 'Do you know Anthony Burgess?'

He looked as if I had hit him, his face vulnerable with the expectancy of rebuttal. 'There's no need to patronise me,' he suddenly spat out. The car was silent. From the first I had been wishing to get rid of him and I knew that he knew it. Perhaps I had been insensitive. I glanced at him; his face was suffused with capillary blood. 'You,' he said, far from amiably, 'have a caring wife, a bourgeois home, you're not going to end in the doss-house. You have one more skin than me. Your wound is hidden, covered.'

Again I felt a sense of needless, irrational guilt. 'People like you,' he accused me, 'people like you, like your neighbour and his safe wife and his dog, people like you, you're God's fortunates: you see a beautiful white ship in daylight. You happen to be around. You have the knack of being in the right place at the right time. But people like me, yes, people like me, we have to imagine that white ship in the dark.' There are occasions when there's nothing to say and it's better not to say anything. We did not speak further until we reached the bus station.

212

There he explained to me, perhaps predictably, that he must have left his Barclaycard in his other jacket at Bristol and it so happened that, alas, because of his mishap at that ridiculous night-club, he had very little ready cash on him.

'Not quite enough for the return journey,' he said, somewhat lachrymosely, 'and at the other end I'll need a taxi.'

I felt in my pocket.

'I'll let you have it back when I send you *The Soussia Review*,' he said.

'Fine,' I said.

He did not refer to the Frolics bill. 'I must entice Anthony Burgess to write for my magazine,' he muttered.

'All the best,' I said, meaning it.

Gene Harvey leaned over to shake hands. He stood there, unsmiling, hesitant, and I glimpsed again, just for one second, one secret, revelatory moment, his mask slipping to expose that vacuous eye, full of endless anxiety. Or was it one of my own reflected eyes that I was looking at? I moved the car forward, deeply unhappy at the realisation that I had behaved, in some unthinking way, more selfishly than he had. I did not look in the side mirror – I guessed he would be standing there helplessly in red shirt, billiard-cloth trousers, dilapidated suitcase at his feet – but drove on to the shopping precinct to pick up some items for Joan before returning to Ogmore-by-Sea where I would resume my lucky life.

I never heard from Eugene Harvey again. So far *The Soussia Review* has not appeared. I doubt if it ever will.

Focus 1986: Ogmore-by-Sea

This morning (4 May) an East wind was blowing so vigorously in Ogmore that our wooden gate had been thrust open. From the bedroom window I could see that a ewe with two lambs had trespassed into our garden. They were munching the daffodils and narcissi, a nice, forbidden, wicked breakfast. I rushed downstairs, still in my pyjamas, to shoo them out.

As I closed the gate behind them I thought more of the East wind than the sheep. Probably it was bearing invisible death-seeds from Chernobyl. Perhaps radioactive raindrops were sipped from the daffodil cups by the ewe and the lambs. Information, so far, is meagre. In any case, who can believe the complacent, stealthy, reassuring voices of experts and politicians? How much has been covered up before, how much will be told to us now? Will radioactive iodine be taken up by small, thirsty thyroid glands? What about my new grand-daughter and all those like her from Ogmore-by-Sea to the Ukraine and beyond where Prometheus is still chained to his rock while the eagle eats his liver?

Last Friday in Cardiff, I visited Llandaff Cathedral. I just happened to be nearby, so popped in as I used to as a boy, passing the yellow celandines beneath the yew tree. Inside soaring spaces of worship – Jewish, Moslem or Christian – I feel not just secular but utterly estranged like one without history or memory. Once more, numb, I observed Epstein's dominating, aluminium dead human figure rising. And it was springtime, springtime in the real world and all seemingly dead things were coming alive again though a cancer sailed in from Chernobyl.

Inside the Cathedral, I ambled towards the Lady Chapel reredos where, on either side of the sculpted Madonna, six niches are filled with gold-leafed wreaths of wildflowers. In Welsh, dozens of flowers are named after the Virgin, as is proper in a nation that reveres the Mam of the family. The marigold is called Gold Mair, Mary's Gold: the buttercup, Mary's sweat; the briar rose, Mary's briar; the foxglove, Mary's thimble; the monkshood, Mary's slipper; the cowslip, Mary's primrose; and the snowdrop, Mary's taper. *Tapr Mair.*

214

If a man believed in a deity, any deity, goddess, god or God, he would, in that Cathedral, have prayed in English or Welsh or no language at all, for the neutralisation of the death wind. And in Ogmore, this morning, as I stood in my pyjamas, while the opera-dramatic clouds, grey, cream, or frowning darker, tracked so visibly westwards, my own lips moved.

The Deceived

I was astonished when I opened my mail. For one letter proved to be from my Uncle Eddie and, accompanying the letter, was a cheque for a hundred pounds. 'The cheque,' he wrote, 'is for Services To Be Rendered by you. Please contact me at the above address.' The notepaper heading was Metatron Hall.

I knew about Metatron Hall. I had learnt about it in the newspapers, how it had become a healing centre because of The Marvellous Girl, Sandra Gibbs. I had read, with some scepticism, how this local young woman had been blind and then how, during a thunderstorm, a miracle had happened. Afterwards, not only could she see, but she had apparently acquired certain psychic gifts. She had appeared on stage for a year before giving up the theatre, and such inconsequential pursuits, to become the saintly, serious, Medicaster-in-Residence at Metatron Hall.

'How did your uncle get involved with that lot?' asked my wife, Joan.

'I don't know,' I said. 'I haven't seen him for twenty years.'

When my mother was alive she called Uncle Eddie, 'a real twister, the black sheep of the family'. I stared at the cheque for one hundred pounds. Uncle had always been disarmingly generous, always quick to put his hand in his pocket – other people's too, according to my mother. Over the years, he had quarrelled with all his numerous brothers, sisters and in-laws. Those still alive spoke with venom about how he had double-crossed them, persuaded them with that glib tongue of his, to invest in one crazy business scheme or another. Even my Uncle Max would have nothing to do with him. 'You have to count your teeth anyhow after you've seen Eddie,' he growled.

The women in the family particularly disapproved of Eddie. For he had abandoned Aunt Hetty, his two daughters and their apple pie home for a succession of gullible women, all wealthy enough to keep him. 'Gone off with another of his chorus girls,' my mother used to exclaim with breathless, condemning fascination. 'What a

216

rotter!' But now he was in his seventies so surely women could no longer think of him as Gorgeous Eddie, even if he called them 'My flower'.

A few evenings later – I happened to be watching the Prime Minister being interviewed on television – I had a follow-up telephone call from Uncle Eddie. Reluctantly, I agreed to go and see him at Metatron Hall. As soon as I'd replaced the receiver I regretted saying 'Yes'. Anyway, there was no point in brooding over it. I returned to the living room and the television screen. There were those who believed that in two week's time Margaret Thatcher would be elected Prime Minister for a third term of office. Entrepreneurs like Uncle Eddie, I thought, thrive in Thatcher's Britain.

The Vale of Glamorgan is studded, not only with the ruins of Norman castles but also with concealed, centuries-old, ivy-hugged mansions that only become visible when you meticulously explore the narrowest, high-hedged, minor roads and turn down some unlikely by-way. That Sunday afternoon in May, after passing several megaphoned cars out electioneering, I drove towards emptiness, down butterfly-haunted country lanes a dozen miles or so from Ogmore before I came to the signpost I was looking for. As soon as I turned into the long drive of Metatron Hall I heard the great clanging bell of the private chapel that adjoined the mansion.

I parked the car just as the sun luminously silvered the edge of a cloud before lighting up the whole landscape, not least the spectacular rhododendron bushes in blood-red flower and the dozen faces of the weary and the sick who were filing into the small chapel. 'They're hoping for a miracle,' I thought as I joined them beneath a flock of noisy rooks wheeling over the chapel.

The chapel itself, inside, was intimate and plain – except for one garish window which reminded me of the coloured glass that decorates so many front doors of older semi-detached, surburban houses. The ceiling had been washed an unconfident blue to match the frayed and fading blue carpet on the floor. A woman at my elbow whispered to me, 'The day of our death is the most beautiful day of our life.' Before I could refute that outrageous statement the service began. I became aware of the sun drizzling through the stained window onto a brassy-gold candelabra and a gold statuette of an angel. The angel Metatron, the heavenly scribe perhaps? There and there blue, the colour of healing; and there and there gold, the colour of money.

After a short service led by an absurdly round-faced clergyman, The Marvellous Girl appeared – she could not have been any other. She was dressed modestly in black, pale of countenance, wearing no make-up, and she laid her hands on those who inched forward. A young father hugged a child in his arms, the child probably not yet three years of age. The little hand was bent on the wrist oddly. It kept on twitching. The Marvellous Girl, Sandra Gibbs, solemnly placed her own two hands firmly on the head of the spastic child and prayed – as did the others in the pews. Then, from outside, I heard some harsh cries. They were the terrible dark sounds of the dozen rooks that must have resumed flying about the roof of the chapel.

Afterwards, behind the pews, at the rear of the chapel, I observed the young father with the child still cradled in his arms. Surreptitiously, he bent down and kissed his little son's head. I saw the naked face of a father, a naked face of a grown man close to tears. He was unaware anyone had observed him. For some reason I felt angry with myself and urgently left the church. I walked on to the mansion.

A young woman with streaky blonde hair led me into a dilapidated, high, oak-panelled room whose long, dust-flecked windows overlooked an extended, tidy lawn on which I could see a man and a woman talking together .

'Your uncle won't be long,' the woman said. 'I'll tell him you're here.'

She closed the door behind her, leaving me alone with the Sunday newspapers on a desk. My small journey from the front door, through the long hall with its peeling wallpaper to this shabby, once elegant room, had given me a glimpse of how tatty and rundown Metatron Hall had become. All the more paradoxical then was the studied tidiness of the mowed lawn outside.

I moved nearer to the window. The two people on the lawn faced each other. They were both exceedingly tall, both very straight-backed. The man in a cream-coloured suit, though athletic looking, was quite old, and the woman probably not much younger. They seemed to be talking earnestly, standing a few feet away from each other, he on my right, she on my left. They were about a hundred yards away from the window so I could not see their faces with great clarity. After a minute, the man moved so that he had his back to me and the woman immediately changed her stance, too, so that now she faced me directly. They stood near a white-painted garden bench but still continued their rapt conversation standing up. Again the man slewed round and the woman followed as in a slow ritual so that the tall, old man was now on my left, the tall woman on the right. 'Sit down,' I thought. 'Why don't you both sit down?'

I turned away, picked up one of the newspapers on the desk and settled in an armchair that was in desperate need of upholstering. Almost at once the door opened and Uncle Eddie came into the room. 'Dan?' he asked. 'Duw, you've changed. I'd never have recognised you in a 'undred year.' He looked pretty sprightly himself, his plastered-down hair with a conspicuous parting was now, unfairly, darker than mine, despite his age.

'I saw you on TV only a year ago. They sure must have made you up,' he said, making me feel the age in my mouth.

'You're looking fine, Uncle,' I said lamely, thinking whatever happened to his glib, buttery tongue?

'TV flatters some people,' Uncle Eddie said, puzzled. 'Anyway, I'm glad you've come.'

He evidently realised he had been less than tactful for he tried to make amends by telling me how he had heard only good things about me, how I was this and how I was that, not like the rest of the family. 'What a shower they are,' he said. Then he took out of the desk drawer a box of Black Magic chocolates. 'See,' he continued, 'I remembered how much you liked these.'

'It was my mother who was keen on them,' I said.

This stopped him smiling. 'Oh, I quite like them too,' I added quickly.

He opened the box and studied the key to the different centres of the chocolates. 'Now, what do you like best?' he asked. 'Turkish Delight? Marzipan? To be honest, I'm fond of the cherry one myself, but if you'd like it you have it...' I selected a chocolate at random. 'What is it?' he asked as I bit on it.

219

'Caramel, I think,' I said. He hunted through the box to select the cherry chocolate. When I looked towards the window I saw that the tall couple had left the lawn.

'I popped into the chapel,' I said. 'I witnessed Sandra Gibbs at work.'

'They don't pay a penny,' Uncle boasted. 'Not one penny. We open up the chapel to the public on Sundays. You were impressed by Sandra, I hope? She has the spiritual blessing, you know, of this Bishop and that – the sanction of the church.'

'I'm a Welsh Jewish secular fundamentalist,' I said.

'I bet you're dubious about The Marvellous Girl,' said my uncle, 'but you haven't witnessed what I have. Sandra's crazy, says little, but when she does speak in that deep, husky voice of hers I've seen a woman fall to the ground, pronto. I've seen a farmer, a very matter-of-fact bloke, having a convulsion so that he had to be held down. She can have an extraordinary effect upon people. She's so mentally fragile, so wistful, so sincere, so possessed by the holy spirit. Some who've visited Metatron Hall have already testified to miracle cures. The place could become a beacon of light for the sick everywhere – like Lourdes. A beacon. And we could make a packet.'

'We?' I asked.

'I mean May Gibbs, Sandra and me. And perhaps, one day, a Medical Director. Why not? The National Health Service isn't much cop these days, is it? All those waiting in queues for ops, they need a place like Metatron Hall, right? If the other marvellous lady is elected again, places like Metatron Hall will do better and better. Mark my words. Listen, Dan, Metatron Hall at present is in an 'ell of a mess. No facilities. No central heating. All fourteen bedrooms in need of repair and decoration. And only two lavs in the whole place. Well, mun, if you're going to charge guests who stay here for The Marvellous Girl's healing touch, you have to offer them luxury, right? Well, we have this idea of building a luxury hotel-nursing-home annexe in the grounds. Out there, beyond that lawn, there's plenty of room for building. But, to be honest, the bank won't lend us more. However, Harri Jenkins is interested in extending his hotel business.'

'Harri Jenkins?'

'Of the Sunset Hotel near Ogmore.'

'I don't know him. I've never been to the Sunset Hotel. That's a bit inland, isn't it?'

'He knows you – of you, I mean. Because of our surname he asked if we were related. He knows you're a doctor. He's very impressed by doctors. He's likely to call on you since you live only a couple of miles away from the hotel. To be honest, that's why I wrote to you. I said that... er... who knows, one day you might consider becoming Medical Director at the Hall. I know it's not your cuppa tea, but I thought no harm in me saying it.'

'It's not my cuppa tea,' I said.

My uncle picked up the box of Black Magic chocolates, then put it down again on the desk. 'I know your mother never thought me to be the bee's knees – because of Hetty. Two sides to everything, right? I'd be much obliged if you'd be very careful if Harri Jenkins asks you anything about me.'

'OK,' I said. 'But I don't need to be bribed.'

I took the cheque he had sent me out of my pocket and tore it up. He laughed. Perhaps he was laughing at me being so dramatically self-righteous. Or would the cheque have bounced anyway?

'Yes, Sandra is sort of remarkable,' Uncle Eddie said. 'Last winter she had a premonition. She had a vivid dream of a car ferry capsizing and sinking outside a French port.'

'The *Herald of Free Enterprise* sank outside a *Belgian* port,' I said.

'Well, it was damned near, wasn't it?' exclaimed Uncle vehemently.

Outside, on the lawn, the tall couple appeared again, this time accompanied by a woman in a blue dress. 'Dan,' said Uncle Eddie quietly, 'it's important to me that this business deal goes through. My last chance maybe. I mean I've buggered up so many things in my life. I'm depending on you being discreet.' He looked towards the window and his face visibly softened. 'There's May Gibbs,' he said, 'in the blue dress.' He came closer to me, too close. 'You know, Hetty was a great whore in the kitchen and a great cook in bed. With May it's the other way round. She's a goer. She keeps me young. She's twenty-five years younger than me but, to be honest, it's good between us. Listen, Dan, I'm telling you that for the first time in my life I care more about another person than myself, know what I mean?'

Vulnerably, he looked out of the window. All three on the lawn were walking towards us. The woman in a blue dress, in her fifties, had a pleasing face, a delicate bone structure, and when young must have been entirely beautiful. Now she waved as she stood at the tall, dusty window, and called, 'C'mon and join us, Eddie. Get some sun.'

'Coming, my pigeon,' he called back.

As we left the panelled room he told me, 'That Llantwit couple with May, they're religious and rich as Croesus but I bet they won't invest in Metatron Hall. They're not so susceptible to May's charms as Harri Jenkins is.'

'And your Marvellous Girl,' I asked. 'I take it she's sincerely religious too?'

Uncle halted. 'She's not a charlatan if that's what you think. She's mad, yes, sort of insane, but not a charlatan.'

After Mrs Thatcher won her third term of office the election posters were taken down. In their stead notices had been put up for miles around – from Ewenny to Merthyr Mawr, from Colwinston to Southerndown. At Ogmore-by-Sea they blazoned forth from the windows of Hardee's, the post office and the village shop: AT THE SUNSET LOUNGE, 21 June 8 p.m. Midsummer Night. One performance only. THE MARVELLOUS GIRL; SANDRA GIBBS IN PERSON. In aid of the Blind Children's Fund.

Harri Jenkins had never contacted me but I had made some enquiries about the Sunset Hotel. Brian Clark, who used to come over once a month to do some gardening at Green Hollows and who lived a stone's throw from the hotel, was far from reassuring. 'The Sunset can't compete with the Craig or Sea Lawns. They're in sight of the sea. I think Harri's up to his neck in debt. As for that show being in aid of blind children, I wouldn't like to bet on that,' Brian said. The more I heard about Harri Jenkins, the more he sounded like my Uncle Eddie!

On Sunday, 21 June, Joan had no wish to watch 'a magic show'. She suggested that if Sandra Gibbs really had psychic powers she could solve the financial difficulties of Metatron Hall by visiting a casino and forecasting which numbers would turn up next. 'Besides,' she remarked, 'I think it would be better if you had nothing to do with either your dubious uncle or the dubious Mr Jenkins.'

She was quite right of course, but I was curious. So I set out to walk the two miles to the Sunset Hotel on my own. On my way I had to pass through the tiny village of Gwylfa. Only very occasionally did a car or a van travel down the narrow winding lane, its hedges filled with so many wild, delicate flowers the names of which I didn't know, this one and that one delinquently incognito. Just before I reached the village I saw a sheep close to the hedge, apparently asleep. When I reached it I realised the creature was dead. It had been hit by a car. I hesitated. There was nothing I could do. I walked on.

The large lounge of the Sunset Hotel, with all its indoor greenery, was crowded that Sunday evening. Soon after I had sat down on a chair in the back row I espied my uncle sitting on the side at the front. I had arrived just in time because the lights were lowered almost immediately. Harri Jenkins came on to the specially raised platform on which had been arranged a couple of chairs, a table covered by a black velvet cloth and, in the background, a blackboard.

'Privilege,' said Harri Jenkins, a middle-aged man with glassy, sparkling eyes and distinctly rosy cheeks that made him resemble a ventriloquist's dummy. 'Privilege,' repeated Mr Jenkins louder so that the humming conversation of the audience began to subside to an expectant hush. He waited dramatically for complete silence before he undid his double-breasted, too tight, purple blazer and continued, 'Privilege for me to introduce the *famous* celebrity, The Marvellous Girl, and her mother, May Gibbs. You've all read about The Marvellous Girl so she hardly needs me, um, to introduce her, oh dear no. Lately I've got to know her and her mother who should be called marvellous too, got to know them both personally. Well, um, many of you here know me, know how good I am at sussing out qualities in men and women. An hotel proprietor does have to be a bit psychic and – '

'Get on with it, Harri,' shouted out Lol, one of the local shepherds, who evidently had had several jars in the bar beforehand.

Harri Jenkins's hands had been raised in the air like a conductor's. He let them drop. 'As I was saying, mun, we have two marvellous women on stage at the lounge tonight. Makes me feel like a glutton,' he added smiling, showing all his teeth. 'As for The

Marvellous Girl herself – just to be near her is to feel a great bronze bell silently ringing.'

'Aw, put a sock in it,' Lol suddenly shouted, amusing some in the audience but embarrassing most.

'Lol?' asked Harri Jenkins, peering into the shadows of the lounge. 'What's the matter with you?'

'I'm pissed,' called back Lol, standing up, swaying a little.

There was a general hum of sighings and tuttings and someone shouted out, 'That man must leave the lounge. He must leave.'

'Go,' said Mr Jenkins, pointing like the Angel who directed Adam and Eve from Paradise. 'If you don't go I'll see you never get another drink at the Sunset ever.'

He stood there with his hand pointing towards the door for a full minute while Lol, obediently, mumbling to himself, made his way past knees to the gangway. At the door, he paused to face the intrepid, pointing Harri Jenkins. 'You're a fart,' he said, then stumbled backwards through the door and disappeared.

Inappropriately, as if he had just heard great good news, Harri Jenkins smiled again at the audience. This absurd, semi-comic prolegomenon was hardly appropriate for the 'mystery show' that was about to follow but the Master of Ceremonies, Harri Jenkins, valiantly continued, 'The stage appearance of The Marvellous Girl is a one-off. She has basically given up stage appearances. Instead she works selflessly at that healing centre, that wonderful healing centre, Metatron Hall in the Vale of Glamorgan. Um. It's the cause of the Blind that brings her here tonight. And my own personal interest in Metatron Hall. Ladies and Gentlemen, please welcome The Marvellous Girl and her marvellous mother.'

The audience applauded and, at once, Mrs Gibbs came on to the stage carrying a lit black candle which she placed on the black velvet cloth, followed by The Marvellous Girl who was wearing bow tie, tuxedo and shiny top hat. Her face had been powdered an unnatural white to emphasise her large, staring eyes. She stood behind one of the crimson chairs while her mother pronounced, 'When the angels descend to this world to fulfil a mission they wear the garments of this world and they take on the appearance of the people of this world. Otherwise they would not be tolerated here on this earth and we, in turn, could not endure them.'

Was Mrs Gibbs suggesting that her daughter was divine? I

recalled my uncle's remarks about Sandra Gibbs that she was 'sort of insane'. Perhaps the mother was too?

The show began. It seemed that the slim, haunted-looking girl in disturbing top hat and in evening-dress suit owned psychokinetic and telepathic gifts. She, at first, did not speak, utter one single word, yet this somehow did not diminish her almost palpable charisma. The mother vocalised everything – quite a joky auctioneer's patter she had too – as Sandra Gibbs, in a kind of cataleptic trance, stared at the flickering lit candle with terrible concentration and made solid objects apparently dematerialise and rematerialise.

After about half an hour of this The Marvellous Girl was blindfolded and a few members of the audience were invited to clamber onto the stage. Each, in turn, was asked to write the name of some real, concrete object on the blackboard. One of my neighbours wrote down 'Tusker Rock', the young woman with streaky blonde hair that I had seen at Metatron Hall chalked up 'Niagara Falls', and Mrs Maddocks, our local wit, started to write the name of the village in Gwynedd fifty-eight letters long. She had got as far as 'Llanfairpwll' when May Gibbs stopped her saying that the village's name, Llanfairpwllgwyngyllgogerychwyrndrobwllllantysiliogogogoch, would be too easy for The Marvellous Girl. 'So give her something more difficult,' urged May Gibbs. After much laughter Mrs Maddocks wrote down, 'Lol, the shepherd' and again everybody laughed.

Sandra Gibbs stood very still, blindfolded, in front of the stage while her mother took a billiard cue and pointed to the words 'Tusker Rock'. 'Concentrate your minds,' commanded May Gibbs addressing the silent audience. 'Bring into your minds a vision of what is written here. Think, think of it, picture it.' She cleared her throat and mumbled something I couldn't hear, then added, 'Ye-es, let it float into your minds. It's coming, it's coming, that's right, into your minds and now it will be seen by The Marvellous Girl.'

The audience waited. The girl with the white powdered face opened her mouth as if to speak but uttered no word. The Sunset Lounge was quite silent. Then, in an unexpectedly deep voice, The Marvellous Girl said, 'Tusker Rock'. And everybody applauded. The same routine was followed before Sandra Gibbs pronounced 'Niagara Falls' and then, with even greater hesitation and more patter from her mother, 'Lol, the shepherd'. Again everybody applauded.

Was this exhibition of telepathy somehow faked? Others followed in similar fashion. Did Mrs Gibbs' patter conceal a code? I suspected so. What did somewhat unnerve me was The Marvellous Girl's remarkable, eerie voice. Deep as a man's. And her clothes were like a man's. Was her evident charisma expressed in the mythic apprehension that man and woman once were one person, a god and goddess dwelling in one body?

'Now, another phenomenon,' May Gibbs solemnly announced after the show had lengthened to almost two hours. She placed a large glass vase on the black velvet cloth next to the one lit candle. 'The Marvellous Girl will now, by a further concentration of psychic energy, shatter this vase into a hundred pieces. She will not, I promise you, touch it.'

Seemingly more white-faced than ever, her eyes hardly blinking and conspicuous beneath her top hat, Sandra Gibbs stepped forward to stand a foot or two from the table. 'Silence, please, utter silence,' called May Gibbs who then raised her right foot on its heel before letting the sole slap down, up and down repeatedly on the floor to evince a regular pattern of noise.

'Slower,' The Marvellous Girl surprisingly objected. 'Slower. The same rate as my heartbeat.'

The foot tapped slower, tap tap tap, about seventy beats a minute, I reckoned. Meanwhile The Marvellous Girl, Sandra Gibbs, passed her hands back and forward horizontally, arms outstretched, above the vase. Suddenly, May Gibbs stopped tapping the floor, the candle flame, which had been increasingly flickering, inexplicably went out and there was a great crash behind me. One of the pictures on the wall had, for no evident reason, smashed down onto the floor. Everybody looked away from the stage over their shoulders and the woman next to me mumbled, 'They say when a picture frame falls down on its own there'll be a death in the family .'

The vase on the velvet cloth remained whole, unshattered. May Gibbs looked dismayed. 'Oh my God,' uttered the Marvellous Girl in her dark voice, 'I'm sorry, I'm sorry. I visited the Void. That was a malefic influence. I'm sorry.'

May Gibbs quickly took the vase away. She told a joke about how things can go wrong that made everybody laugh while Sandra Gibbs sat down again, unsmiling, somnambulistically, on one of the crimson chairs, hands on her knees, palms turned upwards.

'Yes, that picture is of Foxhunting and The Marvellous Girl is an anti-vivisectionist and a vegetarian,' May Gibbs declared.

The audience did not notice, at first, the return of Lol the shepherd. He had abandoned the lounge somewhat tipsy earlier, he was now indubitably quite drunk. As May Gibbs spoke he drifted up the aisle with the obvious intention of climbing up onto the stage. 'You bastards,' he shouted out abruptly. 'You're all bastards.'

Mrs Gibbs looked at her daughter wildly. And as Lol advanced on the stage, Harri Jenkins came forward to impede his progress. 'Leave him alone,' Sandra Gibbs said quietly. 'It will be all right.' Lol had raised his right arm and his right hand had become a fist. He moved threateningly towards Harri Jenkins but Sandra Gibbs stepped forward. 'This way, my dear child,' she commanded in her husky male voice. Lol hesitated. The audience were rapt, quiet. 'This way, my dear one.' Lol changed his direction. 'Come.'

He dropped his fist and, docile, moved towards her. 'Life is so hard for you, I understand,' she intoned quietly. Lol nodded assent. 'What do they know out there,' she said, 'in their comfortable seats, the hardships you have to endure every day. The insults, the injuries, the loneliness. Kneel my child and pray. Afterwards you will feel refreshed, grateful and happier.' Lol sank to his knees, seemingly hypnotised, and uttered, 'Our Father, which art in Heaven, hallowed be Thy Name, Thy Kingdom come... '

While he prayed The Marvellous Girl placed her hand on his head. At the conclusion of the prayer she said, 'Rise now, dear child, and go home in peace.' Lol rose and without stumbling, apparently quite sober, left the lounge. As soon as he had vanished the audience all clapped and Harri Jenkins came forward to conclude the 'show'. His vote of thanks was a masterpiece of hyperbole which would not have shamed the medieval Welsh poets. 'We've seen here tonight, ladies and gentlemen, great inexplicable splendour. We've had torrents of surprises and, um, entertainment. Absolute torrents. The Marvellous Girl has a talent that could put an oak tree into flames. Like the preachers of old she could light the lamp to direct us away from the chasm beyond Hell's gate. As for her mother, an eagle amongst women, we must thank her too. We, of this parish, are truly privileged to have them visit us tonight.'

He diligently continued to extol the virtues of May and Sandra Gibbs before reminding the audience that the evening's takings would be going to the Blind Children's Fund. 'But one should not forget,' he concluded, 'the inspiring, valorous work going on at Metatron Hall. Healing skill they have, money is what they need. So the boxes are going around for notes only, ladies and gentlemen. Remember those who visit Metatron Hall are those the doctors have despaired of. Count your blessings and give in order that these two noble ladies, pure as nuns, may carry on their merciful work. Cheques will be accepted. I deeply thank you.'

I waited until the lounge had cleared before approaching Uncle Eddie who had not moved from his chair. Sandra Gibbs and her mother had disappeared but a few near the door had buttonholed Harri Jenkins. Uncle Eddie stared at me uncomprehendingly when I greeted him. I was curious about the picture frame, how it, deranged, had crashed down unaccountably, surprising – or so it appeared – even those on stage. Had that genuinely been unplanned? I wondered, too, whether the journalist who had originally dubbed Sandra Gibbs 'The Marvellous Girl' had done so ironically, to evoke comparisons with the teenage Thomas Chatterton, that gifted eighteenth-century poet and forger whose deceptions had, for a time, bamboozled the literary world and antiquaries alike, and who had been labelled by William Wordsworth as 'The Marvellous Boy'. But it did not seem the appropriate moment to air my scepticism. Instead I said, 'It went well, Uncle. She certainly has the true hypnotic powers.'

He stood up and said morosely, 'Let's get some air.'

I followed him to the door where Harri Jenkins said to him, 'We'll be leaving in about twenty minutes, Eddie.' But my uncle brushed past him angrily. I remembered how Brian Clark had suggested Harri Jenkins was up to his neck in debt and could hardly invest in Metatron Hall. Perhaps my uncle had become aware of this?

Outside the hotel, the sun was setting so that the trees, drawn in charcoal, barred the width of a streaky coloured sky. Midges, restless specks of energy, had begun their sundown Sisyphus work and, in the distance, doors were slamming shut in the hotel car park. My uncle seemed loath to speak.

'What's the matter?' I asked him.

'The pig, Harri Jenkins, that's what's the matter.'

The cars leaving the car park had their headlights switched on. In the failing light I saw how much older my uncle now looked. 'I don't know what to do, I don't know what to do, I don't know what to do,' Eddie murmured distressingly.

'Maybe someone else will invest in Metatron Hall,' I said.

'That's not the trouble,' Uncle said dismissively as if I were utterly stupid. 'May's persuaded that couple from near Llantwit to put cash in. No, it's Harri Jenkins. Harri Jenkins and May, they're having an affair. He's moving into Metatron Hall.'

'They know you know,' I said, at a loss what to say.

'I've had it,' my uncle said. 'They won't let me stay there much longer. May's the only woman I've ever really cared for.'

He stepped towards the hotel, defeated, then stopped to say helplessly, 'I don't know what to do. I don't know where to go to. All Sandra does is pray, pray, pray. She's doing that now – asking God's forgiveness for giving a show. And May, she's infatuated by that crook Jenkins. Hypnotised by him.'

He stood there without moving. I thought he was going to cry. Instead he added, 'I could kill him.' The deceiver had been deceived. He looked past me, as if into the future. 'What are we here for, Dan?' he asked quietly, 'What the hell are we here for?' before turning to disappear into the Sunset Lounge. His shoulders were round. His back was the back of an old man.

By the time I had walked to the village of Gwylfa it was quite dark. A few desolate sodium lamp-posts lit up a short bend of the road within the village boundaries. Then it was dark again. I expected to see the carcass of the sheep. It had gone. Someone had taken it away. It was as if it had never existed except in my imagination.

Afterword

'Madagascar', the longest story in this novel made up of inter-related narratives, is not set in that island off the African coast but in the much less exotic Canton and Cyncoed districts of Cardiff, the author's home town. Appearances can be deceptive and in this work of "autobiographical fiction" they usually turn out to be so. Madagascar, as a matter of 'fact', refers to the shape of a birthmark on a woman's left buttock. David Pugh, a middle-aged Welsh business man, believes that the woman he has married (the owner of the birthmark) is not his intended but her twin sister. After discovering the birthmark on honeymoon, he locks himself into a room in the Angel Hotel in Cardiff and threatens suicide. The story's narrator, the fictional young Dannie Abse, who has met the beautiful young Australian wife who insists that she is the genuine article, has the problem of deciding what the truth is. Attracted to the wife, the inexperienced Dannie, who is filling in as a locum for his uncle Max, begins by believing her version but before the story ends (inconclusively like most of them) appearances have become very problematic for the newly-qualified doctor.

What is truth? People can't help but see 'reality' through their dreams and beliefs. The eighteen beautifully crafted and related stories in this tight collection explore the mystery of appearances and the difficulty of distinguishing appearance from reality. Dannie's Uncle Max admits to conning his patients "for their own sakes" with his coloured medicines. We never find out whether the birthmark really existed or whether the wife is the right twin. And, as with all the stories, the unexpected and the strange are firmly rooted in the familiar. At the beginning of 'Madagascar', blood drips onto the heads of passengers on the London to Cardiff train. However, the sinister note turns to comic relief when we realise it is only the blood from the narrator's piece of beef, dripping down as it soaks through its wrapper of newspapers up on the luggage rack. Most of the stories are enhanced by this surrealistic quality. When a white ship, apparently crewless like the Marie Celeste, appears off the coast of Ogmore-by-Sea in South Wales, the watchers can hardly believe their eyes, but it steers carefully around the dangerous Tusker Rock and eventually sails safely into the harbour of Porthcawl across the bay. The mysterious, transcendental moment, the watchers realise, belonged to the familiar world after all. In this book, the familiar world of childhood and hometown is forever being visited by the strange.

The puzzling nature of appearances is the central theme which unifies this collection. The last story, about Sandra Gibbs, 'The Marvellous Girl', who is reputed to have remarkable healing powers, ends with the apparent disappearance of a dead sheep: "It was as if it had never existed except in my imagination" is the very last sentence. That the world does largely exist in our imaginations (and yet does not only exist there) is something that fascinates the author. The first story, 'The Pencil Box', tells how the seven year old Dannie stole a beautiful pencil box and suffered guilt until he finally rid himself of it by sailing the box out of his life down the local stream. It seems a straightforward enough story of childhood until Dannie discovers he was not the first thief. The boy he stole it from had himself stolen the pencil box. All was not as it seemed: the foundations of fact and feeling have shifted. As another character says; "It's all dissimulation, pretence, falsehood, deception. Like the stars. How many of those we see are still there?"

The deceptive nature of appearances is not just a central theme, even an obsessional one, in these stories, it also influences how Dannie Abse sees his art as a writer. Sandra Gibbs, 'The Marvellous Girl' in the final story, is directly compared to Thomas Chatterton, 'The Marvellous Boy', the gifted eighteenth-century teenage poet whose deceptions fooled the literary world. These stories are not just about deceptions; clearly Dannie Abse sees the art of the short story as a form of deception too. It is no accident that he writes fiction as if it were autobiography. Nearly every one of these 'stories' is written in the first person, from the point of view of the young man who grows up in Cardiff. The place names are all authentic. The narrator himself appears 'real'; he is honest and straightforward, not given to irony; above all, he is reliable. There couldn't be a better basis from which to spring on the reader those frissons of doubt and deception with which these stories abound. The autobiographical mode is art although it appears to be necessity. It allows the author to give to mystery the authenticity of reality. There is also in the marvellous Uncle Isidore, the speaker of paradoxes, a character who straddles the blurred line between fiction and autobiography; it seems almost impossible to hold him steady in your gaze. Dannie Abse's 'Author's Note' makes his aim clear: "I have deleted my past and, despite approximate resemblances, substituted it with artifice. If I am disbelieved, so much the better."

The autobiographical narrative method might seem natural enough but the structure of the book declares its artifice openly. *There Was A Young Man From Cardiff* is as carefully constructed as a lyric poem. Four of the eighteen pieces (the original publication of 1991 also contained four strategically placed poems) have appeared in two previous books but they still fit naturally into this collection as though written specially for it. The book divides into three clear parts covering the period of Dannie Abse's life from 1930, when he was seven, to around 1989. The second great theme of the book is Time itself and the way our lives are rooted in history: the book's chronological structure and constant references to dates and important events emphasize time passing. The first part, 'The Name of the Story', covers the Thirties, focuses on growing up in Cardiff, relations and friends, and ends with the seventeen-year-old Dannie in hospital at the beginning of the war. The second part, 'Double Footsteps', covers the period after the war when the narrator has grown up and moved away to London. Now Cardiff is somewhere to be visited (hence the title of this part) from places outside, like Bridgend and London. 'Ogmore Elegies', the third part, covers the late Fifties onwards and focuses on Ogmore-by-Sea ("the place I loved best on this earth") where the author had holidayed as a child and where he later bought a house. Cardiff barely figures now amongst the wonderful evocations of the small seaside village and the elegies are for the narrator's relatives and friends as the book moves towards its close.

Although the narrative mode is autobiographical, this is most definitely not an egocentric book. While it celebrates a certain time in very particular places, it also makes us constantly aware of what one of the characters calls "the Tumult of Elsewhere". A remarkable sensitivity to a world apparently outside our own but which nevertheless inevitably impinges on us is one of the strongest features of Dannie Abse's writings whether in poetry or prose. In each of the three parts of this book there are stories relating to the wider world. Perhaps the most powerful is '1938: Vienna' in which an Austrian Jew who has changed his name from Friedman to Friedell finds he cannot hide from his true identity when the Nazis come (a more serious play on the appearance-reality theme). This is a most moving, disturbing story, all the more effective for its brevity.

It would not be difficult to argue that of his prose works *There Was a Young Man From Cardiff* is Dannie Abse's finest book. Its prose is tighter and more lucid than that of *Ash On A Young Man's Sleeve*. It has remarkable structural and thematic unity and should be read consecutively from the beginning. Dannie Abse's voice seems at its most natural and most successful when writing autobiographical fiction and, as he himself says, "An author, despite inadvertently altering the true colours of his life, obliterating this, accentuating that, may ultimately not only give us pleasure but reveal to us more about the world we live in, and more about ourselves."

Further Reading

Novels:
Ash on A Young Man's Sleeve (London, 1954)
Some Corner of an English Field (London, 1956)
O Jones, O Jones (London, 1970)

Prose:
A Poet in the Family (autobiography, London, 1974)
Intermittent Journals (Bridgend, 1994)

Plays:
The View from Row G (Bridgend, 1990)

Poetry:
White Coat, Purple Coat: Poems 1948-88 (London, 1989)
Remembrance of Crimes Past: Poems 1986-89 (London, 1990)
On the Evening Road (London, 1994)
Welsh Retrospective (Bridgend, 1997)
Arcadia, One Mile (London, 1998)